BEIRUT
STATION

CARY REED

Contents

Chapter One

Beirut, 1997

In the shadows of a city where peace teetered on the edge of a knife, Abu Faysal clung to the fleeting scent of jasmine, a tender reminder of his girlfriend's embrace in the claustrophobic quarters of Hamra. Each second of joy was a rare gem in the rubble of his war-weary existence, and he hoarded this moment like a secret as the elevator descended into the bowels of Beirut and the cold anonymity of the underground garage. His life, entwined with the fate of the Lebanese Hezbollah militia, was a testament to the peril that came with power in a country where alliances shifted quickly. This was a time when peace felt more like a harbinger of doom than a promise of harmony.

His safe havens were scarce, limited to Cyla's apartment and this concrete cave. The black Toyota sedan emerged from the shadows as the elevator doors parted, a silent accomplice to his cautious retreat. He moved swiftly into the back seat, the space beside him occupied by his lieutenant, Abdel, the only man whose loyalty was beyond question.

The car's motion wiped the smile from Abu Faysal's face, a change not unnoticed by Abdel. The light banter about love and loss that followed was a thin veneer over the chasm of their reality. "My cousin's place in Achrafiyeh," Abu Faysal commanded, his voice slicing through the early morning silence that blanketed Beirut – a silence that was a double-edged sword, offering passage free from the eyes of the world, yet ripe for an ambush.

Streets scarred by conflict whispered rumors of pacts made and broken as they navigated through the city's skeleton. The ceasefire, a fragile thread in the tapestry of Middle Eastern politics, had so far held; but the specter of Israeli intelligence loomed large, its presence felt in the shadows just beyond the reach of the ceasefire's fragile light.

Abdel's reconnaissance photos, snapshots of an enemy too familiar, were a grim ballet of soldiers in repose, their lives momentarily paused by technology's reach.

"The Israelis are getting soft," Abu Faysal remarked. "See this? They're letting them bring cell phones to the front now."

"Good Jewish boys call their mothers," Abdel said.

All joking aside, Abu Faysal saw an enemy increasingly unprepared, a giant lulled into complacency by the illusion of peace. But the irony of their mirrored existences was not lost on him; both sides caught in a war where the home they longed for was so close at hand.

The quiet of their journey through the streets was shattered by a sound – metallic, ominous, a harbinger of doom that shattered the stillness. The world narrowed to the space inside the car, every sense heightened, the air charged with the electricity of impending disaster.

"Stop the car!"

The urgency in Abdel's voice was a clear signal of the danger that had always been a breath away. But, this time, he was too late recognizing its nature. The streets of Beirut, once silent witnesses to their passage, now echoed with the promise of retribution.

Chapter Two

Something in the night interrupted the few hours of sleep Nava Sarsi could manage. Her eyelids fluttered open in the dim moonlight just in time to catch the haunting dance of her mother's portrait in its frame on the nightstand—a brief, eerie tremor before the world fell back into a deceptive calm. A chilling echo of destruction reverberated through the night, fading into a silence that felt too heavy, too charged. Instinctively, her lips parted, a name escaping them—a plea for reassurance in the darkness.

Calling out to those who could no longer respond had become a sorrowful habit. The empty echoes of her mother's name had once haunted the corridors of her childhood home in Tehran, each call a stark reminder of her loss. Now, in the solitude of her Beirut apartment, it was Farzin's name that slipped through her lips in a whisper of longing and confusion. But her ex-husband was far from this place, likely entwined in the warmth of another's embrace in Tehran, leaving Nava to grapple with the void his absence had carved in her life. The bed they had chosen together, the apartment they had turned into a home, now stood as silent witnesses to the fragments of a life she could no longer claim as her own.

The night air, once a soothing balm, now carried the cacophony of car alarms and the urgent wail of sirens through her open window,

4

piercing the quietude that had settled over her room. Shadows played across her vision as she peered into the darkness, the curtains dancing like specters in the wind. With a heavy heart, she rose, the distance to the window stretching out like a chasm filled with the echoes of her fractured memories. Closing the window against the clamor, she sought to shut out the chaos of the outside world, but the turmoil within was not so easily silenced.

Chapter
Three

Nava's telephone erupted into a piercing ring, slicing through the silence like a shrill fire alarm. The last vestiges of sleep were torn away, those final three minutes of peace stolen from her.

"Get down here as soon as you can," she heard her station chief, Masoud, say on the other end. The urgency in his voice was a rare and unsettling occurrence.

"Your house or the embassy?"

"Embassy," he answered.

The line went dead. It must be something important, she thought, but still... *Three minutes...*

As the dawn crept over Beirut, painting the sky with hues of gold and pink, Nava Sarsi found herself navigating the congested streets of the city in her yellow VW bug affectionately named Dasia. The car, much like Nava herself, was a splash of vibrancy against the backdrop of a city that bore the scars of its tumultuous history.

BEIRUT STATION

Not long ago, Nava found herself in two marriages of different types. The first was a marriage of love to Farzin, and the other was a marriage of convenience to the Iranian Ministry of Intelligence and Security. At around the time they both began, she would never have imagined that it would be the latter that outlasted the former. But her marriage to Farzin had dissolved, and her career, once a means to an end, had become the unlikely bridge to a sense of purpose and belonging.

On this particular morning, her drive was accompanied by the comforting familiarity of a manoushe, a Lebanese breakfast staple. The warm, za'atar-laden flatbread was a small rebellion against the routine of her day, a reminder of the city that had, over time, become a part of her very soul. Beirut was more than just a backdrop for her life; it was a character in her story, a constant companion through her trials and tribulations. Her mother had been Lebanese, raised here in Beirut; and so she had a bond with the city, its vibrancy, craziness, and beauty.

As she weaved through the traffic, a car abruptly cut her off, snapping her out of her contemplative state. "*Ah, shou helwe!*" she exclaimed after narrowly avoiding a collision, then made an obscene gesture with her steering hand before quickly grasping the wheel again. The frustration was fleeting, a momentary break in her otherwise composed demeanor. It was Beirut, after all.

Her phone and pager, the lifelines to her clandestine world, buzzed more incessantly than usual this morning, a reminder of the work that awaited her attention. A message from CLOCKWORK, a source named for the precision and reliability Nava had come to depend on, promised yet another layer of complexity to her evening. A nondescript safe house dubbed The Baker's would be the stage for their clandestine meeting.

The hijab she donned to enter the embassy was a mask, one she shed with relish upon stepping into the freedom of Beirut's streets. In this city, she was not defined by the expectations of others but by her own strength and cunning. Lebanon offered a sanctuary from the rigid norms of her homeland, allowing her the liberty to navigate the intricacies of her identity on her own terms.

The moment Nava Sarsi stepped into her station's offices, an eerie silence greeted her. The early morning buzz that typically filled the space was conspicuously absent. As the largest MOIS outpost beyond Iran's borders, the stillness in Beirut Station was out of character, unsettling. She barely had time to register the anomaly, her bag landing on her desk with a soft thud, before Masoud appeared. His presence was abrupt, his demeanor urgent, signaling that the day ahead was anything but ordinary.

"Follow me," was all he said, and so she did.

The urgency with which he moved was infectious, and Nava found herself caught in the current of his purpose. Their destination, the elevator to B-2, was a descent into the heart of the embassy's secrets. The subterranean conference room, known for its stringent security, was a place where only matters of grave importance were discussed. The weight of the situation settled on Nava's shoulders like a cloak, heavy with anticipation.

"What's happening?" The question slipped from Nava's lips, a whisper in the confined space of the elevator.

"You'll find out at the briefing," was his curt reply.

Amidst the anticipation, a mundane act of checking her nails morphed into a moment of introspection when her eyes caught the glimmer of her wedding ring. The realization that she had adorned herself with it unconsciously brought a strange sense of comfort, a tether to a past life that she hadn't emotionally relinquished... not fully, anyway.

BEIRUT STATION

Flickering fluorescent lights casting long, distorted figures on the walls during their brief journey through the embassy's bowels. As they approached the sealed door to the conference room, Masoud's security card sang the metallic hymn of access granted. The door swung open, revealing a windowless chamber where secrets were both shielded and unveiled, a room that held the promise of answers and perhaps, for Nava, a new mission she could sink her teeth into.

Stepping into the secure conference room, Nava couldn't help but notice a familiar imbalance. Once more, she was the sole woman amidst a gathering of dower, bearded men. This reality, initially daunting during her early days in Beirut, had become a facet of her professional landscape she came to navigate with ease. The deference she once believed was her duty, influenced by the reverence held for her father and his peers, had slowly dissolved with the years.

The room was anchored by a large oakwood table, around which sat the embassy's key figures. Ambassador Gul presided at the head, with his deputies by his side. The military presence underscored by defense attache Colonel Salmani and an unfamiliar IRGC officer. Across from Salmani was Hooman, her office's unlikely star for his landing a source in Israeli Military Intelligence, a feat that overshadowed years of mediocrity. His dual role as deputy station chief granted him a comprehensive overview of operations, further elevating his status.

Nava's designated seat, next to Hooman, positioned her directly across from the new IRGC officer, the desk symbolically dividing MOIS and IRGC representatives. This arrangement was a silent testament to the underlying bureaucratic tension that extended even to Lebanon, a bureaucratic rivalry that occasionally veered into outright hostility. The Revolutionary Guards were just as bullying outside Iran as they were inside.

"Let's begin," Ambassador Gul said once the door was closed.

A technician from her office was operating an overhead projector onto which he placed a grainy photo of Abu Faysal, a prominent commander in the Lebanese Hezbollah militia—Iran's closest ally and proxy force in Lebanon.

"Masoud?" Ambassador Gul called.

"Last night at approximately 2:30 a.m.—"

"Wouldn't that make it *this morning*, Masoud?" Colonel Salmani interjected.

Prick ...

Masoud maintained his composure and answered him, saying, "That's correct."

"So, this morning, then," Salmani said. "Just to clarify."

"This morning," Masoud confirmed. "May I continue?"

"Please."

Whether it was the pitch of his voice or his condescending tone, Colonel Salmani possessed a talent for grating her as few people could. As much love as she had for Iran, it was people like him that had made it nearly unbearable for her. He reeked of malign disparagement and oozed with condemnation. Even with her back to him so that she could see the projector screen, Nava could feel his judgemental eyeballs boring into her. She found herself clenching her teeth and suppressing the desire to turn and yell, "What the fuck are you looking at, you sanctamonious shit?" hard enough to wet his face with her spittle. She imagined that returning just a small fraction of the sanctimonious venom he emanated would be immensely satisfying; but of course, she couldn't allow herself to do it.

"This morning, Hezbollah commander Abu Faysal died in a massive explosion that we suspect was a car bomb," Masoud said, and the technician changed the picture to one taken at night.

It depicted in graphic detail the smoldering, twisted metal shell of a car in the middle of a street. She recognized the intersection. It was less than two kilometers away from her apartment, and her mind revisited the moment her sleep had been disrupted the night before. She imagined the sound of the explosion sending shockwaves through the air, passing over her mother's picture and nearly knocking it to the floor in her bedroom. She guessed that the emergency vehicles she could partially see in the photo were the source of the sirens she'd heard before closing her window. The next photo showed four black bags, lined up very neatly, that she presumed contained the passengers' remains. They appeared to be spaced at precise intervals, as if someone had tried in vain to impose some order on the chaos and devastation that was an all-too-familiar sight in Beirut.

"The Zionists have made their opening move," Salmani said. "God willing, they'll pay dearly for this."

In the brief exchange of glances with Hooman, Nava found some silent solidarity. His eye roll, subtle yet profound, was a clear indictment of the tendency of IRGC officers to let bias cloud their judgment, often leading them to conclusions not grounded in evidence. This silent language of shared skepticism—a language honed through years navigating the nuanced world of intelligence—spoke volumes between them. Nava's expertise in reading the unspoken truths behind people's gestures and expressions had always served her well, allowing her to understand underlying motivations and prejudices. This moment with Hooman was no different; it was an immediate, mutual recognition of their concern over how hatred could distort the pursuit of truth.

She considered Hooman, with his blend of ambition and cool detachment, a study in contrasts. Despite his tendencies toward aloofness, there was an undercurrent of intellectual integrity that Nava respected. His eye roll, a fleeting gesture of solidarity in their shared frustration, was a reminder of the complexities that defined relationships within the embassy. Through these small, meaningful interactions, Nava navigated the intricate web of personalities and politics, her insights a guide to understanding the diverse tapestry of motives and values that influenced the actions of her colleagues. In a realm where trust was both a currency and a commodity, being able to read the room was not just an asset; it was essential for survival.

"The Israelis broke the ceasefire?" the IRGC officer next to Salmani asked.

Masoud turned to Hooman, who swung his chair halfway around and said, "We have no intelligence information that would indicate the Israelis are responsible."

"However," Masoud quickly added, "we've been looking for the other Hezbollah commander in the Beqaa Valley, Yasin Haddad, for several weeks."

"He must know something we don't," a deputy ambassador said to no one in particular.

"Or he's dead," Salmani said.

"Let's not jump to conclusions," Masoud cautioned. "We—"

"Come now, Masoud," Salmani interrupted him, leaning back in his chair. "Be sensible. Be *serious*. Hezbollah commanders are being assassinated! These are Zionist attacks. Ceasefire be damned... If you haven't the spine for calling out their aggression, perhaps this isn't the best posting for you."

Nava felt her face burning. Salmani may have been speaking to Masoud, but he was attacking the entire MOIS station, and in full view of Ambassador Gul, no less. It was bureaucratic backstabbing at its worst.

"I'm sorry," the new IRGC Major said. "You said you've been *looking* for the other military commander?"

"Yes," Masoud answered.

"May I ask why?"

Masoud's gaze briefly met Ambassador Gul's, seeking some unspoken reassurance. The slight nod he received in return was a subtle signal, yet Masoud's hesitation lingered palpably in the air. Nava watched this exchange carefully, fully aware of the gravity that cloaked their conversation. The weight of disclosing sensitive information in such a gathering was not lost on her. In this room, knowledge was as dangerous as it was powerful, and even the most trivial detail could transform into a lethal tool in the hands of those like Colonel Salmani.

With a measured breath, Masoud broke the silence, his voice steady but underscored with the seriousness of the revelation. "Some money is missing from a Hezbollah feeder account," he announced, his eyes scanning the faces encircling the table. "It was meant to buy arms and other equipment. We believe Yasin Haddad appropriated and used it for some other purpose."

The statement hung in the air, a potent admixture of accusation and uncertainty. Nava could sense the ripple of tension that coursed through the room, the weight of Masoud's words settling like a shadow over the assembled officers. The implications were clear, and the potential ramifications vast, underscoring the delicate balance of trust and treachery that defined their clandestine world.

"That sounds as if he stole it," a deputy ambassador said with a little chuckle, as if the idea were so ridiculous that it must have been a misunderstading.

"Stole? How did this happen?" Salmani demanded.

Masoud turned to Nava and held out his palm, indicating that she was the one best positioned to explain.

13

"Prior to the ceasefire, we were flying arms and equipment for Hezbollah into Damascus, splitting them up into smaller loads and transporting them by land into Lebanon," she said. "But for the past year, we've been using intermediaries."

"Why?" Salmani queried, his tone dripping with incredulity, as if the notion was utterly absurd.

Before she could respond, the IRGC Major put a hand up to stop her.

"Apologies," he began, his tone shifting to one of formal introduction. "I'm Major Aydin Khadem."

The offer of his hand, extended toward her, momentarily caught Nava off guard. Such egalitarian manners were rare and distinctly Western, not typically associated with IRGC officers. Yet, as their hands met, the gesture bridged the divide of their respective worlds.

"You have the Hezbollah account?" Major Khadem inquired, his curiosity plain.

"I do," Nava confirmed, her response concise.

His reaction was subtle—a lift of the eyebrows, signaling a grudging respect that did not go unnoticed, even drawing a characteristic eyeroll from Salmani.

Nava elaborated on the operational nuances. "We'vce begun using middlemen for several reasons," she explained, "primarily to maintain plausible deniability. It prevents the Israelis from accusing us of violating the ceasefire by directly supplying Hezbollah with lethal aid."

"Credible deniability," Khadem echoed, his nod conveying a clear understanding of the strategy.

"And the Syrians?" he probed further.

"We haven't communicated this to them," Nava disclosed. "The Syrians used to collect hefty fees for transit and transportation, which we've ceased to pay. After Israel's last engagement with Hezbollah,

Syria's lack of direct support led some within Hezbollah to suspect that Damascus might forsake them for a favorable deal with
Israel—one involving the Golan Heights."

Salmani couldn't resist adding his perspective. "Assad is merely
seeking to ingratiate himself with the Great Satan," he asserted, his
voice laced with disdain. "He would never forsake his support for
Hezbollah."

"Nevertheless," Gul said. "We need to be sure we can supply
Hezbollah without Syrian help."

"So... You provided Hezbollah some money and Yasin Haddad...
what?" asked Khadem. "Ran off with it?"

"The money initially went to Haddad's shell company in Dubai,"
Nava replied. "Then to about ten other shell companies. After that,
we lost track."

"And you think this has something to do with Abu Faysal getting
killed last night?" Khadem asked.

"Haddad has been completely out of contact for weeks," Nava
told him. "But both Haddad and Abu Faysal had been taking extra
measures to conceal their movements for months. We haven't been
able to contact them directly and we haven't gotten any answers out of
Hezbollah leadership, except to say that they're just being cautious."

Hooman finally spoke up, saying, "We do have intelligence, and
I must stress this is from a very sensitive source... We know that the
Israelis can eavesdrop on many Hezbollah cellular telephone calls."

"Many?" Khadem asked. "Not all?"

"Apparently, certain telephones are more difficult than others," he
said. "But if they know the numbers, they can also get geolocation data
within a square kilometer, even if the phone is switched off."

Nava heard gasps from the ambassador's staff.

15

"We passed this information to Hezbollah weeks ago," Nava told them.

"INFERNO?" Gul asked, using the cryptonym of the Israeli source.

Hooman nodded.

"Have we seen any activity in the South that would suggest preparations for an Israeli offensive?" Gul asked.

"No, Mr. Ambassador," Hooman replied.

"Because you're not looking hard enough," a fuming Salmani shot back. "We've been saying all along – the Jews will never keep the ceasef—"

"Forgive me, Colonel," Major Khadem interjected with a measure of deference that seemed almost out of place in the tension-filled room, effectively halting Salmani's burgeoning diatribe. "This context is quite unfamiliar to me. May I pose a question?"

"Of course," Salmani conceded, his response unexpectedly mild.

Nava found the interaction peculiar. Salmani's usual impatience with interruptions, especially from those ranked below him, was notorious. Yet, his reaction was markedly different this time.

"What can you tell us about Abu Faysal?" Major Khadem directed his inquiry towards Nava, signaling a shift in the discussion's focus.

"As Masoud elaborated earlier," Nava began, anchoring her response in the facts previously laid out, "Abu Faysal was a key figure within the Beqaa Valley, aligning with Hezbollah shortly after its inception. He has been instrumental in developing the military wing into an effective fighting force."

Khadem delved deeper, shifting the conversation towards a more nuanced territory. "What about his politics?"

"Abu Faysal wasn't outspoken about his political views," Nava replied. "Of course, Shiite nationalism is common in Hezbollah; but he was among the few who endeavored to extend its influence beyond sectarian lines and appeal to a broader Lebanese demographic."

Intrigued, Khadem probed further. "If I were to ask for a name, the first that comes to mind, in response to 'Who killed Abu Faysal?' what would you say?"

Again, Salmani couldn't resist interjecting. "Isn't it obvious?" he scoffed, a harsh laugh betraying his contempt. Slamming a palm onto the table for emphasis, he declared, "The Zionists were targeting them, and we must respond."

Nava, undeterred by Salmani's assertion, countered sharply. "This is Lebanon, Colonel," she retorted, her words laced with a mix of frustration and resolve. "Navigating the layers of complexity and ambiguity is part of the terrain here. If that's beyond your grasp, perhaps this isn't the best posting for you."

Salmani's reaction was immediate and visceral. He straightened with such force that it seemed as if an electric current had jolted through him. His eyes narrowed into a glare directed at Nava, the intensity of his gaze palpable across the table. The hand he had slammed down now clenched into a fist, a physical manifestation of his simmering anger. Nava, for her part, struggled to maintain a professional demeanor, the corners of her mouth twitching in suppressed amusement at Salmani's theatrical display of outrage.

Out of the corner of her eye, she noticed Major Khadem's discreet attempt to mask his own amusement, his gaze fixed on his lap as if the answer to some profound question lay there. Nava braced herself, anticipating a scathing retort or a formal reprimand from Salmani, perhaps even an audacious move to dismiss her from the meeting for her boldness.

However, before the tension could escalate further, Ambassador Gul intervened with a gesture that seemed to physically separate the brewing conflict between Nava and Salmani. "Let's all just take a breath," he urged, his voice a calm amidst the storm, holding his hands in the air as if to push them from one another.

Salmani's response was reluctant, his glare lingering on Nava with undisguised animosity before finally acquiescing to Gul's command, his fist slowly uncurling as a sign of grudging compliance.

Gul then shifted the focus to a matter of graver importance. "Tehran is proceeding with the belief that the Zionist regime has violated the ceasefire," he disclosed. "They've asked me to provide them with options for retaliation."

The weight of his words hung heavily in the room, a somber reminder of the potential for escalation and the fragile peace at stake. Nava's mind raced through the likely scenarios: rocket attacks into Israel, ambushes against Israeli forces—each action inevitably leading to harsh retaliation. The cycle of violence, she feared, would resume in full force, plunging Beirut once more into chaos and conflict.

Gul, acknowledging the complexity of the situation, inquired about the timeframe needed to investigate the alternative theories they had discussed. Masoud's estimation of a month was met with Salmani's incredulous reaction, a testament to the urgency and pressure they faced.

"I can give you a week," Gul stated, a compromise that underscored the critical nature of their task. Beyond that, the decision would be out of their hands, leaving them to navigate the consequences of actions set in motion far beyond the confines of their meeting room.

Chapter Four

J ust outside the conference room, Major Khadem caught up with Nava before she could make her way to the elevator. He invited her for a coffee in his office—a proposal she was wont to decline, given the urgency of gathering information on Abu Faysal's assassination. However, Masoud's directive to accept the invitation was clear and non-negotiable.

"He's a protégé of Soleimani's," Hooman murmured discreetly into her ear, his words carrying a weight of significance as the elevator doors parted. The ride to the third floor, where the IRGC offices were housed, passed in a charged silence, each floor's passing marking their approach to a realm where the influence of Qasem Soleimani loomed large. Soleimani, a figure of considerable strategic and tactical acumen, was widely regarded as a potential future leader of the IRGC's elite Qods Force, a testament to his prowess and influence in the corridors of power in Tehran.

Upon exiting the elevator, Masoud's parting words, "Meet me on top afterwards," hung in the air as Nava accompanied Khadem. Their conversation during the walk to his office was light, touching on his recent arrival in Lebanon and his family, contrasting sharply with Nava's own status—a personal detail she disclosed with a hint of resignation.

The opulence of the IRGC's domain, far surpassing that of Beirut Station, always astonished and annoyed Nava. The disparity was evident in the allocation of private offices, a luxury afforded to each IRGC officer, including Khadem, whose spacious office stood as a stark reminder of their resources and influence.

Settling into the relative comfort of Khadem's office, the conversation took a turn towards the ideological. Over cups of aromatic Arabic coffee, Khadem sought to dispel the stereotype of IRGC officers as unyielding hardliners. "I just wanted you to know that we're not all knuckle-draggers," he stated, signaling his alignment with the Islamic Republic's policies while simultaneously distancing himself from the more extreme caricatures attributed to its supporters.

As their conversation unfolded, Nava's attention was drawn to a book on Khadem's desk, "The Rise and Fall of Great Powers" by Paul Kennedy, its cover adorned with a globe and a sequence of national flags depicting the shifting sands of global dominance. The U.S. flag was positioned at the zenith of power, yet on the brink of descent, followed by the British flag, symbolizing a prior decline. Notably, the Japanese flag was depicted in ascent, but Khadem had taken the liberty of adding a small Iranian flag trailing just behind Japan's, a hopeful amendment to the narrative of global power dynamics.

Nava couldn't help but smile at the sight, a gesture partly for Khadem's benefit should he be observing her reaction. Inwardly, she harbored reservations about the optimism such an addition implied. The narrative of the U.S.'s decline had been a recurring theme among its adversaries, and even within its own borders, echoing through history from its inception and resurfacing with every perceived failure, including the recent fiasco in Somalia. Moreover, the book's pre-1991 publication date cast its prognostications in a dubious light, given Japan's economic struggles in the years that followed. Nava considered

Iran's potential ascent contingent on a delicate balancing act with the West, a nuanced dance of cooperation and contention, particularly regarding regional conflicts and occupations.

Khadem's demeanor throughout their discussion was effortlessly engaging, a blend of charisma and calculation that Nava found not entirely disagreeable. As they delved into the complexities of Lebanon's political landscape, she sensed Khadem was adeptly gauging her perspectives on a range of contentious issues—from the Syrian presence to the fragile ceasefire with Israel and the intricacies of Hezbollah's internal dynamics. His approach seemed to mirror her own method of engaging sources, a strategic empathy designed to foster a sense of security and openness. This tacit acknowledgment of shared understanding, of being truly listened to, had a disarming effect, encouraging a candor that might otherwise remain guarded.

"Look, I know there is a lot of... collegial rivalry between our organizations back home," Khadem began, acknowledging the unspoken tension that often marked the interactions between their respective agencies.

Nava offered a polite smile but chose not to engage further on the topic. The fundamental divide between their organizations was no secret; the IRGC reported directly to the unelected Supreme Leader, whereas the MOIS was under the control of the popularly elected President. This structural difference underscored the complexities of their cooperation.

"I want to leave all that back in Tehran," Khadem expressed earnestly. "Out here, we're two intelligence officers serving the Islamic Republic."

As they spoke, Nava felt the discreet buzz of her pager against her side, a silent intrusion that drew her hand to the device hidden beneath her clothing. She glanced at the screen with practiced nonchalance, noting the code '78920' without letting her gaze linger, though her mind raced to place its significance.

Khadem, meanwhile, shifted the conversation to a more personal terrain. "I understand your mother was Lebanese," he remarked, his tone casual but his scrutiny evident.

"She was," Nava confirmed, acutely aware of his watchful gaze. Though his approach was ostensibly friendly, Nava sensed an underlying motive, a desire to glean insights about her under the guise of casual conversation. Her experience in the field had honed her awareness of how seemingly innocuous exchanges could serve as fertile ground for intelligence gathering, reminding her that in their line of work, information was always more than mere conversation—it was a tool, and sometimes, a weapon.

"You've been here for, what... seven years?" Khadem's question seemed casual but was laced with implication.

"Correct," Nava affirmed, her guard up, sensing the conversational minefield she was navigating.

"You must have a deep affection for Lebanon," he ventured, laying the groundwork for a probe she anticipated with ease.

"Not as much as my love for Iran," she countered smoothly, mentally chiding him for the transparent attempt to get her to admit to dual loyalties.

"Do you visit Iran often?" he pressed.

This was another calculated move. Since her last trip to Iran had been primarily to finalize her divorce, her visits had been anything but regular. Khadem, like many IRGC officers, likely harbored an idealized vision of Iran—a nation unified in piety and submission to authority, vastly removed from the complex reality many of its citizens experienced.

"Not as often as I'd like," she offered diplomatically.

Khadem's polite smile marked the end of his probing, at least for the moment. He then shifted the discussion to a more professional matter. "Look, Nava... The IRGC is highly invested in the results of your investigation into Abu Faysal's murder. The ramifications could significantly impact Qods Force activities here."

"I understand the stakes," Nava acknowledged, maintaining her composure.

"I've discussed this with Colonel Salmani, and we believe the investigation would benefit from my involvement," Khadem revealed, suggesting an unexpected collaboration.

"That's a matter for Ambassador Gul," Nava redirected.

Khadem's response revealed a hint of frustration. "The problem is, the ambassador, much like those in Tehran, prefers to pit us against each other. You know? What I'm proposing is more of an... informal partnership."

Nava glanced at her watch, signaling the conversation's end. "I'm due elsewhere, Major. It was a pleasure meeting you, and thank you for the coffee."

"Can we count on your cooperation?" he inquired, rising to see her out.

"I'll discuss it with Masoud," she assured him, noncommittally.

"I was hoping to arrange this directly with you," Khadem pushed, seeking a more personal commitment.

"Beirut Station operates with a certain level of formality," Nava stated as she opened the door to leave, her polite refusal clear. "I'm sure you can understand."

But Khadem's displeased expression told her that he didn't.

Chapter Five

E ight years ago, on the cusp of marriage, Nava made the decision
to quit smoking. If her divorce had a silver lining, she mused, it
was no longer needing to conceal a vice she so enjoyed. Despite being
acutely aware of its health risks, she found a certain solace in smoking. The rooftop sessions at the embassy with Masoud had become a
valued sanctuary. There, amidst the panoramic embrace of the city's
eastern sprawl and the vast expanse of the Mediterranean to the west,
she found her reprieve. This spot was unique, allowing her to momentarily forsake her hijab without facing censure and offering privacy
from the omnipresent surveillance—a haven for speaking freely, away
from the prying ears that monitored their own.

"You saw your father while you were in Tehran?" Masoud asked
her.

"Briefly," she answered. "As always."

"How was he?"

She shrugged and lit her cigarette.

Years ago, in a different chapter of her life, her father and Masoud
had shared a posting in Paris. Back then, Nava's acquaintance with
Masoud was cursory at best; but over the last seven years, he had
evolved from a mere colleague of her father's into an exceptional mentor to her. The enduring friendship between Masoud and her father

was a fact Nava had seldom pondered. In her eyes, her father was a solitary figure, the type who traversed life's complexities without the companionship of friends.

"Oh..." she said, opening her bag and beginning to rummage through it. "I forgot... He gave me something before I left."

She retrieved a small wooden box and held it up for him with a wry smile.

"Open it," he told her.

"I can't. At least not yet."

"Why not?"

"It's a puzzle box," she said, sliding a panel out and putting it back in place.

"Ah ..." he said, clearly more amused than she was.

"My father got them for me all the time when I was young," she told him, dropping it back into her bag. "He used to put sweets inside them for me and little notes telling me how clever I was to figure it out."

"Sounds very nice."

"Of course, he'd reuse them from time to time," she said. "When he thought I'd forgotten how to open it."

"Would you?" he asked. "Forget, I mean?"

She smiled a little and said, "I pretended to."

Masoud puffed his pipe a while before abruptly changing the subject.

"What did you think of Khadem?" he asked her.

"He's a slick one."

Masoud grunted and said, "Don't let the charm fool you. Any protégé of Soleimani is bound to be as ruthless as he is."

"It's a good thing he's on our side, then," she said.

"Khadem is counterintelligence."

As she glanced at him, Masoud's eyebrows lifted briefly—a subtle reaction that, to Nava, seemed insufficient for the gravity of his revelation. Her British peers back at Oxford would have described Masoud as a "cool customer," a man with a calm disdain for unnecessary drama. This made his marked sense of urgency earlier that day all the more striking, a deviation from his usual demeanor that hinted at the seriousness of the situation.

Turning to gaze over the Beirut skyline, Masoud allowed Nava a moment to process his words. Before them, the city sprawled in a chaotic tapestry of architecture. Sand and limestone high-rises jostled for space with flat-roofed yellow and brown buildings, their ramshackle appearance belying the vibrant life within. Observing this mosaic, Nava felt the pulsating energy of Beirut seep into her very being, a reminder of why she held this city so dear. Yet, amidst this love, there lurked a dread at the thought of seeing its streets and buildings once again marred by the ravages of conflict.

"Why is he here?" she asked Masoud.

He took a handkerchief from his pocket and wiped the beads of sweat from his shiny bald head with a shrug.

"Do they think there's a mole in Beirut Station or something?" she asked.

Masoud's response was tinged with resignation. "I can't claim to know their thoughts, Nava," he admitted, his gaze drifting towards the distant eastern horizon, a soft curse in Farsi escaping him. "Mole or otherwise, the IRGC will undoubtedly seize any opportunity to wield whatever they discover as a cudgel against us, especially given the missing Hezbollah funds. Our perceived alignment with President Khatami's reformist agenda only sharpens the divide, casting us against the hardliners in IRGC."

"Do they intend to target Khatami directly?" Nava ventured further.

"Their aims are political, of that I have no doubt," Masoud affirmed, the smoke from his pipe curling into the air as he spoke. "The real question is the lengths to which they're willing to go to undermine him."

The tone of his voice carried a weight of concern and conflict, underscoring the gravity of the situation.

"During my meeting with Khadem, I received a message from a source," Nava disclosed, shifting the conversation towards a potentially significant breakthrough. "It seems I might have a lead on Yasin Haddad's whereabouts."

Masoud's attention snapped to her, the urgency of the moment etched on his face. "Where?" he asked urgently, the prospect of actionable intelligence momentarily cutting through the morass of their political entanglements.

"I think he's in Ansar."

"Ansar? What's in Ansar?"

"A safe house," she said. "It's off Hezbollah's books ... The ones they've shown us, at least. We're calling it 'The Gulag.' Haddad's the only one we know who uses it. Most of the time, it's empty." She held up the pager and showed him the code. "But this means it's in use right now."

"You need to set up surveillance on it," he said. "Immediately."

"Immediately?" she echoed him. "As in ... today?"

Chapter Six

N ava ferried two MOIS technicians in Dasia down Route 51 before veering east onto the A5. Within the hour, they arrived at their destination on the outskirts of Ansar, the Hezbollah safe house they codenamed the Gulag.

Like many towns in southern Lebanon, Ansar was predominantly Shiite. Although not exactly a bastion for Hezbollah, the town was nonetheless peppered with sympathizers and active members of the group. Aware of the potential for local informants, Nava recognized the urgency of establishing an observation point swiftly and covertly. She managed to secure a rental for two hundred thousand Lebanese pounds—approximately 130 U.S. dollars—for an apartment offering an unobstructed view of the Gulag. The space was modest and its antiquated refrigerator emitted decades worth of odors, but its vantage point was unparalleled, save perhaps for the building's roof.

Upon arrival at the nondescript four-story building, the team waited in Dasia for Dhuhr, the midday prayer, to commence. Silence enveloped them, punctuated only by the distant sounds of daily life in Ansar—children's laughter, the communal chatter of returning shoppers, and the camaraderie of men sharing jokes and cigarettes. Despite the vibrancy of the town's routine, a palpable tension lingered, heightened by the scrutinizing glances of passersby. Nava's attention was fixed on the mosque's minaret, her focus so intense she half-believed she could detect the electric buzz of the awaiting loudspeaker.

"Should we—" Hassan, one of the technicians began, but Nava quickly shushed him.

Observing the townsfolk's nonchalant demeanor, undisturbed by the impending call to prayer, Nava wrestled with her expectations. The rhythm of daily prayers was a constant, yet today, of all days, her anticipation seemed misplaced. As the second hand on her watch swept forward, marking the relentless passage of time without the expected call, Nava felt her impatience grow. The minutes ticked by—one minute past noon, then two, inching towards three—each moment amplifying the tension of their wait.

"Allāhu 'akbar ... 'Allāhu 'akbar ... 'ašhadu 'an lā 'ilāha 'illā -llāh ..."

The streets swiftly emptied, leaving Nava and her team an unobstructed path. They got the dolly on loan from the building's superintendent to transport the styrofoam-insulated metal boxes from Dasia's trunk up to the rented apartment. A young girl, curiosity evident in her gaze, watched from a slightly ajar door as they moved their equipment inside. Nava held onto the hope that this child would remain their sole observer—the stakes were high, as espionage among allies carried risks even greater than watching foes.

Inside, the technicians quickly set up the main camera on a tripod, positioning it to overlook the Gulag's entrance from their vantage point. Connecting it to a monitor, Nava watched the scene come alive on the screen.

"Nice shot," she commended. "They won't spot the camera, will they?"

"Not unless they're looking very closely," Caspar, one of the technicians, assured her before. "Boss, do you mind handing me that black sheet in the box?"

Nava sifted through the equipment, found the sheet, and tossed it to him. Together, the technicians discreetly concealed the setup, ensuring only the lens remained exposed. As Caspar adjusted the shades to minimize visibility and Hassan donned headphones to operate a directional microphone, Nava's gaze returned to the Hezbollah militants absorbed in their prayers.

"I can catch the sounds from the street," Hassan reported, "but that's it."

"Nothing from inside at all?" Nava pressed, her disappointment palpable.

Hassan shook his head, and Nava silently considered her next steps. She needed to compensate her informant, a teenager with an affinity for Manchester United, who had provided the tip. This intel had revealed the Gulag's reactivation after months of dormancy, a fact they might have missed without his keen observation. Visual surveillance was a start, yet without the ability to eavesdrop on internal conversations, their intelligence would be incomplete. Nava resolved to delve deeper, understanding that the real task lay in piercing the walls of the Gulag to uncover the secrets held within.

Chapter Seven

C LOCKWORK was a good source, however skittish. Barely
nineteen, his gangly frame and youthful appearance belied the
gravity of his role as driver and sometime courier for Hezbollah General Secretary Sayyid Hassan Nasrallah, granting him proximity, if not
direct access, to the organization's most closely guarded secrets. Nava
couldn't help but think that his attempt to appear older, marked by a
mustache ill-suited to his youthful face, only underscored his youth.

Ensuring she wasn't being followed or monitored took both time
and diligence, a necessary precaution before she could safely venture
to an apartment block housing an MOIS safe house known as "The
Baker's." As she neared the building, her path intersected with that of
a young woman pushing a stroller. Too late to alter her course and too
crucial a moment to shy away from, Nava steeled herself. She lowered
her gaze, the weight of her own private grief pressing down on her,
until the moment of passing was nearly at hand. Lifting her head,
she mustered a warm smile and exchanged brief pleasantries with the
woman. The encounter, fleeting as it was, tugged sharply at the scars
left by her infertility diagnosis. The presence of the child, unseen and
unheard within the stroller, invoked a sense of diminishment in Nava,
a stark reminder of her longing and sense of loss.

"Did anyone follow you here?"

The voice gave Nava a startle. She drew a sharp breath and turned in the speaker's direction with clenched fists. CLOCKWORK's familiar face emerged from the shadow of the building, eyes darting and probing this small part of the quiet neighborhood of Geitawi. She breathed a heavy sigh of relief and silently reprimanded herself for letting something as silly as a baby distract her.

The safe house here wasn't called the Baker's for any relationship with or proximity to a bakery. It was chosen at random, as cryptonyms that regularly changed usually were. But "CLOCKWORK" wasn't random. He was one of the few people in all of Lebanon who strictly kept to a schedule. As early as she was for their meetings, CLOCKWORK was usually even earlier. Even with the doubling back and other techniques she employed to ensure she hadn't been followed, she was still over five minutes early, and he'd been here waiting for her.

"Did anyone follow you?" he asked again, and she noticed his voice was tenser than usual.

"No!" she said in a hushed voice, but he continued to look around the neighborhood as if her answer didn't satisfy him. "If someone had, I wouldn't have shown up."

"Of course, of course," he muttered, rubbing the back of his neck.

"Were *you* followed?" she asked, unlocking the front door to the apartment building. "Did you follow the protocol that I—"

He mumbled something, causing her to stop and ask him to repeat it.

"I think I lost him," he said; and before she could ask who, he slipped past her through the door.

CLOCKWORK typically found his calm once the tea was brewed and he was indulging in some ba'alewah from the café near Nava's apartment. However, this evening, he remained distinctly unsettled, fidgeting as he sipped his tea and nibbled on the sweet pastry. Nava observed the rhythmic bounce of his leg, a clear sign of his inner turmoil, as his eyes fixated on the void between the kitchen and the door.

Breaking the tense silence, he confessed, "I don't know if I can do this anymore."

Nava leaned back and adopted a posture of ease. "We don't usually start off with such heavy statements," she remarked, hoping her calmness would be contagious. "Is this about the secretary-general? Do you think he knows about our arrangement?"

"What? No! No ... It's the Syrians! Don't you know?" he blurted out, his agitation palpable.

"The Syrians? What about them?" Nava pressed, her curiosity piqued as she took a measured sip of her tea.

Exasperation washed over CLOCKWORK's youthful features as he revealed, "They killed Abu Faysal! The Syrian Mukhabarat."

The term Mukhabarat, referring to the General Intelligence Directorate, was a common name for intelligence agencies across several Arab nations, including Syria. Nava's understanding of the intricate ties between Iran, Syria, and their operations in Lebanon was thorough. She was well acquainted with a Syrian GID agent, a man she knew as "Rafiq." Despite Syria's hesitance to stick its neck out and support Hezbollah during Israeli offensives, their collaboration remained significant.

CLOCKWORK had always been a reliable informant to Nava, never knowingly deceiving her. Yet, she was acutely aware that even the most trusted sources could err, driven by misinterpretation, haste to judgment, or the simple human penchant for exaggeration on topics beyond their grasp.

"Nasrallah said this?" she asked.

"No one needed to *say* it, Sabi," he answered, using the name by which he knew Nava. "But everyone *knows*. You know Abu Faysal never slept in the same place two nights in a row for the last six months? Even Nasrallah didn't know where he was at least half of the time."

"Alright... so tell me why the Syrian *Mukhabarat* would want Abu Faysal dead."

At the mention of the Syrian intelligence agency, CLOCKWORK visibly tensed, the name alone seeming to instill fear. "Abu Faysal was convinced the conflict with Israel was nearing its end," he revealed. "He believed that once the Zionists retreated, Hezbollah's utility to Syria wouldn't last much longer. We'd shift from allies to rivals for influence in Lebanon, and Syria would not hesitate to act against us."

"And the Shura Council?" Nava inquired, referencing Hezbollah's decision-making body.

"Losing Abu Faysal would have been a significant blow," CLOCK-WORK explained, his nerves seemingly settling as he delved into the rationale. "Nasrallah and the Council feared you might expel Abu Faysal from Hezbollah to maintain the alliance with Syria. Unity in our struggle against Israel was easy, but the ceasefire is changing things. The council turned a deaf ear to Abu Faysal's warnings about Syria, yet..."

His voice faded, leaving his sentence hanging as he lost himself in thought once more.

"What changed?" Nava pressed.

Puzzled by her question, CLOCKWORK hesitated, "What do you mean?"

"If, like you said, the council was ignoring Abu Faysal," she clarified. "What prompted the Syrians to act against him now?"

CLOCKWORK's response was uncertain, "I'm not sure," he admitted. "But maybe... *maybe* the Council started listening."

———————

A tiring but fruitless day tapping her sources for information about Abu Faysal's assassination preceded an evening full of exhaustion without sleep. Nava laid flat on her back in bed, staring at the ceiling with CLOCKWORK's words from the night before running through her head. The more she thought about how Syria failed to come to Hezbollah's aid last spring, during the fiercest Israeli offensive in years, the more it made sense that the Shura Council was reconsidering its reliance on Syria as a transit point for its supplies from Iran. If Syria was not helping them, it was just another occupying power.

She felt almost relieved when her cellular phone rang. It was nearly 11:00.

"Boss?" she heard Caspar's voice call into her ear. He was on nights at the observation point they had set up across from the Gulag.

"I'm here," she answered.

"You'd better get here when you can," he told her. "Something's happened."

———————

As the clock approached midnight, the streets of Ansar descended into a profound silence, the kind that spoke of anticipation and unease. The secretive nature of Hezbollah's operations never fully shielded the local populace from the repercussions. Whether through direct actions or the inevitable Israeli responses, the lives of Ansar's residents were intertwined with a fragility born of constant uncertainty.

Nava's frustration was palpable when she returned to find Caspar, defying the late hour and the exhaustion of a twelve-hour shift, alert and buzzing with an energy that clashed with her desire for rest. The prospect of retreating to the solitude of her apartment held little appeal, yet the need for rest was undeniable. Her own weariness made Caspar's usual vibrancy, often a source of motivation, feel overwhelming and tiresome tonight. As she set about preparing tea for herself, Caspar busied himself with the technical setup, adjusting one of the trio of video recorders linked to their surveillance camera, his focus undiminished by the hour.

"What exactly are you working on?" Nava inquired, her curiosity piqued despite the fatigue clouding her senses.

Caspar, absorbed in his task, gestured towards the setup hidden beneath the black tarp. "We're actually monitoring through three cameras here," he began, his voice carrying a hint of excitement. "There's a standard telescopic lens, a night vision, and a thermal imager. Here, let me show you."

As he settled back into his chair, Nava's attention was drawn to the monitor as it flickered on, revealing an image quite unlike any regular surveillance footage. Displayed were two human-like forms, defined by their warmth against the cooler backdrop, each with a pair of small, bright dots that seemed to hover nearby. The screen's corner also featured a timestamp marking the scene at around 10:00 PM.

"What am I looking at here?" sha asked just before a yawn escaped her.

"Sorry," Caspar responded quickly. "This is a view of the front courtyard. Let me switch to the standard lens for a clearer picture."

With a press of a button, the scene momentarily disappeared into darkness, only to be replaced by a dimly lit view of the Gulag's entrance. Now, two figures could be discerned moving near the gate, their presence marked by the faint glow of red from their cigarettes. The surrounding features—the building, its enclosing wall, and the gate—came into sharper focus.

"Those figures are guards," Caspar pointed out, indicating the barely visible men on the monitor. "Their dark clothing makes them hard to see, but those cigarettes are pretty clear."

Switching back to the thermal view transformed the scene once more, rendering the guards as luminous figures against the night, the tips of their cigarettes now blazing points of light in the thermal spectrum.

"Keep watching," Caspar urged, advancing the footage.

The guards lingered by the gate, the monotony of their vigil broken only by the casual drift of smoke. Nava, still uncertain of the significance, watched as the timer neared 10:30. Just then, an expansive white shape emerged on the screen, moving deliberately towards the guards, eventually positioning itself squarely between them.

"That's a car arriving," Caspar told her, shifting the footage back to the standard view for a clearer perspective. As shadows began to detach themselves from the vehicle's interior, Nava found herself leaning in, her gaze sharpening as she peered over Caspar's shoulder. She watched as three doors snapped shut in succession, leaving the rear passenger-side door ajar. A guard leaned into the car, withdrawing a figure obscured by a dark void where the head should be. Caspar froze the frame at that moment.

"If it weren't for the hood, we'd likely have a clear view of the face," he remarked, his finger tapping against the screen where a face might have been visible. "We have to be looking at a prisoner."

Switching the display back to thermal imaging, the detailed contours faded, leaving only the vague outlines of the scene.

"The thermal imaging doesn't penetrate the hood," Nava observed, a hint of frustration in her voice. "We still can't identify them."

"Right," Caspar agreed, "but watch this..."

As they maneuvered the prisoner towards the door, the shape appeared to slim down on the screen. Caspar again paused the video, highlighting a profile view of the figure.

"Look at this silhouette," he directed, his voice subdued. Nava leaned in, her eyes narrowing as she focused on the part of the image he indicated—a protrusion on the figure's front.

It took a moment, but realization dawned on her with a clarity that made her question her initial oversight.

"Breasts," she whispered, the word barely audible.

"The prisoner is a woman," Caspar confirmed softly.

Nava's attention was unwavering, the revelation on the screen igniting a flurry of thoughts. A captured Israeli soldier? Who else could the prisoner be? Despite her exhaustion, the speculation coursing through her mind was invigorating.

"What are you up to, Haddad?" she murmured to the empty room, half-expecting the silence that would have met her question even if Haddad were present. Suddenly, a sharp noise shattered the quiet, causing her to snap to attention, her body tensing.

"It's just the tea kettle," Caspar said, noticing her reaction.

A chuckle escaped her. Still, her pulse raced, leaving her senses sharpened and body primed for action.

"Boss... What's going on?" Caspar inquired, his voice laced with concern and confusion.

Nava could only offer a silent shrug, her mind still grappling with the implications of their discovery and the myriad questions it raised.

Chapter
Eight

M asoud preferred to host morning briefings at his expansive residence in Dahieh, a suburb just south of Beirut. Given the choice, Nava favored it to the formal confines of the embassy, not least for its proximity to her favorite café, which opened early and served her cherished mint tea just the way she liked it: piping hot. This morning, she arrived armed with a steaming cup in one hand and an envelope filled with surveillance prints from the Gulag in the other. She anticipated the warm welcome of Masoud's wife, Samira; but was met with Masoud's stern countenance framing the doorway.

"Where's Samira?" Nava inquired, momentarily taken aback.

"Good morning," he replied, his tone a gentle chide on the manners befitting any greeting.

Chastened, she echoed the salutation as she entered. "Good morning. Apologies. It was a long night."

"Samira is visiting her mother in Iran," Masoud informed her, shutting the door and leading the way to his office.

"Don't you lock your door?" she asked him.

"Not when I'm home. Why?"

"You're a spy, Masoud," she pointed out, a mix of concern and incredulity in her tone.

Masoud's response was a soft chuckle and a dismissive wave of his hand. Concious of the gravity of the documents she carried, Nava took it upon herself to secure the door behind them.

Masoud's home office, a stark contrast to the embassy's austerity, boasted both space and comfort. A majestic desk sat before an east-facing Palladian window, draped with sheer curtains that filtered the morning light to cast a serene glow across the room without unwanted heat. Masoud could often be found behind this desk with pipe in hand while visitors were invited to relax in two plush leather chairs set before him—so comfortable, in fact, that Nava often joked about the risk of dozing off during prolonged discussions. Hooman had already claimed one of these coveted seats before she arrived.

"Hooman was just saying that he shares your doubts," Masoud said as he tamped some tobacco into his pipe's bowl.

"Doubts?" Nava asked, turning to her colleague.

"I don't think the Israelis killed Abu Faysal," Hooman said, his elbows resting comfortably on the chair's arms and his long, slender fingers tented in front of him. "Not just because they're not preparing for retaliations, but they're actually tasking assets to find out what happened to him."

"You've confirmed this with INFERNO?" Masoud asked him, referring to his prized source.

"Both human and electronic sources," Hooman answered him. "It *could* be a deception, but they just seem to be trying to figure out what's going on."

Masoud lit his pipe and raised his eyebrows.

"For what we're paying him, I expect more concrete insights," he said.

"Speaking of financial matters..." Hooman said, shifting in his chair.

"*Mashallah!*" Masoud said with a shake of his head. "How much now?"

"Through the end of the year, including the safe house—"

"How much, Hooman?" an impatient Masoud interrupted.

"Another fifty thousand, USD," he said.

The response elicited a barely audible curse from Masoud, followed by a weary sigh.

"Alright, fine," Masoud conceded, albeit with a palpable sense of reluctance as he busied himself with the papers on his desk, signaling his grudging acquiescence.

"What about the Syrians?" Masoud asked, looking back and forth between them.

She glanced at Hooman, hoping that he'd proffer an answer before she had to; but she saw him looking back at her, perhaps with the same hope.

"What about the Syrians?!" Masoud asked, obviously annoyed for having to repeat the question.

"Do you mean check to see if the Syrians know anything?" Nava asked him. "Or to see if they... if they did it?"

"Both," Masoud said. "Either."

"They didn't have a good relationship with Abu Faysal," Nava said. "Some would even say slightly hostile."

This revelation piqued Hooman's interest, prompting a surprised, "Really?"

"Source?" Masoud asked.

"CLOCKWORK," Nava confirmed, the significance of her informant not lost on Masoud, who acknowledged the importance of the information with a raised eyebrow. "Approaching them could easily be perceived as an accusation rather than a conversation, given their, um... history with car bombs as a method of expressing displeasure."

Masoud grunted and took a few puffs from his pipe.

"See what Al-Laqqis says about this," he told Nava, referring to her official liaison in Hezbollah.

"I heard you met with Khadem yesterday," Hooman said to Nava.

"I did," she said. "He's trying to muscle in on the Abu Faysal investigation, probably to make sure the Israelis are blamed no matter what."

Hooman gave a sardonic laugh and shook his head.

"IRGC Neanderthals," he said. "We should get the ambassador to send him back to Tehran."

"Try to play nice, Hooman," Masoud told him. "A pissed-off Khadem in Tehran might be more dangerous than a placated Khadem in Beirut. At least we can keep an eye on him while he's here."

"Are you certain who's keeping an eye on who in this situation?" he asked, and Masoud answered with a crooked smile. "You know well what kind of political animal the IRGC is, Masoud. He's here for political reasons. You need to stand up to him."

"I have been," Masoud assured him. "He already tried to get me to replace Nava. I already made it clear that I have absolute confidence in her. He seems to have given up... for now, at least."

Hooman nodded in recognition and appreciation. "Good to hear," he said.

"Enough time spent on them," Masoud said. "What have you got from the Gulag, Nava?"

She opened the large brown envelope and spread three enlarged photos from the surveillance footage on the desk in front of them. After she told them about the prisoner, Masoud set back in his chair and looked at the pictures warily, puffing on his pipe.

"It's rare that we get something this early into a surveillance," Hooman said. "But you believe this is important?"

"I do," she replied.

"What do you think it means?" he asked her.

"I think whatever Haddad is up to, he's doing his best to keep it from us."

Masoud tapped the image of the female prisoner and said, "We need to find out who this is and why Haddad is keeping her."

She sipped her tea and tried to gauge Masoud's mood. Like any intelligence officer, what her boss wanted more than anything was *information*. The perpetual desire for it was tempered only by the readiness to embrace the risks involved in uncovering it. Observing Masoud, with his thoughtful posture and the tension in his gaze fixed on the photographs, she sensed a willingness for a bold course of action, provided it promised to yield the crucial insights they sought.

"I have an idea," she said. "But I'll definitely need approval."

"Let's hear it," Hooman said.

"We passed Hezbollah the intel about the Israelis intercepting their cellular phone calls," she said.

"Sure."

"Can we use it as a reason to get them new cell phones – ones that we can use as microphones, even if they're not using them?"

Masoud leaned back, smoking his pipe as he took a moment to mull it over. Both his subordinated fixed their gazes upon him, awaiting his answer.

"Hmm," he said to Nava's frustration.

"Hmm, yes?" she asked. "Or hmm, no?"

"It's risky," he said.

"It may be the only way we can get sound from that house," she countered.

He looked to Hooman, who nodded back at him.

"Okay," Masoud said. "I'll see what I can do."

43

Chapter Nine

Nava's morning was spent chasing leads that bore little fruit, save for a visit to her uncle in the Lebanese Internal Security Forces, who spoke about the placement of the bomb that killed Abu Faysal—a detail that nagged at her.

"Israelis strike from above," he told her. "Sometimes at street level. That's because Hezbollah's security men always check under the carriage and hood. But this time the blast came from under the car."

"What does that tell you?" she asked him, and her uncle had sighed.

Though they were alone, he lowered his voice to just over a whisper. "It tells me whoever killed him was either extremely skilled," he said. "Or it was someone he trusted."

That was the highlight of her morning, for what it was worth.

In the afternoon, she had a meeting with her official liaison in Hezbollah, who was also the organization's treasurer. She'd have to bring up the missing funds that Haddad had withdrawn unless she got some explanation from Haddad himself. Just like the previous twenty or so times she had called, however, Haddad didn't answer.

Nava dreaded eating meals by herself, though she had grown accustomed to it ever since Farzin had left. Alone in her apartment, the void his absence created was far heavier than it was anywhere else in the city. She needed to move... and get new furniture. Everything here was to Farzin's taste, and she hated it—even the chair on which she sat to eat her *hashweh*. She stood up, holding the plate in one hand and her fork in the other, and looked at it. The ugly, gnarled piece of wood studded with iron and covered with a cushion in some hideous shade of yellow stared back at her. *Why even have an entire set?* She kicked it over, and it fell flat on its back with a dull thud and lingered there like an overturned turtle with its stubby, ugly limbs in the air. It was strange, but seeing it in that kind of distress somehow made her feel the slightest bit better.

She took a few more bites and strolled around, looking at the place with new eyes. It wasn't hers and Farzin's any longer, so why was she treating it as something other than what it was? Why was she living in the tomb of a dead marriage? Everything was evidence of the dominance Farzin formerly possessed over her as a husband. While all the stuff he liked and she hated was here, it was as if he still had power over her. She cleaned them, washed them, maintained them, and housed them; but she didn't want them.

She gently placed the plate she was using on the kitchen counter, grabbed one of its twins from the cabinet above, and smashed it on the tile floor. The sound of the shattering ceramic and the sight of the pieces shook her at first, but it felt good. She did it again, and again... One at a time – plates, bowls... and when the dishes ran out, the cups and glasses. One by one, like links in a chain, she broke them apart; grimacing, then screaming, and finally breaking down and sitting on the floor of her kitchen, staring with puffy and teary red eyes at the mess she'd made.

Hassan Al-Laqqis, not yet forty years of age, bore the countenance of a man sculpted by the relentless grind of war. With an education that polished his urbane sensibilities and a role pivotal to Hezbollah's veins of procurement and logistics, Al-Laqqis was as enigmatic as he was indispensable. His intricate dance around the fringes of Hezbollah's operational secrets made him an elusive yet invaluable font of knowledge. But, to Nava's chagrin, his revelations seemed always just shy of complete transparency.

Their rendezvous points were typically nestled within the labyrinth of Hezbollah's discreet sanctuaries in Dahieh. However, in need of a veil of anonymity away from prying Hezbollah ears, Nava opted for a divergence from their usual haunts. She chose a café in Hamra, nestled in a bustling street where the city's heartbeats were most audible. Enclosed by aged stone walls, the café's entrance was adorned with a mosaic of colorful tiles, each piece a testament to the rich cultural tapestry that was Lebanon. As Nava stepped inside, the aroma of freshly ground coffee beans mingled with the sweet scent of jasmine and tobacco from the sheeshas, enveloping her in a cloud of sensory delight.

Outside, the café's garden was an oasis of tranquility amidst the urban chaos. Lush green vines climbed the stone walls, and pots of blooming flowers added splashes of color to the verdant space. The outdoor tables were set under a canopy of grapevines, providing a shaded retreat where patrons could enjoy the gentle breeze and the occasional song of a hidden bird.

Nava settled at a table that offered a clear view of the entrance, yet was secluded enough to afford privacy. The garden around her buzzed with the subdued chatter of other guests, a background symphony to her swirling thoughts. She ordered an iced mint tea, the glass sweating in the warmth of the day, and fruit-flavored sheesha that arrived with a ceremonial flair. As she inhaled the fragrant smoke, she watched the life of Beirut unfold around her—a tableau of diversity and resilience.

Cloaked in a hijab and behind the anonymity of dark sunglasses, Nava navigated unwelcome advances with the grace of a seasoned diplomat, weaving a narrative of awaiting her husband's arrival to deter persistent young men.

Her pretense of engrossment in an article about a missing American diplomat served a dual purpose, masking her vigilant surveillance of the café's patrons. The specter of Israeli intelligence loomed large over the assassination of Abu Faysal, seeding Beirut with the potential presence of agents seeking information—or, just maybe, their next Hezbollah mark. Amidst the glances cast her way, discerning sinister intent from lustiness or idle curiosity proved a challenge, with the café's transient guests weaving a tapestry of motives and desires.

The sudden intrusion of her cell phone's ringtone, bearing the weight of her father's caller ID, sliced through the ambient hum of the café.

"Did you open your gift?" he asked her.

Gift ... What gift? That stupid box?

It was still in her bag, closed. She plucked it out.

"This isn't a good time," she told him and put it back. "I have to work."

"I'll be quick," he promised. "But I need you to listen to me."

"Fine," she answered.

"Take what's in it and put it somewhere safe," he told her. "*Not* the embassy. Understand?"

"Wha—" she started, but she stopped herself. She didn't have the energy to argue, and she didn't care enough to ask more. "Fine."

"You might not hear from me for a while," he said. "But don't worry. Just... keep it safe. Will you do this, Nava? Tell me you will."

"Yes, yes," she answered him. "*Baba*, I have to go."

There was silence on the other end, and she thought they might have been disconnected.

"*Baba*?" she called to him.

More silence followed, and she was about to call to him again when she heard his voice answer softly.

"I'm sorry," he said, and the line dropped.

"*As-salaam 'alaykum*," Al-Laqqis greeted her, his arrival at the table marked not just by his words but by a brisk pace and a brief, cautious glance over his shoulder as if the weight of unseen eyes lingered upon him.

"*Wa 'alaykum as-salaam,*" she returned the greeting as he settled across from her.

"Our time is pressed today," he said.

It was a departure from the norm, where dialogues traditionally wove through the tapestry of familial and communal updates before meandering to the realms of business. Al-Laqqis, while typically more indulgent of these cultural exchanges, now seemed ensnared by the immediacy of matters at hand, his feigned interest in personal affairs notably absent.

"I know you've been looking into Abu Faysal. This line of inquiry will prove fruitless, I assure you," he cautioned, his voice carrying the weight of finality. "Hezbollah is under no illusion—his blood is on Zionist hands."

"And this is Nasrallah's belief?" Nava probed, seeking to peel back the layers of his assertion.

"What Hezbollah holds to be true transcends individual conjecture," he responded, the ritualistic preparation of the waterpipe momentarily pausing as he addressed her query.

"Hmm... The thing is, I heard that he had it in for the Syrians."

Al-Laqqis scoffed quietly and asked, "And who has been spinning these tales?"

"It's just the word on the street," she said.

Now it was his turn to study her, but she was good at showing exactly what she wanted someone to see—nothing more, nothing less. The sunglasses helped.

"He was not in favor of them staying after the Zionists leave," he admitted. "But that was his opinion and his alone."

"There was no discussion of breaking with Syria in the Council?" she asked him.

"Of course not!" he answered with a little too much indignation.

"I just need to know," she told him. "It's just... politics."

The word seemed to have some deleterious effect on his energy. Al-Laqqis nodded and let out a heavy sigh, easing back into his chair.

Nava shifted the conversation to the subject she was more eager to hear about. "My concern today lies with the whereabouts of certain funds," she ventured.

The mention jolted Al-Laqqis, his composure momentarily fractured by the implication. His query, "What funds?" was laced with a blend of confusion and apprehension, a testament to either ignorance or a meticulously crafted facade. She watched as Al-Laqqis's fingers began an erratic dance upon the tabletop, a visual echo of his growing discomfort. His eyes, once steady, now flitted away, evading hers as if the truth lay hidden in the avoidance.

"The funds meant for Monzer Al-Kassar," she told him. At the evocation of the arms dealer's name, Al-Laqqis's disdain was palpable, his veneer cracking further under the weight of the revelation.

"Al-Kassar!" he sneered. "The mangey dog! He, um... told us he found another buyer. The money is still in the account, yes?"

"Withdrawn," Nava informed him. "By Yasin Haddad."

Nava's gaze lingered on Al-Laqqis's face, deciphering the subtle interplay of emotions beneath his beard—a fleeting blend of surprise and indignation that he swiftly cloaked under a veneer of calm.

With a hesitant affirmation, he elaborated, "Ah, yes, Yasin, he, um ... rerouted the funds through an intermediary. It's all temporary; the situation will be rectified shortly."

"Can you assure me of that?" she pressed "Because Yasin seems to be operating with an unusual level of autonomy."

A brief tightening of his jaw, a fleeting dart of his eyes—a silent testament to the layers of concern he harbored beneath his composed exterior. "Haddad operates under the Council's directives," he began, his words measured, yet a hint of hesitance betrayed his assurance.

Nava noted the slight falter in his conviction. "So, there's no chance he's pursuing some... personal agenda?" she pressed, her inquiry delicately poised between curiosity and accusation.

Al-Laqqis paused, the briefest lapse in his façade revealing the depth of his concern. He leaned forward, his voice lowering to a conspiratorial whisper. "Hezbollah has grown very large, very quickly," he confided in her. "It's challenging to keep every thread tightly woven. Haddad has become... ambitious."

The weight of his admission hung in the air, a silent acknowledgment of the precarious balance within Hezbollah's ranks. Al-Laqqis quickly recovered, straightening his posture as he added, "But rest assured, the Shura Council maintains oversight of all significant actions.

Any deviation from our strategic goals would be quickly and decisively addressed."

Nava watched Al-Laqqis closely, each guarded answer and each carefully masked expression adding to her suspicion. The tension in his posture, the evasion in his eyes—every sign pointed to a truth far more complex and potentially dangerous than the facade of unity Hezbollah presented to the world. Haddad's activities, whether fully sanctioned or marginally tolerated, hinted at a fissure within the organization—a fissure that Al-Laqqis, despite his assurances, seemed genuinely concerned about.

"I still need to speak with him."

"Don't worry," he told her. "We'll make sure he finds you."

Chapter Ten

Nava's evening was spent amidst the remnants of her earlier tempest, gathering shattered porcelain and glass, each piece a sharp echo of her fractured emotions. The task completed, she retreated to the sanctuary of her bedroom, her gaze settling on the puzzle box sticking out of her bag. Once a source of delight, the intricate wooden contraption now seemed an emblem of her isolation—a tangible reminder of the distance that had grown between her and her father.

Lying back on her bed, she allowed her fingers to trace the familiar grooves and panels of the box, her movements automatic as memories flooded back. The joy these puzzles once sparked had been extinguished, replaced by a profound sense of loss. Her father, once warm and present, had receded into a shell of himself after her mother's illness, leaving Nava to navigate her grief alone. The hope that following in his professional footsteps might rekindle their bond had faded into resignation.

As she manipulated the box, attempting different sequences to unlock its secrets, images of her father's detached demeanor merged hauntingly with the memory of Farzin's resigned expression on that devastating day at the doctor's office. The realization that she might never forge the connections she yearned for with either man ignited a raw, simmering anger within her. The desire to hurl the puzzle box, to shatter its wooden facade against the indifferent masks worn by Farzin, her father, or even herself, surged powerfully.

But then, with a subtle shift and a soft click, the box yielded, revealing its hidden compartment. Inside lay a black floppy disk, its existence as unexpected as the label it bore: "Ergensbank Zurich 7356-39550-30." The stark, impersonal digits offered no clues, no immediate understanding, only deepening the mystery of her father's cryptic parting words.

Thump-thump-thump.

The rapid succession of knocks echoed through the silent apartment, each thump resonating with an ominous foreboding. For a fleeting moment, Nava's pulse stuttered, her breath hitching in her throat. Perhaps it was the lingering shadow of CLOCKWORK's ever-present anxiety, or the acute awareness of her solitude—a stark contrast to the life she shared with Farzin. Now, that solitude felt like a tangible presence, amplifying every sound into a potential threat. Her 9mm PC-9, a constant companion on her nightstand, suddenly seemed more an emblem of her vulnerability than of protection. Its magazines lay empty beside it, a testament to a life where the immediacy of danger was a distant thought, until now.

The knock might well be the herald of Haddad's retribution. The thought that his operatives had traced her, perhaps even compromised the Gulag observation, sent a visceral shiver through her. Images of her technicians under duress, their loyalty bought by pain, flashed across her mind. Silence became her shield, a fragile hope that the intrusion was a mistake, soon to be corrected.

Yet, the knock persisted, propelling her into action. Grabbing the weapon, she stumbled in her haste, the bullets slippery and rebellious in her trembling hands. The echo of the pistol's chamber accepting its first round seemed to thunder through the apartment, a sound she cursed for its indiscretion.

"Miss Benham?" The voice was muffled but unmistakable in its enquiry, invoking an alias familiar yet distant. Her response was automatic, even as her fingers fumbled to ready the weapon, her movements betraying her turmoil.

The voice on the other side of the door, calm and devoid of malice, did little to quell her unease. The sight that greeted her through the peephole was incongruous with her fears: a solitary figure, youthful and unassuming, marked by the mundane uniformity of a courier, the logo of KGL emblazoned across his cap—a symbol of normalcy, yet alien in the context of her expectation.

"What do you want?" Her voice was a blend of caution and command, masking the torrent of adrenaline coursing through her.

"I have a delivery here from Mr. Bin Zahan," the voice replied.

The mention of Yousef Bin Zahan, one of the identities Masoud used, was a balm to her frayed nerves. With the recognition came a release of the breath she didn't realize she was holding. Concealing the weapon with practiced ease, she cracked open the door, a sliver of space through which trust and suspicion warily met.

"Miss Benham?" the smiling young man asked. The courier's query was met with Nava's cautious acknowledgment, her senses heightened by the late-hour interruption. "I have your cell phones here," he announced, his foot gently tapping the enigmatic black box that now piqued Nava's curiosity. His attire, consisting of khakis and a casual polo shirt emblazoned with the KGL logo, was unusual for Lebanon.

"Cell phones?" Nava echoed, her confusion mirrored on her furrowed brow.

Unfazed, the courier consulted his clipboard once more. "Ten Nokia sixty-one-tens and one receiving station," he said.

"A receiving station?" Nava pressed, her intrigue deepening.

The young man's response was to offer the clipboard, urging her to sign. Yet, Nava's request for clarity persisted. "Can you open it, please?" she asked, her voice steady, betraying none of the turmoil churning within.

"Sure," came the obliging reply, and as the seals were cut and the box revealed its contents, Nava's gaze was drawn to the ten blue Nokia phones nestled in their foam beds, accompanied by an object that resembled a small laptop computer.

"I don't have any money," she told him.

"They're already paid for," he assured her. "Just sign here."

With a hesitant hand, she signed the form and then watched, a silent sentinel at her window, as the truck retreated into the night, leaving behind a trail of unanswered questions and a box filled with enigmatic technology.

"Bizarre," she whispered to the empty room, the word hanging in the air like a ghostly echo, a testament to the strangeness of a world where the mundane and the mysterious danced a delicate pas de deux.

Chapter
Eleven

"Salam, Nava," greeted Darian, the station's intelligence collection management officer, as she stepped into the bustling office.

"*Wa alaykum salam*, Darian," she replied, her voice steady despite the undercurrent of tension that seemed to permeate the air.

She dropped her bag onto her desk, her gaze instinctively drawn to Masoud's office. The door was shut, an unusual sight at this hour.

"Is Masoud in?" she inquired, her curiosity piqued.

"No, he's been at Ambassador Gul's office for a while now," Darian informed her, his eyes briefly flicking towards Masoud's office before returning to his paperwork. "Khadem's taken over his office for now."

"Khadem?" The name left a sour taste in her mouth.

Darian nodded, his expression a mixture of wariness and irritation. "He's been summoning us one by one," he said, his voice low.

Nava's heart sank. "The inquisition has begun."

Darian let out a dry chuckle.

The door to Masoud's office creaked open and Hooman stepped out, his usual composure replaced by a hint of bewilderment. Nava caught his eye, offering a silent nod of solidarity. He managed a brief, strained smile before hurrying to his desk, his shoulders tense.

"Nava," Khadem's voice sliced through the room, his figure looming in the doorway. "Your turn."

She squared her shoulders, bracing herself for the onslaught of questions that awaited her. The office felt smaller somehow, the walls closing in as she made her way to the lion's den.

Khadem's smile widened as he gestured for Nava to enter Masoud's office. She cast a glance back at Hooman, who was massaging his temples with a look of distress. Nava braced herself, knowing that as a woman, she might face even more scrutiny from Khadem.

The weight of her colleagues' stares bore down on her. She sensed that everyone now knew of his counterintelligence role, casting a shadow of suspicion over the entire station. They knew that any minor slip-up could be exploited.

"You and Masoud have a long history, don't you?" Khadem asked, settling into Masoud's chair with an ease that irked Nava.

She nodded, keeping her response brief. "He's been my superior for about seven years."

Khadem's casual demeanor as he sipped his tea and probed further into her relationship with Masoud put Nava on edge. She remained guarded, offering only the most necessary information.

"Has he ever asked you to do anything unusual?" he asked her.

"Nothing in this job is normal," she told him cooly.

"Fair enough," he said. "Anything that might violate the laws of the Islamic Republic?"

"Aside from not wearing a hijab?"

"Aside from that," he said, unfazed.

"No."

The interrogation continued, with Khadem's questions weaving between personal and professional lines, clearly aiming to catch her off guard. Nava maintained her composure, providing vague responses to his probing. The tension in the room thickened as Nava's impatience grew palpable. "Is there much more, Major Khadem?" she pressed, her voice edged with a growing desire for escape from the stifling atmosphere of suspicion.

"Why? Are you in a hurry?" Khadem retorted, a hint of challenge in his tone.

"There's a lot that requires my attention at the moment," Nava replied, her professionalism masking her irritation. "As I'm sure you know."

Khadem leaned back, a thoughtful expression crossing his face. "It seems I'll need to allocate more time for our next meeting," he mused.

Nava's brow furrowed. "Is that really necessary?" she asked him.

His eyes narrowed slightly. "Do my questions unsettle you?"

She sighed, choosing her words carefully. "It's just... as I said, we're very busy at the moment. May I be excused?"

He held her gaze for a moment longer before nodding. "One last inquiry. When did you last visit Jezzine?"

The question caught her off guard. "Jezzine?" she echoed, puzzled. "I believe it's been a few years."

"And you're sure of that?" he pressed.

Before she could delve into why Jezzine was of any interest, Masoud appeared at the door, his expression stern. "My apologies for the interruption," he said to Khadem before addressing Nava. "Join me upstairs,
he said. "Immediately."

She rose, eager to leave the room's oppressive atmosphere. "We'll pick this up another time," Khadem assured her as she exited.

The rooftop of the embassy offered a reprieve from the stifling tension of the office below. Nava observed Masoud's unusual agitation as he struggled with his lighter, a clear sign that he was shaken up about something. "I was bumped last night," he began, indicating an unexpected encounter with another intelligence service. Nava knew such events were not uncommon in their line of work, but Masoud's demeanor suggested this was no ordinary encounter.

"Which agency?" she inquired, trying to gauge the gravity of the situation.

"CIA," he replied, the mention of the American agency adding a layer of complexity to the unfolding scenario.

Her thoughts immediately turned to the mysterious shipment of cell phones she had received the night before. "Is this related to the phones you sent?" she asked him.

Masoud seemed momentarily confused by her question, but he quickly regained his composure. "What? No, no... that's unrelated. That's a new service we're trying," he explained, dismissing the connection with a wave of his hand. He handed her a newspaper, the same one she had been reading at the café with Al-Laqqis. The headline screamed about the kidnapping of an American diplomat in Jordan.

"They believe it's our doing," Masoud said, his voice heavy with concern. "That we've taken an American hostage through Hezbollah."

Nava scanned the article, absorbing the details of the brazen abduction. It must be who Haddad was holding at the Gulag. The implications were clear: a conflict with the United States could reignite regional hostilities. "What do they want from us?" she asked.

"They want their diplomat back," Masoud said, pacing restlessly. "Emily Lynch. Look, to them, we're indistinguishable from Hezbollah. They think we can simply wave our hand and secure her release."

Nava felt the weight of the situation pressing down on her. The delicate balance of international relations teetered on the edge of a knife. "Has Haddad reached out to you?" Masoud asked, his gaze piercing.

"No," she replied, her mind racing with the potential fallout of Haddad's actions.

Masoud paused, finally facing her. "I've discussed this with Ambassador Gul. The risks are too great. Haddad's operation, sanctioned or not, could drag us into a war. We need to act quickly to prevent escalation."

"Okay. What's our move?" she asked, ready for whatever directive Masoud had in store.

"We need to secure the release of the hostage," he said, his expression grave.

"You want me to tell Haddad to—"

"No!" he said, raising his voice to nearly a shout before taking a breath. "No. We don't know what's going on. No... *do not* confront him or anyone else in Hezbollah with this. Understood?"

"Why?"

"Because we don't know who Haddad is working with," he said. "So we can't afford to tip our hand. If Haddad is acting with the blessing of someone in Tehran, confronting him could put us all in grave danger. Remember what I told you about factionalism. It's very real, and very dangerous; especially for us."

"What, then?"

He extended a small cellular phone toward her. "This connects to a company of some sort in Austria," he explained. "The Ministry has them on retainer for just this sort of thing. You'll liaise with a team they're sending. Set them up at The Butcher's safe house and share what we know about the Gulag, but nothing more."

Nava took the phone, her mind already plotting the logistics. "And they'll handle the extraction?"

Masoud nodded, a grim certainty in his gesture. "The cell phones you received," he continued, linking the pieces together. "They came from some sort of an associate company. It's all connected."

She couldn't help but marvel at the efficiency. If they didn't have them on hand, it would've taken at least a week just for the request to get to MOIS headquarters in Tehran and be considered. They may have gotten half the number of phones they requested, all of which would be in shoddy condition if they worked reliably at all, in about two months. This company got them the same day, shiny and new, delivered right to her door.

The conversation shifted, a momentary lightness in the air as they contemplated the rapid turnaround. "Maybe there's something to this 'outsourcing' thing," Masoud mused.

Nava nodded, a hint of a smile playing on her lips despite the gravity of their situation. "It's just the delivery that was weird."

Masoud's agreement was punctuated by a thoughtful puff of smoke. "Brace yourself," he warned her. "From what I've seen, it's going to get a whole lot weirder."

Chapter
Twelve

The instructions from the woman on the phone had been precise: a time, a place, and a passphrase for Nava to identify her
contact. Amidst a day spent testing cellular phones for Haddad and
his lieutenants and chasing elusive leads on Abu Faysal's assassination,
the thought of the upcoming meeting lingered in her mind.

As the sun dipped below the horizon, Nava navigated her way
to Saifi Village, a chic district in downtown Beirut now quieting as
shops shuttered for the evening. The upscale setting led her to fanta-
size about the type of operatives she might encounter—perhaps the
sophisticated spies of cinematic lore, arriving in sleek luxury cars. Her
imagination conjured an image of an elegant Aston Martin pulling up,
its debonair driver stepping out to greet her.

Reality shattered her daydream with a jarring cacophony—a sound
part squeal, part screech. It heralded the arrival of a vehicle so battered
and ancient, it seemed more suited to a junkyard than the streets of
Beirut. As it jerked to a halt before her, with a hubcap making a bid for
freedom down the street, Nava's instinct was to retreat. It was absurd,
almost comical, yet her curiosity anchored her in place. The vehicle, a
relic from a bygone era, felt out of place, as did the young man behind
the wheel with blond locks. His bright eyes met hers and he grinned.

"Hey, lady! You wanna ride in my car?" he asked suggestively.

"*Mashallah* ..." she gasped, as that was, in fact, the phrase she had been told to expect.

"Well, come on in," the boy said, leaned over, and popped open the heavy passenger-side door, which seemed to groan as it swung on its rusted hinges.

Nava pulled the door the rest of the way open, revealing the surface of a seat that seemed to consist mostly of duct tape. After closing her eyes and mouthing a quick prayer, she eased herself inside and secured the door. The boy winked at her, which she found very strange and a bit creepy. She also saw there was another boy in the back seat whom she guessed was about the same age as the driver but who had a much darker complexion and a goatee.

They pulled away from the curb and Nava tried to roll the window up. The handle, however, didn't budge.

"Great..." she muttered to herself.

"So, I guess we should introduce ourselves," the driver said. "I'm Han Solo, Captain of the *Millennium Falcon*. Chewie here tells me you're looking for a passage to the Alderaan System."

The driver glanced at her several times, and she could hear the boy in the back chuckling. The thought crossed her mind that this was all part of a strange, elaborate joke Masoud was playing on her; though to what end, she had no idea.

"You're supposed to say, 'Yes, indeed ... if it's a fast ship,'" the driver told her, only adding to her confusion and sense of unreality. "Not a *Star Wars* fan, huh?"

"What are you talking about?" she asked, narrowing her eyes.

"Name's Scott," he said, extending his hand toward her. "Everyone calls me Scottie."

"Sabi," she responded, her handshake bridging the gap between them.

"My brother, Christian," Scott said, tilting his head toward the back seat. "We call him 'Chin'."

From the shadows of the backseat, Christian offered a genial wave.

Nava was taken aback by the casual introduction, its normalcy strikingly out of place against the backdrop of their clandestine meeting. 'Scottie,' she repeated in her mind, her skepticism tinged with a hint of amusement. 'Chin.' This was not the kind of introduction she had anticipated. It was disarmingly ordinary, as though they were about to set off on a mundane adventure rather than engage in a high-stakes operation.

"You're with the company I called?" Nava inquired, her gaze flitting between them.

"Janissary Solutions," Scottie affirmed with a hint of pride. "We're Janissaries."

"You're what?" she asked, opening her bag to look for her cigarettes.

"Janissaries," Scottie reiterated with a patient smile, pointing first to himself and then to Christian. "Janissary. Janissary. We're Janissaries," he clarified, his gestures underscoring their collective identity.

Lighting her cigarette, Nava allowed a stream of smoke to curl into the air, her nod signaling understanding even as her mind wrestled with the reality before her.

"You, uh, mind rolling down the window?" Scott asked.

She looked at him sideways, and she could see him grin.

"Seriously, though," he said. "Those things'll kill ya."

"Right now, this the only thing stopping me from panicking," she said, holding up the cigarette.

"Panicking? About what?"

"Oh, let's see... That the fate of a country seems to be in the hands of two fraternity boys," she said; and while she was very serious, they seemed to find her answer incredibly funny.

"How old are you?" she asked, her patience wearing thin.

"Twenty-three," Scott answered. "You?"

As close as she was to thirty, she suddenly felt ancient.

"None of your business," she snapped back.

"It's *five* frat boys, by the way," Christian said from the back seat. "Actually, four boys and a girl. We're a man short right now, so we had to borrow her from another—"

"Just... Please tell me the rest of you are older," she said.

Scottie's response was a gentle letdown. "We're all pretty much the same age," he admitted.

The car groaned ominously as Nava rested her elbow against the window frame, a reminder of their precarious surroundings, and she quickly withdrew it.

"Is age going to be a problem or something?" he asked her.

"I don't know," she said. "Does your *mother* know you're in Beirut?"

The exterior of the building was a stark testament to Beirut's turbulent history, its facade a mottled canvas of concrete and scars, standing on the city's fringe like a forgotten relic of conflict. To the untrained eye, it was nothing more than a derelict structure, a grim monument to past strife. Yet, beneath its war-torn exterior lay one of Beirut Station's most secure sanctuaries. Masoud had purchased this erstwhile post office, its upper stories obliterated by an Israeli airstrike, transforming it into an unassuming fortress hidden in plain sight. The remnants of destruction served as the perfect camouflage, concealing a meticulously fortified interior only accessible through what was once a service bay for postal vehicles.

Nava, leading the Janissaries into the safe house dubbed "The Butcher's," illuminated the expansive space with the flick of a switch. The stark halogen lighting revealed a functional, open area, devoid of any ornamentation save for the essentials of clandestine operations: foldable furniture, a lone refrigerator, and a quartet of monitors surveying the city from their perch on the eastern wall.

"We call it 'The Butcher's'," Nava told the two Janissaries, who looked around at the room lit with halogen work lights. "Cots are in the corner and there are some tables and chairs over there."

As she pointed them out, Scott whistled, obviously impressed.

"You like it?" she asked them.

"This place is incredible," Scott told her. "I think we can get like two, maybe three kegs of beer in here. What do you think, Chin?"

Christian gave her a wry smile and said, "He's joking."

"Security cameras cover all four sides of the building," she said, turning each of the monitors on for them. The images of the streets and alleyways surrounding the building faded into view. "The cameras are hidden in the rubble."

"Pretty slick," Christian said. "As Scottie said, this is much better than we usually get, so don't worry. We'll bring in everything else we need. What's with this map?"

"We're here," she said, pointing to a black spot mark on the map of Beirut. "There is another safe house about six blocks north from here. That is called 'The Baker's'."

She pointed to a blue spot on the map a little north of their location.

"It's a second-floor apartment, two-zero-two," she said. "If something happens to this place, The Baker's is where I will meet you."

She pointed to the big red dot far to the south.

"This is the target building," she told them. "The Gulag."

"Cute," Christian remarked. "Any checkpoints on this highway or around the neighborhood?"

"Not since the ceasefire," she said.

"Right... Anything else we need to know?"

"Don't use the loading bay in the daytime," she told them. "There's a better way in and out, here." She opened a door next to the bathroom and hit the switch, illuminating a staircase leading down.

"Where does it go?" Christian asked her.

"To the alley behind a small grocer across the street," she told them. "There's a door to the alley from there. There's water in the refrigerator. Do you have food?"

"We'll take care of it," he said.

She sighed heavily and said, "Okay... I'm probably going to regret this, but I need to get back to my car."

Each time they went over a small bump or hole, Nava heard something under the car scrape the pavement until the ancient squeaky shocks returned the rusting hulk to its idiosyncratic equilibrium. She found herself wondering if it was the muffler or catalytic converter but then told herself it didn't matter since no part of a car should be dragging along the road. Scottie, however, seemed completely unconcerned as he steered the car through the streets of Beirut.

As they drove, she caught him stealing furtive glances at her. She thought that he was just curious at first, but then she caught him staring at her chest. He looked away and blushed a little, and she found herself smiling for the first time in... how long had it been? Days, at least. Maybe weeks...

The smile quickly faded, however. He just saw an attractive figure, she thought; but if he knew the truth about her, he would look at her just as Farzin had that day at the doctor's office.

"Where did you get this car?" she asked him.

"This baby? Courtesy of KFS."

"What is that?"

"Khan Fleet Services," he told her. "Khan Enterprises is a sort of a... preferred vendor. They give us some hoopties, but they usually run pretty well. The worst part for me is this..."

He pointed to the radio in the console.

"What?"

"No CD player," he said. "Not even a cassette deck. Nothing to play my jams, you know?"

"Music is that important to you?" she asked.

"I *love* music," he told her. "All kinds of music. Rock, folk, grunge, alternative, R 'n B, classical... Lately, I've been all about Superchunk. You know, the whole Chapel Hill scene is really in right now. Plus, I've had this huge crush on Laura Ballance for like two years now. What about you?"

"Where is the rest of your team?" she asked, ignoring the question. "Christian said there were five of you."

"They'll be here," he said. "Hey, you know someone's following us, right?"

"What?"

Sure enough, she spotted it. But how had she not spotted them before this boy had?

"How long have they been there?" she asked.

"About a half mile from the safe house," he said. "What do you want to do?"

She cursed under her breath and tried to think. The only thing of which she was certain was that keeping the location of the safe house secret was her current priority.

"Do you know if they were there on the way to the safe house?" she asked him.

"Nope, they weren't."

She could try to lose them; but in this car, what were the chances? She could try going to the embassy. They couldn't follow her through the gates there. Of course, that would mean being recorded driving around with a mercenary, and only God knew what was in this car to be found. Drugs, weapons...

Still going over the options in her head, she heard Scott say, "Hold on, okay?"

"What? Hold—"

He stepped on the gas, and the car accelerated faster than she expected, pinning her in her seat. Before she could ask what he was doing, Scott turned as sharply as possible to the left, making a U-turn in the middle of the road. She heard something snap, and her door fell away from the car to the street. She braced her hands against the glove compartment, arms locked, screaming in terror. The car went up onto the curb with a jolt, then plopped back down onto the road and bounced as they got back underway to a hail of car horns from angry and frightened drivers. Soon, Scott took a violent right turn down a side street, then pulled to the side and stopped.

69

She turned, mouth and eyes wide in horror, but the blond boy had the same easy smile on his face as if nothing at all had just happened.

"Well, now," he said, motioning to where the door had been. "That's a first."

Chapter
Thirteen

"If I didn't know better, I'd think it was some sort of prank," Nava confided in Masoud as they navigated the corridor toward Ambassador Gul's office early the next morning. The events of the previous night played in her mind like scenes from an absurdist play.

As they approached the door, Masoud's light chuckle only served to fuel her frustration.

"They're basically children," she whispered sharply. "We can't possibly entrust something this important to—"

"Just support them as needed," Masoud instructed, his tone attempting to balance firmness with reassurance. "Focus on finding who killed Abu Faysal."

"The stakes are too high," she countered. "We should send them back where they came from. Let me deal with Haddad directly."

Masoud remained silent until they paused at the threshold of the ambassador's office.

"I'll consult Tehran," he finally conceded.

Grateful for his consideration, Nava nodded. They were greeted by the ambassador's secretary, whose attention remained squarely on her computer monitor.

"He's behind schedule," she informed them dismissively, gesturing towards the office door. Nava couldn't help but wonder if Western intelligence agencies had a clearer window into Ambassador Gul's deliberations than his own station chief.

"You're heading out?" Masoud inquired, eyeing the backpack she had momentarily forgotten she was carrying, its contents crucial for the operation at the Gulag.

"That's the plan."

Masoud leaned closer, his voice dropping to a whisper. "Some of the funds have resurfaced."

"How much?"

"Half."

"Where did it come from?"

"Back from the same channels it vanished into," he explained, suggesting a possible vindication of Al-Laqqis's insights.

"But that doesn't clarify the situation at the—" She caught herself before mentioning the Gulag, wary of the secretary's prying ears.

"I'm aware," Masoud admitted with a sigh of resignation. "You should get moving. I'll brief him."

"And our hired help?" she probed, seeking reassurance.

Masoud's smile returned, exuding confidence she found both vexing and comforting—vexing because she couldn't fathom how Masoud, with his wealth of experience and deep understanding of the stakes involved, could place such trust in those she saw as barely out of adolescence and lacking the gravity their mission demanded; comforting, because his assurance suggested a depth of strategy and insight she had yet to grasp.

"Just keep an eye on them," he told her. "They might yet surprise you."

Only a teenager, Dasia was dead; for the moment, at least. At first, the 17-year-old little yellow VW Golf had seemed determined to start, whatever may have been bothering her. She clicked and sputtered when Nava cranked the key, giving the engine as much gas as she dared without flooding it. Most of the time, her pleading triggered Dasia's sympathy, and the car would cough to life on the third or fourth attempt, but it seemed her mileage was finally overcoming her spirit, and it nearly drove Nava to tears right there on the street outside the embassy.

Reluctantly, she made the call to have Dasia towed, a decision that filled her with sadness and anxiety. More than just a car, Dasia was a companion on many covert operations, a silent keeper of secrets. The immediate problem was more practical: securing a ride under the radar. An embassy vehicle was out of the question, of course. The thought of reaching out to the only acquaintance with a vehicle arguably more decrepit than Dasia was a bitter pill to swallow, but she did it nevertheless. The security of her destination depended on it.

Seeking refuge and a momentary escape from her predicament, Nava retreated to a nearby café. The brief respite was shattered when Major Khadem spotted her from across the room. His recognition was immediate, cutting through her anonymity even in the absence of her embassy hijab, marking the continuation of Nava's streak of misfortune.

"May I get you something?" Khadem offered, his tone casual yet carrying an undercurrent of insistence that Nava found irksome.

"No, I'm just waiting for a ride. Car problems," she replied, keeping her voice neutral to mask her irritation. The last thing she needed was Khadem's company, but she recognized the precarious balance she

73

had to maintain. Rejecting his offer outright could rouse his curiosity, a risk she couldn't afford. Her mind raced, hoping Scott's entrance would be as unremarkable as possible.

"I'll wait with you, then," Khadem said, settling into the seat across from her with a comfort that seemed to claim the space as his own. Nava felt the edges of her patience fray but maintained a composed exterior, her hands folded neatly on the table to keep from fidgeting.

"Still trying to get on your calendar for our little chat," Khadem continued, leaning back slightly in his chair, the smirk on his face suggesting he enjoyed this game of cat and mouse far more than she did.

"You should be prepared to wait a while longer," Nava retorted, her tone laced with a firmness intended to deter further prying. Yet, as she heard him snicker at her response, a wave of annoyance washed over her.

"I heard that about you," he said, his voice carrying a hint of admiration or perhaps mockery—Nava couldn't be sure. "Always very direct."

"Well, if I shock you, I apologize. My parents tried their best," she quipped.

"I can see that," Khadem conceded, his tone softening ever so slightly. "No, I appreciate directness."

"Even in a woman?" Nava challenged, her eyebrow arching inquisitively.

He answered only with a coy smile, a non-committal response that left her questions hanging in the air, unanswered. The ambiguity of his expression frustrated her, adding yet another layer of complexity to their already tangled interactions.

As they were speaking, Nava barely registered a soft rumble in her ear and chose to ignore it. It took her a moment before she realized that Scott was outside now, looking through the glass at her, sitting upright on a motorcycle.

She heard herself curse under her breath and felt blood rushing to her cheeks. The sight left her speechless and horrified. He was clad in blue jeans and a t-shirt with aviator sunglasses. His blond hair spilled out as he took his helmet off, and it occurred to her that he couldn't look more American if he were wrapped in the flag of the United States.

"*Mishnasish*?" Khadem asked her. *Do you know him?*

Trapped between the need to respond and the absurdity of the situation, Nava found herself momentarily voiceless. She shook her head in disbelief as she rose to confront Scott directly.

"Hey, pretty mama!" he greeted her.

"What the fuck are you doing here like... like this?" she asked him.

"Whoa! Language!" he said. "Where did you learn that word?"

"I went to Oxford," she said through clenched teeth as he offered her a helmet. "I know all kinds of fucking words."

"Who's the stiff?" he asked, motioning to Khadem, who bore an expression that was equal parts concern and suspicion.

"None of your business," she snapped and snatched the helmet from him.

No sooner had they merged into traffic than Nava's trained senses tingled with the unmistakable feeling of being followed. A few glances behind her confirmed her suspicion: a nondescript sedan, its presence too constant to be coincidental, was shadowing them with practiced subtlety. She tapped Scott's shoulder, signaling him to take the next turn.

What followed was a high-stakes game of cat and mouse through the winding streets of Beirut. Scott maneuvered the motorcycle with a blend of recklessness and precision that both terrified and exhilarated her. They darted through narrow alleyways, skirted around bustling markets, and sped down main thoroughfares.

The true test came as they approached a notoriously busy intersection. The light was against them, a steady red eye that promised to halt their escape. Nava's heart pounded in her chest as she weighed their options. Turning back was not a choice; they had to lose their tail here and now.

She leaned close to Scott's ear, her voice steady despite the adrenaline coursing through her veins. "Run it," she instructed, her tone leaving no room for hesitation.

With a nod, Scott edged the motorcycle forward, positioning them at the head of the waiting traffic. When the tiniest break in the traffic appeared, Nava braced herself, and Scott twisted the throttle. The motorcycle leaped forward, cutting across the intersection with mere inches to spare from oncoming vehicles. Horns blared and tires screeched in their wake, and they took full advantage of the confusion they'd left behind. Scott aggressively wove through traffic as Nava's eyes constantly scanned their surroundings, searching for signs of further pursuit, but the sedan was nowhere to be seen.

Upon entering the safe house, Nava was immediately struck by the meticulous setup dominating the space. A detailed model of the Gulag and its surrounding area commanded attention on a large table. The model was annotated with a complex system of colored tape arrows and fan-shaped overlays indicating lines of sight and potential sniper positions, each detail meticulously plotted for maximum strategic advantage. The wall boasted a large map of Ansar and Beirut, overlaid with a transparent sheet filled with symbols and annotations in various colors, transforming the map into a dynamic planning tool. Against one wall, several black cases were neatly stacked, one open to reveal the sleek form of an MP-5 submachine gun, its flash suppressor hinting at the seriousness of their mission.

"You... you did all this?" Nava ask Scott, her voice tinged with a mix of surprise and admiration.

"We work fast," came a reply, not from Scott, but from another corner of the room. A young Latino-looking man stood, his gaze sharp and assessing.

"Jake," he introduced himself, his demeanor shifting seamlessly from professional to guarded as he shook her hand. "Janissary Twelve team leader."

He crossed his arms in front of him, his posture and slight tilt of the head conveying a silent appraisal that left Nava feeling oddly scrutinized, as though she were being weighed and measured by some unseen criteria.

The only other person present was a woman, her blonde hair drawn back in a practical ponytail, revealing the lean muscle of her arms and shoulders. Engrossed in a conversation on a rugged-looking satellite phone, she exuded an air of focused competence. "... Yeah ... An electronics package, as well ... Hang on a sec ..." she said, before tossing the phone to Scott and indicating that the call was from KEI.

Her brief smile towards Nava hinted at an unspoken camaraderie, or at least a recognition of the unique challenges they faced in this male-dominated sphere. She introduced herself as Erica.

As Scott departed, presumably for another task, Nava, Jake, and Erica gathered around the table. The model of the Gulag's vicinity, the centerpiece of their makeshift command center, now served as a focal point for their collaboration. As they settled into a discussion, the dynamic in the room shifted subtly, a reflection of the serious nature of their undertaking and the shared commitment that bridged their diverse backgrounds.

"This is just the beginning," Erica stated firmly. "We're going to need a lot more information."

Nava, feeling the weight of their gaze, nodded. "Okay," she acquiesced, her tone open yet cautious. "What do you need to know?"

"Whose place is this?" Jake asked.

"I'm not authorized to disclose that."

Jake's reaction was immediate, his features tightening into a scowl, his eyes narrowing—a visual manifestation of frustration, or perhaps it was his default state.

"Why does it matter?" she challenged.

He leaned in, his posture aggressive, a clear attempt to assert dominance in the conversation. "It's critical," he pressed. "How they're armed, how well trained they are, if they can call a quick reaction force, if they have air assets, if we need to take the hostage out of the country..."

Nava, feeling cornered yet defiant, responded sharply, "Look, I don't know why you were chosen for this task, but my role here is solely to safeguard my country's interests."

"And those would be?" Jake pushed, not relenting in his interrogation.

Matching his forward lean with her own, Nava's response was pointed. "To ensure you don't fuck this up."

His smirk at her rebuttal didn't mask the tension in the air. "Okay," he conceded, shifting gears. "Let's start simple. What's your name?"

"I already told you."

"Your real name," he clarified.

Nava's laughter at the request was spontaneous, a release from the intensity of their exchange. Jake, however, remained unamused, steadfast in his demand.

"You're serious?" she asked, incredulous. Despite knowing their operational names, she hadn't considered the exchange of personal information.

"You know our names," he said. "Why shouldn't we know yours?"

"What's your last name?" she asked him.

He took a passport from the pocket of his cargo pants and put it on the table in front of her.

"We don't have them," he said. "Not really. But, right now, it's Espinosa."

She didn't bother calling his bluff and looking at the passport. If this company really was connected to the one that had supplied her with the bugged cellular phones, as Masoud told her, she had no doubt they were able to manufacture an Austrian passport with whichever name they wanted on it. She remained silent as his cold green eyes stared back at her expectantly.

The tension in the room escalated as Jake laid out the crux of their predicament, his words laced with a mix of desperation and caution. "We're short on time for thorough intelligence preparation," he said. "I'm about to take those I hold most dear into something based solely on information you give us. If you withhold even the simplest truths about yourself, how can I trust anything you say?"

"Because I want this to succeed," she answered. "Else we wouldn't be paying you. Trust doesn't figure into this transaction."

Jake's response cut deep, challenging her commitment. "Really? How much do you want this to succeed? Would you tell us if you thought only half of us would make it out of there alive?"

Their eyes locked, each assessing the other's resolve. Nava considered this a critical moment to gauge Jake's reaction to pushback—a test of sorts before they plunged into the operational chaos that awaited them. His sudden smile, the first genuine one she'd seen from him, marked a shift in the atmosphere, prompting her to relax slightly in response.

"Look, lady ..." he said.

"Sabi," she told him.

"Sabi," he said. "You seem pretty normal."

"Did you think I wasn't?"

He snickered at the question, then said, "I mean, you're Iranian, right? You could be all..." He began a mock ululation followed by an explosive gesture, crudely mimicking a suicide bomber. Nava was taken aback, her offense palpable in the silence that followed. Erica's suppressed amusement only added to the discomfort, leaving Nava to wonder what exactly she found funny: Jake's blatant stereotype or Nava's reaction to it. The moment laid bare the complexities and challenges of their collaboration, a reminder of the diverse perspectives and biases they each brought to the table.

The sudden ring of her cell phone interrupted the charged atmosphere. The screen displayed an unfamiliar number, an anomaly in her carefully curated contacts. With a cautious step aside, Nava answered.

The voice that greeted her was unmistakably deep and smooth, a stark contrast to the in which tension she'd just been enveloped. "I heard you need to speak with me," it said, its calmness belying the storm it represented.

Recognition dawned slowly, each syllable from the caller echoing through her with a mixture of anticipation and dread—Yasin Haddad.

Moments after ending the call on her StarTAC, Nava faced Jake's discontent with a composed demeanor. "I need to get to Ansar," she stated, her voice carrying a blend of urgency and expectation.

Jake's response was terse, a mix of sarcasm and detachment. "Call a taxi," he suggested, as if the weight of her request bore no significance.

"We're compensating you," she reminded him, her patience thinning.

"Oh, well I'm afraid transportation services fall outside our contractual obligations," he retorted.

"That was our hostage taker," she told them.

"And?" he asked with a shrug.

She knew that she had to trust them with something, but she was still determined to share as little as possible.

"I need to speak with him... in person," she said. "It's directly related to getting more intelligence from the safe house."

"Am I supposed to just take your word for it?" Jake asked her, lifting the corner of his mouth.

She sighed in frustration and pushed her hair back over her head to get it out of her face. "I get it," she said. "I need to give you more details. I'll talk to my boss."

"I'm not working with your boss," he said. "I need you to trust us, and I need to trust you."

"I'm going to get sound from the safe house," she told them, motioning to the model on the table.

"You're going to bug it?" Erica asked, her tone incredulous.

"No," she said, holding up her phone, indicating her conversation with Haddad. "He's going to do it for me."

Chapter Fourteen

E rica drove Nava in a dark van that was thankfully in much better shape than the vehicle whose door had rotted off its hinges. The vehicle hummed steadily southward towards Ansar, carrying Nava and a cache of technology critical to the operation that lay ahead of them.

"I don't think your boss likes me very much," Nava mused aloud, her voice tinged with a mix of curiosity and resignation.

Erica's response came with a smile, a subtle curve of her lips visible beneath the rim of her blue-tinted aviator sunglasses. The glasses, which Nava had always thought of as masculine, now seemed nothing short of fitting on Erica, who wore them with an effortless grace. It seemed like part of some enviable ability of hers to redefine what strength looked like, blending toughness with an undeniable feminine allure.

"Well, he's not exactly my boss," Erica clarified, her voice carrying a hint of pride. "I lead my own team. Most of the time, anyway."

"Your own team?" Nava echoed, her interest piqued.

"Janissary Five-Zero," Erica revealed, the name spoken with a reverence that hinted at the depth of her commitment. "And don't worry about Jake. He's a real dick, but he's also a real professional."

Nava couldn't help but laugh, a sound that felt foreign yet fitting in the moment. It was a laughter born of shared understanding, of the recognition of the absurdity and complexity of their situation. As they approached Ansar, however, the laughter faded, replaced by a somber contemplation of the dangers that awaited.

"Thank you for not asking me why I'm meeting with the people I'm asking you to attack, by the way," Nava told her.

"I figure you'd tell us in your own time," Erica replied with a congenial smile.

"This whole thing must seem strange to you."

Erica shrugged a little and shook her head slightly. "I'm not like Jake," she said. "I don't need everything to be clear and straightforward."

"Are they, usually?"

"Shit, no," Erica replied. "Why do you think he's always pissed off? Look, it's all good. I know life can be... complicated."

"Especially here," Nava told her.

They stopped well short of their destination, the van idling in the shadows of what was to come. "All set?" Erica asked, her voice a gentle probe.

Nava took a moment, her thoughts a whirlwind of anticipation and fear. After a deep breath, she took a business card from her pocket and scribbled Masoud's number on the back. "If you don't hear from me in two hours, go back to the Butcher's without me and contact Beirut Station."

"Okay... They know where you are, right?"

"Yes," Nava told her.

"Then why do we need to—"

"To replace me," she said.

83

Erica's eyebrows arched slightly over the rims of her sunglasses, a hint of surprise—or perhaps admiration. "Okay," she murmured with a nod, took the card, folded it carefully and tucked it away. For a moment, the barriers of rank and duty seemed to dissolve between them, leaving two individuals bound by the harsh realities of their clandestine world. "I hope it doesn't come to that," Erica finally said, her voice low.

"So do I," Nava replied, offering a small, determined smile.

As she stepped out into the balmy air of Ansar, the afternoon sun cast long shadows that seemed to stretch toward the unknown. She closed the door softly behind her, sealing her resolve with the soft click of the latch.

"Good luck," Erica called out from the driver's seat.

Nava nodded her thanks before starting down the sidewalk, her strides measured and purposeful, steeling herself for what lay ahead.

As Nava approached the Seahorse Café, the weight of the mission pressed upon her with each step. Clutching a shopping bag filled with brand-new cellular phones, still encased in their sterile packaging, she couldn't shake the feeling of being watched. A white Yugo shadowed her, its occupants a mystery. Despite the unease this surveillance stirred within her, she pressed on.

"*Mudira!*"

The voice cut through the ambient noise of the street, pulling Nava's attention across the roadway. It was Marwan, a figure from Haddad's inner circle, whom she'd encountered on rare occasions. His use of "boss" to address her, a nickname overheard and adopted after a brief interaction with one of her technicians, brought a fleeting smile to her face. The last time she saw him, Marwan was due to marry some woman from a village near the Syrian border.

"My friend, the newlywed," she greeted him as he trotted across the street between passing cars.

He wore an especially big smile as he approached.

She could tell that remembering that detail about his life had endeared her to him, if only a little. If she had a special power that made her a better agent than most, it was making people feel seen and heard. She was constantly surprised at how fast someone would open to her, even pour their heart out, when she appeared to care about their lives.

"Your family is well?" she asked.

"Very well, thank you," Marwan replied, his respect evident in the slight bow of his head.

The moment of cordiality was brief, as the white Yugo that had been trailing her came to a halt nearby. The offer to enter, presented with a gesture towards the open rear door, filled Nava with a deep sense of foreboding. The interior of the car, shaded by curtains, seemed less a refuge from the sun than a coffin. But showing even a slight hesitation about climbing inside might have already made them suspicious.

Their journey through the streets of Ansar was a delicate dance of normalcy against the backdrop of their purpose. Conversations about Marwan's expecting wife and the speculative excitement of their family over the unborn child's gender were interspersed with Nava's careful avoidance of any direct interest in the Gulag, even as they passed by it.

Arriving at a nondescript apartment block, they ascended to a third-floor dwelling. They were greeted by a woman about her age but whose life seemed a world away from the clandestine nature of Nava's visit. The warmth of the apartment, filled with the rich aroma of lamb stew, momentarily transported Nava to memories of her own family. The innocent curiosity of two young girls playing in the living room served as a stark reminder of the stakes at hand.

On the small balcony, the scene was set for the meeting. Around a modest table adorned with a simple tea service, the man who held so many threads of their fate in his hands awaited her. This was the moment Nava had prepared for, where strategy and humanity would intersect, and the course of their mission could be altered with a word, a gesture, or the silence in between.

"*As-salaam 'alaykum*," Haddad greeted her, and Marwan disappeared into the apartment.

"*Wa 'alaykum as-salaam,*" she replied, and they began speaking in Arabic. "You've been very difficult to reach lately."

"I apologize for not returning your calls earlier," he said. "We've been taking some extra precautions since Abu Faysal. Things have been... unsettled. You understand."

"Of course," she said in the most understanding tone she could muster, and he motioned for her to sit. "Maybe we should speak English," she said in English.

He glanced inside the apartment, where Marwan was sitting on the floor with the two girls having a "tea party" of their own.

"I have nothing to keep from him," Haddad replied. "But I can always use the practice."

"You went to college in America, didn't you?"

"MIT," he said with a nod and brought the cup to his lips. "Three years."

"You could have been an engineer," she said. "Building rockets to the moon."

He smiled at the notion and said, "God had another plan."

Nava observed Haddad with a practiced eye, understanding that every gesture and expression offered insights into the mind of the man before her. His posture was relaxed, yet there was a latent tension in the way he held himself—like a coiled spring, ready to release at a moment's notice. This was a man accustomed to command, whose calm exterior belied a strategic mind always at work.

As they spoke of his family, Nava noted the slight softening in his demeanor, a glimpse of the person behind the soldier. Yet, when she mentioned his brother, Seyyed, she saw a brief flicker of discomfort cross Haddad's face. His body stiffened almost imperceptibly, and his eyes darted away—a clear sign of a topic he wished to avoid. Nava recognized this as indicative of the complex dynamics that often exist within families, magnified here by the pressures of their involvement in Hezbollah's military activities.

She knew Seyyed was also in Hezbollah, but he hadn't risen through the ranks as quickly as his older brother. She only knew that he was something of a hothead, and Yasin kept him back from the front lines. In any case, he wasn't important enough for her to know all that well.

"He's well," he told her with a forced smile. "So... I understand you want to ask me about allocations."

"I was hoping you could shed some light on what happened to the deal with Monzer Al-Kassar," she said.

Haddad grunted and looked at the floor. It was as if she'd shown poor taste in broaching the subject with him.

"It was a lot simpler when you sent everything we needed through Damascus," he lamented. "Now there's all these... accounts to manage and slimy middlemen. It didn't take long for one to betray us as soon as he found a better buyer."

"That's not what Al-Kassar said."

"That's the problem," he said with some anger in his voice. "You're listening to some arms dealer and not me."

"Until today, he was the only one talking," she replied.

She saw his jaw clench before he managed a fake smile and a nod, conceding the point.

"The money will be back into the account by the end of the month," he told her. "You have my word."

"That's all I needed to hear," she told him.

Haddad motioned to her shopping bag.

"You brought me gifts?" he asked. "I'm ashamed I neglected to get you anything."

"Poor civil servants like me can't afford things like these," she said, taking a Nokia out and showing him. "There are ten just like this in the bag for you and your lieutenants. We have good reason to believe the Israelis can't intercept calls made on these."

He took the phone from her and looked at it as she glanced around the courtyard. A single tree grew bravely in the only corner that got decent sunlight next to a rusting swing set. Birds were incessantly chirping from the clotheslines strung between buildings and from nests that were built in rain gutters.

"You think the Israelis found Abu Faysal by his phone?" he asked her.

"It's a good possibility," she said. "We do know they can at least eavesdrop on the Motorolas that you've been using. These have better security."

He nodded in understanding, put the phone in his pocket, and slid the bag to his side of the table.

"Well," she said, "I've taken enough of your time."

"Not at all," he said as they both stood. "I always have time for my friends from Tehran, from whichever agency."

Now for the big finish. She began to turn toward Marwan.

"Oh... one other thing I needed to ask," she said, turning back to Haddad. "The American that was taken in Jordan... Do you know anything about it?"

"No," he said, shaking his head. He broke eye contact and looked at the tea set resting on the table. "Why do you ask?"

He crossed his arms in front. Even if she hadn't known it already, she would have known now that he was hiding something.

"The Americans believe we have her," she told him.

"The Americans are always up to something," he returned with a smirk. "All warfare is based on deception, right?"

"We're not at war with the Americans," she said.

"Maybe you should check in with Tehran about that," he said half-facetiously. "Anyway, I wouldn't worry about it."

"Oh? Why is that?"

"She'll turn up soon," he said. "Either in person or... on CNN, I would imagine."

Nava gave one last forced smile before saying her goodbyes, then turned to see Marwan make way for her to enter the aromatic little apartment ahead of him. She walked, doing her best not to shake too visibly. No one was inside—not the two little girls or their mother, though the food was still cooking on the stovetop. Like when she was approaching the curtained backseat of the car that brought her here, a sense of dread seemed to squeeze her chest, forcing her to draw quick, short breaths as she traversed the main room. This was where they would put a bullet in the back of her head, as they'd done to so many whom they suspected of collaboration with the Israelis. Approaching the door, she fought the strong urge to lunge for it. The knob was there, seeming to retreat as she approached it. She felt Marwan's eyes on her. Had he looked back at his boss for a signal? Just a nod... a simple nod from Haddad to this boy and it would be over. The last thing in this life she would see would be that damned door that seemed to pull itself away from her. The bullet would send skin, brain, and blood onto the walls and ceiling, a dripping red mess of gore...

"Hadia!" she heard a tiny voice shriek, and the sound nearly stopped her heart. "I want to play with Hadia!"

One of the little girls ran from the hallway and passed Nava as if she weren't there at all, then picked up her beloved doll and clutched it tightly.

"It's supper time!" her mother said, emerging from the hallway with the other little girl in tow. "Don't touch that doll! Now you'll have to wash your hands again!"

She gave Nava a polite smile as she passed by her, then began what promised to be a lengthy negotiation with the little girl.

Nava felt herself breathe deeply again as she looked back at Marwan, who smiled and shrugged at the girl's stubbornness. As he stepped past her and opened the door for her, she looked back and saw Haddad out on the balcony with his back to her.

Erica's van seemed like a mobile sanctuary when she finally picked her up near where she had dropped her earlier. She didn't truly feel safe until they were inside and taking a circuitous route back to the apartment overlooking the Gulag.

It wasn't until they were safely on the return trip to Beirut that Nava told her everything that had happened in the meeting with Haddad.

"Damn girl!" Erica said when the story ended. "You got balls."

"Balls?" Nava asked, bemused by the word.

"Guts," Erica tried. "Courage."

"That one, I know," Nava said, resting her head back on the headrest.

"The boys are going to be pretty impressed."

"They are?" Nava asked though she hadn't the vaguest idea of why she would even care what they thought of her.

"You bet."

It was a good feeling—exhilarating, even. She didn't know if she'd come close to death, but she at least felt as if she had just defied it.

"Can I tell you something, though?" Nava said, rolling her head on the seatback to look at the pretty blonde American.

"Yeah."

"On the way out, I think I peed myself a little."

Erica burst into incandescent laughter so hard that Nava felt like taking the wheel from her. She might have, if she'd been able to stop laughing herself.

Chapter
Fifteen

Ambassador Gul took longer than it should take to read through the message to Tehran, which signaled to Nava that he reread it, and perhaps more than once. When he finally finished, his chair groaned as he sat back in it, as if it carried the weight of Gul's position as well as his physical mass.

"This source..." he said, holding his arms in front of him. "He's solid?"

"He's never lied or fabricated anything," Nava replied, a little concerned with Gul's body language. She told herself he might just be trying to maintain his objectivity, but she was worried that he had already made his mind up about what to tell Tehran for political reasons, and the report was unwelcome news.

Gul sighed heavily and rubbed his face. The long hours were beginning to wear on the man, who was pushing 70.

"Masoud?"

"I think it'll buy some time," Masoud proffered. "Hopefully allow us to lower the temperature."

Gul's gaze flitted between them before he said, "I agree. Until this situation with the American is resolved, I don't think Tehran will want to stir the pot with the Israelis, anyway. The problem is, the IRGC will disagree with this; and they'll send their own report back."

"Does the IRGC know about Haddad's prisoner?" Nava asked.

"Let's hope not," Gul replied. "But, assuming they don't, the longer this goes on, the more chance they have to find out and intervene. So let's keep this moving, yes?"

"Yes, sir," they answered nearly simultaneously and left Gul to his next meeting.

"I spoke with your father," Masoud said when they were out in the hallway. "I take it you've opened your gift by now?"

"That stupid computer disk?" she snorted.

"Hey..." Masoud glanced around them nervously. "Lower your voice," he told her.

"So you're in on whatever little game my father is playing, too?"

"You could say that," he said, his eyes again scanning the halls ahead.

"What is it?" she asked.

"Just... Know it's important," he told her.

"You want to go up for a smoke?" she asked him.

"I have another meeting," he said. "Keep it somewhere safe. Not your apartment. Not the embassy. Okay?"

"Fine," she said, rolling her eyes.

They parted ways at the elevator. Luckily, an empty one came quickly. Unluckily, Khadem caught the door just before it closed.

"Headed out?" he asked her when the doors closed.

"I am," she answered, avoiding eye contact.

"Not going to see Yasin Haddad again, are you?" he asked.

It got her attention. She snapped her head around to see Khadem grin knowingly.

"How did you..." she began.

"You refused my offer of cooperation, so I had to rely on my own sources," he told her. "The IRGC has many, many contacts in Hezbollah, Nava. I thought you would know that."

"Of course," Nava replied tersely, diverting her eyes back to the floor indicator.

"So I take it your business with him has concluded," Khadem asked.

"I think so," she lied as the doors opened.

"That's good," Khadem said, holding the door for her as she exited. "Because the Revolutionary Guards made Hezbollah, Nava. It's *ours...* and we don't appreciate Beirut Station sticking its nose where it doesn't belong."

He let the door go, pressed a button and disappeared behind the closing steel doors.

***

As slow as it was, she took the bus to the Butcher's safe house rather than risk another ride from Scott. The only good thing about having to change buses so many times for counter-surveillance was that she was able to get a complete update from her technician, Caspar.

"This equipment you got is fantastic!" he told her over the phone. "Do you know everything it does?"

"What do you have, Caspar?"

"Well, I was going to say..." Caspar replied, a little annoyed but still enthusiastic. "It can tell you how far each phone is away from the monitoring station if they're close enough. Very cool, right?"

"Go on," she said.

"Anyway... Haddad must have gone straight back to the Gulag after you left," he told her. "He had someone waiting for him there—someone the Hezbollah people there called *Majnoon*. Who is that?"

"It's not a name," she said. "It's a word. Like, um ... lunatic."

"Right. Well, they had this 'lunatic' guy locked in some room downstairs. Haddad says he'll be there in a minute, then I hear him climbing the stairs up to the second floor. Some guy recognizes him, opens a door, then this..."

There was a short pause before the sound of the recording reached her ear.

"You're being treated well?" she heard Haddad's voice ask in English.

A distinctly feminine voice answered in American-accented English.

"All things considered, yes," it said.

"Boss," she heard Caspar say, "that has to be their prisoner."

"I agree," she said, trying to sound as neutral as possible.

"So, I got the distance reading from the monitoring machine," Caspar said, excitement creeping into his voice. "That was less than sixty meters away. I did the math, and even within the margin of error... Boss, she *has* to be in the southwest corner room."

"How sure are you?"

"I'd bet a month's salary," he told her.

"Great work, Caspar," she said. "I'll pass it on to the..."

"The help?" Caspar asked as if 'help' were some cryptonym.

"Them," Nava told him.

"That isn't all," he said. "Boss, you're not going to believe this. I'm not sure I believe it myself."

"Just tell me," she said, exiting the bus to switch routes again.

"Haddad meets with the prisoner, asks her how she's doing, tells her she's going home soon ... Then he goes downstairs and tells someone to take him in to see the *Majnoon*. Listen to this ..."

"Go ahead," she said, finding a spot next to the bus stop.

She heard Haddad exchange greetings with someone in Arabic, then the scuffling of chairs on the hard floor of the Gulag as they settled in to speak.

"A gift from the *sheikh*," the man said.

"This is the same *sheikh* that called us... what was it? Apostates or heathens or..." Haddad replied. "You can take it back to him. I'm only interested in his money."

"You will have the amount we agreed upon," the man told him.

"That is no longer sufficient," Haddad answered, followed by a beat of silence. "I have the Iranians breathing down my neck, now."

"How is that our problem?"

"They don't care for you," Haddad told him. "You aren't worth trouble with them... not at this price."

"I see," the man replied, his tone resigned. "I suppose we'll have to take our business somewhere else. We'll expect our deposit back by the end of the day."

Nava heard a chair slide back on the wood floor, then footsteps of more than one person before Haddad asked, "You want to learn to make a car bomb without blowing yourself up? You want it powerful enough to destroy the face of a building from hundreds of feet away? You need to learn target reconnaissance? Counter-surveillance?"

There was a pause before Haddad told the stranger to sit back down. They haggled over a price, finally settling at 900,000 USD. Haddad expressed some doubt over the mysterious "*sheikh*" and his ability to deliver payment.

"Word is your enemies overran Jalalabad," Haddad began before the man cut him off.

"He is but part of the struggle," he said. "We have many sponsors among the faithful. You will get your money."

After the meeting ended, she heard Marwan's voice.

"We should kill them," he said, and then she heard Haddad laughing. Marwan, however, sounded deadly serious. "What if they use what we teach them to attack us?"

"You worry too much," he told Marwan. "These guys don't go anywhere in Lebanon without us knowing."

"They're fucking crazy," Marwan said.

"That's why they might be useful to us."

"How?"

"If we have to get rid of the American," Haddad said. "Her blood will be on their hands."

Nava's grip on the phone tightened, the plastic creaking softly under the pressure of her fingers. As Haddad's words echoed in her ear, a cold realization seeped into her consciousness, stark and foreboding. It was as though the shadow of a cloud had passed overhead, casting an unanticipated darkness over her thoughts. The idea that the hostage's life, and by extension the fate of both her countries, hung so precariously on the outcome of their plans, left Nava feeling a profound unease. The gravity of the situation settled in her stomach, a leaden weight that reminded her of the delicate intricacy of their operation Tehran had inexplicably put in the hands of five people she knew then she needed to trust if there was any hope of getting that woman out alive and defusing this bomb before it blew up in their faces.

Upon entering the Butcher's, Nava's attention was immediately captured by a figure who stood out not just for his height but for an allure that seemed to fill the room. Ridley, as he introduced himself, carried the kind of charm that seemed to echo off the walls, making him not only the most visually striking member of the Janissary team but perhaps the most captivating man Nava had encountered in her life. She fought the instinctive rise of color to her cheeks, managing a measured smile in response.

"What's your role on the team?" she asked him.

"I'm the engineer," he told her.

"So, you build things."

"I mostly blow them up."

"Oh."

"Are you married?" he asked her, and she realized that she'd put her ring on this morning yet again.

"Oh... no," she replied. "Divorced, actually."

He winced.

"That's too bad," he said. "We could've had some fun."

She furrowed her brow, wondering what he possibly could have meant. Ridley evidently found that amusing, as a broad grin came across his face. Something in his face at that moment, as attractive as it was, utterly repulsed and horrified her. It was as if that beautiful mask slipped just a little, but enough to show something hideous behind it.

"Ridley," she heard Jake call from behind him, and Ridley turned his head toward his team leader. "Breaching kits."

"On it," he answered, and the mask was back on when he turned his head back. "Nice to meet you."

The encounter left her disquieted. She found it especially strange that, of all the perilous encounters she'd had, this was the one that left her the most shaken. It wasn't that he looked through her like Jake or saw her as a threat like Haddad. There was something much darker about him.

"Hey," Jake called to her, snatching her away from her ruminations. "Erica told us you got us sound in the target house. Good work."

His eyes were a little softer now, but not by much. She found his disposition oddly comforting. He came across as cold and aloof, but also highly professional. He went over the plan for assaulting the Gulag with her, exuding competence that belied his age and seemed to indicate absolute confidence in himself and his team's abilities.

"So... Are you ready to tell me who this is?" he asked at the end of the brief.

She took a breath, preparing to go against her instincts and training to put her trust in, of all people, an American-born mercenary.

"It's Hezbollah," she told him. "Specifically, a militia commander. His name is Yasin Haddad."

Jake called Christian over to them and told him what she had just said.

"You're attacking your ally?" he asked, stroking his goatee. "Are we stepping into like a ... factional war or something?"

"All we know is he's taken a hostage without getting approval," she answered. "Not from us, at least, and probably not from the council that governs Hezbollah."

"Uh-huh."

Christian stopped rubbing his chin and put his hands on his hips.

"We heard that a Hezbollah guy was assassinated a few days ago," he said.

"Abu Faysal," she said with a nod. "Do you know something about it?"

"No," Jake answered. "But could this have anything to do with that?"

"I don't know," she answered. "I do need to find out who killed him, but I haven't gotten far on that yet."

Christian looked to Jake, who shrugged.

"I guess this is the American diplomat that went missing in Jordan," Christian said.

"American?" Jake asked, his interest piqued.

She nodded.

"What do you think is his reason for doing this?" Christian asked her.

"I don't know," she answered.

"Well, I probably don't need to tell you that people usually take hostages for leverage," he said. "Maybe if you find out what he wants, you could get her out without a fight."

Jake turned his attention to the table.

"Where's the next nearest Hezbollah facility that you know of?" he asked her. "Somewhere with a lot of armed militiamen?"

"Beirut," she told them. "That's why we call it the Gulag. It's away from all the places Hezbollah has the heaviest operational presence."

"Security in obscurity," Christian mused. "Makes our job easier, anyway."

"They could still have people in that town," Jake said.

"Spies, definitely," she told them. "Not soldiers."

"*Sawubona,*" she heard Scott say from behind her.

"*Shiboka,*" Jake and Christian answered him nearly simultaneously.

"Sup, girl?" he greeted her.

"Sup?" she replied. "Is that English?"

"It's American," he told her. "Good news – I got the hooptee a new door."

Hassan, the technician on the day shift at the Gulag observation point, called as he was speaking. She stepped aside to talk to him.

"Boss," he said. "Haddad is meeting someone tonight. I couldn't hear well enough to say exactly who, but ... I think ... I don't know for sure, but ..."

"What?"

He almost whispered his answer, as if it was too embarrassing to speak aloud.

"I think it's with the Israelis."

Chapter
Sixteen

That night, Scott drove Nava in the same terrifyingly decrepit car that he had picked her up in at their first meeting to the quiet town of Jezzine. It was here that Haddad was to meet with a contact named "Isaac."

As soon as she'd heard where the meeting was taking place, Nava thought of Khadem asking her about Jezzine. She heard the name of the little town in the mountains perhaps twice before that day in Masoud's office. Now she heard it twice more within the span of a few days, and it bothered her.

Before they left, they stopped at the Baker's, where she hid the floppy disk that her father had sent her in a smoke detector. She knew that she had to talk with him about it at some point, but it would have to wait. For now, it was enough that she did what he asked.

They hadn't left the city before Nava fell dead asleep. She remained that way the entire two-plus hour ride despite how uncomfortable that car was. She dreamt of eating something delicious... and no wonder. She hadn't eaten since breakfast. When she awoke on a tree-lined street in Jezzine, it was to a rumbling stomach and the smell of something rich and greasy.

"Hey, you're up!" Scott said, his voice muffled from gorging himself on something he was holding in a tinfoil wrapper.

Nava blinked her eyes open to see the lights from small shops and restaurants flickering like fireflies beyond the windshield, creating a warm, inviting glow that contrasted with the dark, wooded hills encircling the town. She inhaled deeply, moving past the smell of food to take in the cool and fragrant air scented with pine from the surrounding forests.

"Where are we?" she asked.

"Not sure," he said. "I saw some sign back there, said Saint Joseph Square. Everything else is in Arabic."

He pointed to a small hotel down the street.

"Our boy, Haddad, went in there about an hour ago," he said. "That's his car."

"What are you eating?" she asked him.

"Hmm? Oh... chicken shawarma," he told her and took another bite as she continued to salivate. "Pretty good."

"You just got one?"

Scott stopped chewing abruptly and turned to her with the look of a child caught sneaking a treat before dinner. Nava groaned a little, cradling her stomach and curling herself into a ball on the uncomfortable chair and telling herself not to be disappointed. Another selfish guy. She seemed to be a magnet for them.

He handed her the wrapped sandwich he'd been hiding, and she heard him chuckling as she snatched it from him. She greedily devoured the sandwich, dripping sauce and tiny bits of shredded lettuce onto the duct tape-ridden car seat. Finished, she sat back, immensely satisfied, and gazed over at Scott.

"Where did you get that?" she asked.

"At a stand up the road," he said, motioning behind them. "Took a while, but I think he got what I was saying."

"You speak some Arabic, then?"

"No," he said. "Russian, yes. Ukrainian, Polish, Romanian, and German."

"What language was that I heard back at the Butcher's?" she asked him. "Saw ... Sawa ..."

"*Sawubona,*" he said. "It's Zulu."

"You speak Zulu?"

"God, no ... Only that," he said. "It's how Janissaries greet one another. *Sawubona* means 'I see you.' You respond with *Shiboka*, which means 'I am here.' Pretty cool, right?"

"It is," she agreed. "Why do you say that to one another?"

"We had a friend, way back when we were in training," he told her. "Zulu was his first language. A lot of us spoke more than one. Anyway, he was the first one of us that died in training. It hit us all pretty hard. We decided that we'd always greet one another in his language, to remember him."

"When did that happen?"

"Ten years ago," he said.

She did the quick math, but it seemed too incredible to be correct.

Whether it was completely true or not, the story made her see him in a slightly different light. The impish boy seemed replaced by a young man that had seen much in his short life. He was no 'old soul,' but he had definitely seen more than she'd given him credit for when they first met.

"What do you think Haddad is doing?" she asked him.

"He has a girl up there," he said.

"You think?"

He held up her cell phone and said, "Your technician, Caspar, called and said Haddad was in amorous congress."

She took the phone from him, asking "Amorous... what?"

"You know," he said. "Bumping uglies. Laying pipe. Playing hide the salami. No one says 'knockin' boots' anymore but..."

"Okay, I got it," she said, holding up her hand for him to stop.

"He'll call us when they're done," he told her.

She took a sip of her soda and asked, "Can I ask why you volunteered to bring me here?"

"Because I think you're hot and wanted some time."

His directness surprised her, and she nearly choked on her soda. Instead, it came spraying out of her nose.

"Are you okay?" Scott asked her, chuckling a little.

"I'm ... yes, I'm okay," she said, trying to dab away soda from her jeans and shirt. "Just keep watching the hotel, Romeo."

"Yes, ma'am," he answered.

She hadn't finished cleaning herself up and formulating a response to his come-on before she heard him say, "There."

She looked out at the shadow of the hotel entrance and saw the slightest movement in the darkness. From this distance and in this light, all she could see was that it was two people in dark clothing headed up the street.

"Why didn't Caspar call?" she whispered.

"Find out," he whispered back, and she dialed the number.

"Boss?" she heard Caspar on the line.

"Why didn't you call when he left?"

"All I hear from his phone is the shower running," the technician answered.

Nava cursed and ended the call. "He left his phone in the hotel room," she said.

In the hush of the Jezzine night, Nava and Scott made their exit from the car with a purpose that belied the casualness of their movements. Scott, with the practiced ease of a man who had done this many times before, slung a small black backpack over his shoulder—a "Go Bag" filled with the sundry equipment necessary for surveillance. They set off through the streets and alleys of Jezzine, a labyrinthine dance of shadow and light under the watchful eyes of ancient buildings.

Their quarry, Haddad and his companion Marwan, moved with the assurance of men on their own turf, yet burdened with the caution of those who know they are hunted. Haddad, with his guerrilla's intuition for surveillance, wove a path through Jezzine that would have thwarted less skilled followers. But Scott and Nava were not so easily deterred. They matched his steps with a silent choreography of their own, a thread of tension drawn taut between them.

Haddad paused, a sudden interest taken in a shop window. It occurred to Nava perhaps half a second too late that it was not the wares inside he sought to inspect but their reflection. Luckily, Scott had seen it and reacted quickly by pulling Nava close, using his body as a shield between them and the glass that could betray their presence. For a moment, pressed against him in the dim light, Nava felt her heart quicken, a rush of adrenaline or perhaps something more, making her breath catch.

The danger passed as Haddad moved on, hopefully none the wiser; but the moment lingered between them, unspoken.

"Let's go," she said, the breathiness in her voice surprising her.

They continued their pursuit, the distance between them now charged with an unacknowledged tension. The streets of Jezzine, with their secrets and shadows, had become the backdrop to a different kind of dance, one of risk and revelation, where the stakes were not just the success of their mission but the uncharted territories of trust and proximity.

Their journey led them to where the town's ancient architecture gave way to the natural world. The destination to which Haddad led them was seemingly innocuous. Luckily, Scott's bag had a pair of night vision goggles. In the green-tinged world, Nava observed some sort of entryway—a gaping maw set against the ancient stone, its edges softened by the passage of time and the encroachment of creeping vines. The archway loomed like a portal to another world, its darkness absolute, swallowing the faintest hints of light.

"What's there?" Scott whispered to her.

Nava could only offer a shrug in response as Marwan and Haddad melted into the shadows. With practiced fluidity, Scott slipped on the night vision goggles and drew a silenced pistol from the bag.

"Stay close," he whispered.

Approaching the entrance, they descended the ancient steps with caution, entering what appeared to be an old cistern, long abandoned. The air hung heavy with an unspoken tension, their movements a silent ballet among the shadows. Every step was a balance between haste and stealth; too fast, and they might stumble upon their targets unprepared, too slow, and they risked losing them entirely. Scott led with the precision of a predator, halting at a bend with a hand signal for Nava to stop. She froze, her breath held tight, ears straining for any sound in the enveloping silence. Ahead, the soft echo of footsteps and the cadence of a distant conversation whispered through the dark, a delicate thread of sound in the vast quiet.

Scott, ever vigilant, eased the bag to the ground without a sound, his focus never wavering from the unseen corner. Nava watched, her heart a drumbeat in the silence, as he silently retrieved an object from the bag and handed it to her with a gesture towards his ear, then turned back to survey the darkness ahead.

In the dim light, Nava fumbled with the tiny receiver, her fingers clumsy with tension. As she attempted to tuck her hair behind her ear to place the device, it slipped from her grasp, landing with a betraying clink against the stone floor. Panic surged and her body coiled to flee or fight. Time stretched into an eternity as she awaited the consequence of her mistake.

But the voices continued, a muffled but distinct murmur of conversation. Relief washed over her as Scott retrieved the fallen receiver and placed it securely in her ear. Now, with the voices clear and discernible, she caught the exchange, a vital snippet of dialogue unraveling in the quiet of the cistern.

In the quiet of the night, their breaths shallow and hearts racing, Nava and Scott absorbed every whispered word with bated anticipation. The voice, laced with authority and a hint of menace, spoke in Arabic, recounting a tale of devastation. "...brother was making bombs for Hamas, one of which obliterated a bus, claiming nine innocent lives in Haifa."

Haddad's response was a vow wrapped in velvet steel. "You won't see him outside Lebanon again. You have my word."

A silent exchange of approval passed between Nava and Scott in the form of a thumbs-up. She could hear them well. They began their cautious retreat, their roles momentarily reversed as Scott's eyes and weapon remained locked on the unseen meeting.

The conversation took a sharp turn, unveiling a nexus of terror that sent a chill down Nava's spine. "There's another matter," the unknown interlocutor pressed. "We know there's an al Qaeda cell in Beirut. Are you in contact with them?"

"Yes," came Haddad's admission, stark and chilling.

"What are they doing here?"

"Training," Haddad said. "To build a car bomb and detonate it remotely."

"Where?"

"You don't get something for nothing," Haddad countered.

"How about this?" the man replied. "You tell us where they're training, and we won't leak what really happened to Abu Faysal."

Caught off guard by the mention of Abu Faysal, Nava nearly stumbled in the dark, her focus momentarily shattered. Emerging into the lesser darkness of the night, she heard someone say something about a bluff, then, in her other ear: "Sabi..."

Her codename, uttered so close, snapped her attention back with the intensity of a whip crack. Her hand instinctively reached for her concealed PS-9, and she whirled to face the shadows. They stepped forward, one showing his hands, the other with a pistol pointed at her.

"We need to talk," declared the one showing his hands, stepping into the dim light. It was Rafiq, her colleague from Syria's General Intelligence Directorate, his face a mask of solemn intent.

"Do you mind putting that away?" he asked her, his gaze shifting between her and his companion. "Easy. We're all friends."

"Did you kill him?" Nava blurted out, and Rafiq's brow furrowed.

"Kill who?" he asked.

"Don't fuck with me, Rafiq!"

He extended his right palm toward her—a plea for calm that she ignored.

"We didn't kill Abu Faysal, if that's whom you're asking about," he said. "And we don't know who did. Just put the gun—"

"Why have you been following us?" she demanded.

"Who's 'us'?" he asked in reply, and the question surprised her. "Or are you the only one allowed to ask questions? Where's your friend? Is he still down there?"

The man with the gun peered into the entrance to the cistern for a second before quickly turning his attention back to her.

"Why are you following me?" she asked.

Rafiq shook his head and threw his hands up as if the question were absurd.

"Well, let me see, Sabi," he said. "You stopped sending arms shipments through Damascus, Hezbollah is training an Al-Qaeda cell, and now you show up in a town with an active Mossad cell. You're freaking us the fuck out! Now you mind telling me what's going on?"

"I'm trying to find out who killed Abu Faysal and why," she said, her tone still terse. "My source named *you*, and they haven't been wrong yet."

Rafiq's bewilderment seemed genuine, but she couldn't trust it just yet.

"Well ... You should cut that source loose because we had nothing to do with it," he said. "Not that I know of, anyway."

She wanted to believe him, but it was difficult. All day she felt danger closing in on her, and now the Syrians show up out of nowhere just days after she found out about their possible involvement in Abu Faysal's death.

"Listen," Rafiq said. "We knew Abu Faysal was trying to convince the *Shura* Council to stop working with us, but we also knew Nasrallah and his advisors weren't receptive. At worst, we thought Abu Faysal would split off from Hezbollah and start his own movement, but that was years from now at the soonest. When you stopped sending arms to them through us, we started to think that you might be seeing if you could support Hezbollah without our help. It seemed like you were cutting us out. We're just trying to make sure we still have a seat at the table. That's all. *Wallah*, I'm telling the truth."

Before she could answer, there was a loud thud and the *Mukhabarat* agent beside Rafiq collapsed, falling face-first onto the ground. She saw a flash of movement in the darkness behind where the agent had stood, brought her pistol up, and aimed in that direction; but the only thing she saw beyond the front sight of the pistol was empty darkness.

Chapter Seventeen

Nava glanced at her "captive" as Scott sat him in the passenger's seat, never taking his silenced weapon off him. She could feel Rafiq's eyes boring a hole in her skull as Scott climbed in the back seat.

"We have to move," Scott told her once he closed the door. "Like *now.*"

She pulled a U-turn and drove into the night, trying to think of a way to explain all this to Rafiq ... If he lived through it.

"Did you kill my friend?" Rafiq asked Scott in English.

"He'll be fine," Scott told him. "Worry about yourself."

She could feel Rafiq giving her the side-eye, even if she couldn't look directly at him.

"Whatever this is, it's not going to turn out well for you," Rafiq told her.

"Let's just ... Calm down," she said, though she felt on the verge of panic. She had to find a way to resolve this before they got to Beirut, where they would have to let Rafiq go.

In the rearview mirror, she saw Scott lower his weapon, though she didn't doubt that it was now pointed squarely at Rafiq's back rather than his head. Nava's mind was a tumult of conflicting emotions as she faced Rafiq, the weight of her decisions pressing heavily upon her.

The dim interior of the car, lit only by the passing streetlights, cast their faces in a dance of shadows and light, highlighting the tension in the air. Her hand, though steady on the surface, betrayed a slight tremor, a physical manifestation of her internal struggle between duty and the dire necessity of trust in this precarious moment.

"*Meen hayda?*" Rafiq asked her in Arabic. *Who is he?*

"He's ... helping me," she said.

"He's an asset?"

She bit her lower lip and nodded, though she could tell Rafiq wasn't completely sold. He still looked at her with suspicious eyes, and rightly so.

"You were spying on Haddad," Rafiq said. "We followed you following him. Why are you in such a shitty car, anyway?"

"It's ... a long story," she answered him, glaring at Scott's reflection in the rearview mirror.

"This has something to do with Janta, doesn't it?"

Janta was one of several training facilities Hezbollah ran in the Bekaa Valley, and one of the largest in Lebanon. Like everything else in the Bekaa Valley, it belonged to Haddad.

"Why do you say that?"

Rafiq scoffed, shook his head, and looked out at the pitch-black road ahead of them. He wouldn't offer anymore. Nava tried to remember what he said before Scott intervened. Her anger with him for putting her in this situation was consuming nearly all her conscious mind, and the rest was dedicated to driving the lethargic car.

"What were you doing in Jezzine?" he asked her.

When she didn't reply, he shook his head and laughed bitterly.

"Is something funny?" she asked him.

"Yes!" he told her. "This! This is funny. Fucking spies ... We don't trust anyone, especially not each other; even when we really need to."

She saw Rafiq glance in the rearview mirror, undoubtedly looking at Scott.

"Is he American?" he asked her.

Her mind raced for a response, and a snippet of conversation she shared not that long ago came to her.

"He's Russian," she said.

Rafiq looked in the rearview mirror and asked, "*Vy Russky?*"

Scott said nothing, and she immediately suspected that he'd lied to her about knowing Russian. She could see Rafiq giving her the side-eye again.

"*Vy—*" he began, but Scott snapped at him.

"*Zatkniss! Pridurok ... pogovorii s damoi.*"

Rafiq raised his eyebrows and said, "He's very rude. He's Russian, alright."

Nava looked in the mirror and saw Scott wink at her, but it did nothing to assuage her anger with him.

"Aren't you going to say something?" Rafiq asked her.

"Why should I?" she replied.

"Are you seriously asking the guy you just kidnapped to show some good faith here?"

"You were the one following me," she said.

"Fine," he said. "We weren't following you. We got electronic intercepts indicating a Mossad cell in Jezzine. We think two, maybe three agents. It's a heavy tourist town, mostly Christian, so it's a permissive operating environment for them. We think they might be staying at an apartment building on the street where you parked. That's what we were watching. We only started watching *you* when you drove up. I was going to put a tracker on the car, but it's hard to tell which part of this thing isn't about to fall off. That's when I saw you. We followed you following Haddad."

"Why were you following me yesterday?"

"We weren't," he told her, and she heard the confusion in his tone. "Now do you want to tell me why you were in Jezzine?"

For the second time in less than twenty-four hours, Nava was being asked to ignore her training and instincts and lend something she had in short supply – trust. In both cases, the very nature of that person's existence was an argument against investing her trust in them. Between the anguish of having to relinquish secrets and her anger with Scott for putting her in this position, she missed the faint ring coming from Rafiq's pants.

"May I answer it?" Rafiq asked her. "It's probably my boss."

Rafiq's request to answer his phone seemed almost mundane in the context of their high-stakes encounter, yet it pierced the silence like a siren, jolting Nava back to the immediate reality. His voice, while steady as he spoke to his superior, carried an undercurrent of urgency that resonated with Nava's own sense of urgency.

"Yes ... No, it was just a misunderstanding. I'm with her now. He's fine? Good ... Hold on ..."

He put his hand over the microphone and looked at her.

"Are we going to discuss this?" he asked. "Or am I going to say that I don't know why you were parked a hundred feet from a suspected Mossad safe house, attacked a Syrian intelligence officer, and kidnapped another?"

She sighed and nodded in resignation. He left her little choice.

"Yasin Haddad was meeting with an Israeli," she told him once he'd ended the call with his boss. "We were trying to find out why."

"That's easy," Rafiq said. "The Israelis have his brother, Seyyed."

"How do you know that?" she asked.

"You don't read the Israeli papers?" Rafiq asked and shook his head. "He was arrested in an IDF sweep in Gaza. Had quite a bomb factory there, from what I understood."

"Why would he go to Gaza?" she asked

"I was just as surprised as you are," Rafiq said. "I mean, all that money we put into vocational training for Hezbollah, and what does one of their bombmakers do when a ceasefire puts him out of work? He goes looking for someone to pay him to make bombs! The ingratitude is galling."

Nava glared at him, but it didn't stop him from having a little laugh at her expense.

"What did he offer the Israelis?" he asked her.

"A hostage," she said.

"Host—Are you talking about the missing American?"

Telling him that, she decided, was over the line. For one, the information would be just that much more widely known, and the chances a secret would cease being a secret went up exponentially with each person that knew it. Then there was what Masoud had warned her about. If this was an attempt by the hardliners in her own government to undermine the reformers, the Syrians might well stand with the hardliners.

"No," she lied to him. "An Israeli soldier, we think."

Rafiq still seemed shocked at the news. He slouched in his chair with eyebrows high and exhaled a long breath through pursed lips.

"Wow," he said. "I thought that ... Well, I don't know. After Abu Faysal, things were tense enough. Now grabbing an Israeli? It starts to look like tit-for-tat. Wars have started over less."

Nava saw what she believed was genuine anxiety on Rafiq's face. He didn't say anything else until they reached Beirut. They were well short of the exit for the Syrian embassy when he told her to get off the

116

highway at the Tariq El-Jdideh neighborhood, where he told her to park on a side street.

"There are people on all sides that want this ceasefire to be done with," he said.

"How do you feel about it?" she asked him.

"I feel that how I feel about it doesn't make a damn bit of difference," he answered her. "I do what I'm told. It could change, but right now I'm told to keep the ceasefire in place. What about you?"

"The same," she lied again. She didn't have any instructions regarding the ceasefire, likely because Tehran was of two minds about it. She had little doubt that the same was true of Damascus and Tel Aviv.

"Haddad's a wild card," he said. "Even if this thing with his brother gets fixed, he'll still have to be reigned in."

He paused, perhaps to allow her to raise any objections. She did neither, figuring the best thing to do was keep her options open. He pointed to a nondescript apartment block facing the highway.

"The sixth floor," he said. "Is an Al-Qaeda cell. Haddad has been training them at Janta for about a week."

She looked up at the mostly darkened building with incredulity.

"What do you know about Al-Qaeda?" he asked her.

"Not much," she answered. "They're in Sudan, I think."

"Bashir kicked him out of Sudan," he said.

"Him?"

"Osama Bin Laden," he said. "He moved his operations to Afghanistan."

She made a face, scrunching her nose and furrowing her brow.

"It's the last place I would go, too," he told her. "But he feels right at home there. They're a lot closer to Iran now, anyway. They're paying Haddad nearly a million U.S. dollars, according to our source."

"How many are there?" she asked, motioning to the apartment building.

"At least eight," he said. "We only know one of them – an Egyptian we know as Seif Al-Adel. We were tracking him as a member of Islamic Jihad, but sources say he's hooked up with Al-Qaeda. The rest are Saudis, we think."

Rafiq turned to face her as much as the seat allowed.

"This isn't going to fix itself," he told her. "We had nothing to do with Abu Faysal; but if you or the council don't reign Haddad in, we *will* get in the business of liquidating Hezbollah commanders."

Nava got back on the highway and headed toward the Syrian embassy.

"So, uh ... This guy's a mercenary?" he asked her, jerking his head toward the back seat.

"What makes you say that?"

"Ever since the Soviet Union broke up, they've been showing up all over the place," he told her. "Ex-Spetsnaz, ex-KGB, GRU, plus Eastern bloc guys. South Africans, too. End of apartheid and all that. Suddenly a lot of thugs are all out of work. Is he from something called the Russian Business Network?"

"No. Why?"

"We're thinking of using them on some missions," he said. "Overseas, of course, like you. We both have plenty of thugs at home, don't we?"

"That, we do."

After dropping Rafiq at his embassy, Nava drove Scott in silence to her apartment. She was aware that Masoud would soon hear what happened. So, too, would the ambassador. She was almost certain that a man would be given the benefit of the doubt. They would say he took a bad situation and brought it back under his control, demonstrating his crisis management skills. As a woman, however, she would probably be blamed for creating the problem in the first place.

She pulled the clunker over to the side of the road, yanked the door open, stepped out, and slammed it shut. She didn't even care that it failed to stay closed, bouncing back from the frame and creaking open as she stormed toward her apartment building's entrance.

"Hey ..." She heard Scott call to her as he climbed out of the car. Ignoring him, she kept walking until he shouted, "You're welcome!"

She whirled, looked at the boy with blood in her eyes, and spat his words back at him. "You're welcome?!"

"Yeah," he said, clearly taken a little aback.

"You fly into a situation you know nothing about, almost end my career, and I'm supposed to be grateful?"

"I assessed the situation and did what I thought necessary." He tried to close the driver's door, but it kept opening. "Great ..." he said, motioning to the door.

She fumed as he began to dig through the car's glove compartment. "I don't even know why I'm mad at you," she said.

"Neither do I," he retorted, emerging with a roll of duct tape.

"You don't know a thing about this place!" she said, waving her hand in the air as Scott walked around to the passenger's side. "And you think you can 'assess a situation'? I should be mad at myself for taking you with me in the first place. I should have known you'd come in like a cowboy waving your gun to save the helpless woman from—"

"I never thought you were helpless," he said. "I thought you were in trouble, so I tried to help because that's what I do for my friends, Sabi."

He got in the car and began tearing strips of duct tape off the roll. She stepped up to the open passenger-side window and stooped over to yell at him.

"You're not my friend, Scott!" she rebuked him. "You're the help, and from now on you do what I tell you to and nothing else. Do you understand?"

"Yeah, yeah ..." he said. "Can you at least give me a hand?"

"What are you doing?"

"Just ... hold the door closed, please." She stepped around the car and pressed the door closed, but it popped open. "I said hold the door closed!"

"Fine!"

She closed the heavy door and stayed in place. It took considerable effort on her part, forcing her to lean into it and bring her head close to the window while Scott taped the door to the frame. It brought their faces close to one another – close enough that, if when he finished and looked up at her with his vibrant blue eyes, she could have brought her lips to his with the lightest of efforts, and for a split second she forgot about her anger until he drew his head back inside the car.

"That's not going to fix it," she told him.

"What do you care?" he asked. "I'm just the help."

She didn't know why, but it stung having the very words she'd spoken to him flung back at her. As much as she wanted to apologize, she felt herself in the right. Instead, she just stepped back as he started the car and drove off without another word.

Chapter Eighteen

Masoud's face remained impassive through most of Nava's account of the previous evening. Puffing on his pipe in his comfortable home office, he reacted only twice—once when she first mentioned Jezzine, when he grunted and shook his head; then after she told him about Scott's intervention in her standoff with the Syrians, he chuckled a little. By the time she finished, she felt exhausted.

"I mean it, Masoud," she said. "I want their contract canceled. This is an internal matter, and they already know too much about it."

"You don't think they can be trusted?"

"Not in the slightest," she answered, sipping her favorite mint tea and marveling at how it was still warm even half an hour after buying it.

"Someone above both of us disagrees," he told her. "But I'll pass your recommendation up again."

"Thank you."

He shifted in his chair, searching for a more comfortable position. It was what he did when he was uncomfortable with the conversation.

"What do you propose we do about the hostage, then?" he asked.

"We wait to see if the Israelis trade Seyyed Haddad for her," she suggested.

"And if they don't?"

Nava sipped her tea, buying her a few seconds of thought. She'd already considered the alternatives the previous night, on the taxi ride from her apartment to the café, and the walk to Masoud's house. There was no third way that the hostage came out of this alive.

"You heard the conversation from the Gulag," she said. "Haddad will give her to al Qaeda, and they'll gladly take credit for killing her. It'll be all over CNN within hours."

"And you think the Americans will accept that?" he asked her. "Even if Hezbollah was the one that took her in the first place? They still blame us for Khobar Towers."

Nava threw her hands up with a shrug and shook her head.

"Look, it's a policy question now," she said. "I don't know what the Americans will do. Even if they did think we did Khobar Towers, they didn't do anything afterward."

Masoud leaned back and puffed on his pipe, turned his chair a bit toward the grand window behind him, and looked through the sheer curtains at the early morning pedestrian traffic outside. Nava checked her watch.

"I have to go," she told him and stood to leave. "I'll be late for another interrogation with Major Khadem."

"Forget Khadem," he said. "I'll take care of him for you. Do whatever else you need to do to get them ready. Tehran wants them ready to go in tonight."

At the Butcher's, she found only Erica in the main room, making Turkish coffee. The others, she said, were either sleeping or out preparing for the raid.

"Going to rain tonight," Erica told her.

"Is that good or bad?" Nava asked, flopping down on a chair at the table with her. Neatly lined up against the wall, she saw several black tactical vests, various assault rifles, a sniper's rifle, and pistols.

"It'll help," Erica said, then yawned. "But it's bad for the helicopter. The plan is to hold her here until it can fly, then bring her to the LZ."

"It sounds like you have it all figured out," she said.

Erica placed a small cup of thick cardamom-infused coffee in front of her.

"I heard you had a long night," Erica said. "Sorry about Scottie."

Nava propped her head up, pushed her black hair out of her face, and took a sip.

"It wasn't completely his fault," Nava admitted. "I would probably apologize if he was here. This is really fucking good."

"I try," Erica replied with a sly grin.

"Can I tell you something sad?" Nava asked her. "I got divorced last month."

"Seriously?"

Nava nodded.

"Fucking *bummer*!" Erica said, making Nava laugh a little.

"I think it's harder because I haven't had anyone to talk to about it," Nava went on. "My family moved around a lot, and I got married right after college. I never really had a lot of friends. I guess I just never really thought I needed them."

Erica offered nothing in reply, other than a sympathetic smile. Nava decided to change the subject. "You said you had your own team?" she asked her.

Erica nodded, but her eyes were dull; almost sad.

"I did, anyway," she said. "The truth is we might get broken up. Fucking McBain might have me do this from now on."

"McBain?"

"Jack McBain. Our CEO."

"How long have you worked there?"

Erica's forehead wrinkled and she shifted in her chair. It was the first time Nava had seen her uncomfortable with talking about something.

"Janissaries... people like me, we were part of a program," she said. "It started when we were very young. When exactly we became what we are is a little ambiguous."

"A program?"

"Yeah... like a government program," Erica replied. "The deal was if we made it all the way through, they paid for college wherever we wanted to go."

"Made it through?"

"It was tough," Erica said before her gaze fell to the floor and she entered a contemplative trance. She seemed to snap herself out of it quickly, though; and Nava was left to wonder what she'd been thinking or remembering. "Anyway..." she said. "We were never supposed to be a private company. When the government decided they didn't need us anymore, they just wanted us to go away."

The hurt in her voice, no matter how she tried to conceal it, was visceral. She sounded nearly like an abandoned child.

"You should go home," Erica told her. "Get some rest. It's going to be a long night."

Chapter
Nineteen

Nava's attempts to reach Masoud by phone throughout the afternoon were met with silence, leaving her in a state of escalating concern. It was uncharacteristic for Masoud to be unreachable.

When he finally responded to her call late at night, his tone was brisk, devoid of any explanation for his absence. He issued her orders with an air of finality before abruptly disconnecting. The directive was straightforward: position the Janissaries strategically and await further instructions from Tehran.

Nava understood the gravity of the situation, aware that such decisions likely escalated to the highest levels of government. She mused over the complexities of authority within the government's covert operations. In times past, under Ayatollah Khomeini's leadership, decision-making had been more centralized, more straightforward. Masoud often reminisced about those simpler times, contrasting them with the current fragmentation of power. The Revolutionary Guard had aggressively stepped into the void left by Khomeini, yet her ministry, along with the presidency, still wielded significant influence. President Khatami, in particular, represented a democratically elected counterbalance to the more entrenched powers of the IRGC and the supreme leader, underscoring the inherent tension within an absolute regime's disregard for public opinion.

As the mission start time approached, Nava's thoughts briefly wandered to Scott, wishing for a moment of camaraderie before the operation commenced. Instead, she departed with Jake and Erica, leaving Scott behind. She was reassured, however, to find Caspar beginning his shift. His dual expertise as a skilled technician with a keen understanding of operational dynamics was a rare and valued asset in their line of work, providing a sliver of comfort in the uncertain hours that lay ahead.

The clock had edged past 3:00 a.m. when the team initiated their final communications check, a precursor to the operation hanging in the balance, waiting for Tehran's approval which Nava was tasked to relay. To facilitate this, Erica handed her an additional headset, integrating her into their network of callsigns that echoed the names of legendary figures from Greek mythology: Achilles, Ajax, Hector, Odysseus, and Athena. Nava was dubbed "Helen," a nod that carried a touch of irony. Though she may not have incited a war of epic proportions, she was undeniably the catalyst for their current assembly in Beirut's rain-soaked night.

"Are Abbott and Costello still on stage?" came Jake's voice through the headset, a light-hearted reference to the aliases they had assigned to the visible militiamen.

From her vantage point, Erica, under the callsign Athena, scrutinized the scene through the lens of a sniper rifle, poised on a tripod for stability and precision. The task of reconfiguring the room to accommodate their operational needs – rearranging cameras and furniture for an unobstructed view of the target, ensuring Erica's shooting angles were clear, and preventing any monitor light from impairing her night vision – had been intricate. Yet, for Nava, observing the meticulous preparation, she considered it a minor hurdle in the grand scheme of their mission.

Peering over Caspar's shoulder, Nava glimpsed the grainy figures on the monitor, mirroring what Erica surveyed through her scope. The targets were clustered under a makeshift shelter of corrugated tin, precariously propped and offering scant protection against the elements. Erica's confirmation, "Affirmative," came crisply through the headset, signaling readiness and a shared focus on the task at hand. The operation was a go, tethered to the hope of Tehran's imminent green light, under the cover of Beirut's warm summer rain.

"I have eyes on Chong," Jake's voice filtered through, poised and ready, a harbinger of the impending action. "Waiting for the light."

Erica's soft hiss for attention drew Nava closer. "Take a look," she urged, gesturing towards the sophisticated equipment before her.

Navigating the nuances of the rifle's thermal sight proved more challenging for Nava than anticipated. The darkness initially seemed impenetrable until a faint glow—a solitary beacon in the night—captured her focus. With careful adjustments, a form emerged from the void, its outline punctuated by the bright ember of a cigarette. The realization dawned on her; the guard was making his rounds, oblivious to the watchful eyes that marked his every move.

"That's the point of no return," Erica's voice, laden with gravity, broke the silence. "When you signal us to proceed, Jake will neutralize the guard. Then, the entire area will plunge into darkness."

Nava, pulling away from the scope, sought clarification. "Why is that?"

"Ridley's tasked with severing the power supply," Erica explained with a strategic calm. "He's also prepared to deploy a breaching charge near Abbott and Costello as a backup plan. Meanwhile, Scott and Christian will execute the main assault from the opposite end, eliminating any immediate threats and paving the way for Jake and Ridley to infiltrate through the main entrance... You understand the sequence?"

Nava nodded, her mind racing through the implications of each move in this meticulously choreographed operation.

"But we can't initiate and then hesitate," Erica's tone was instructive, underscored with a seriousness that anchored Nava back to the gravity of the moment. "We can't risk alarming them to the point they relocate the hostage."

Nava acknowledged with a swift nod, her breath caught in a tight chest. The pulse of adrenaline had stealthily woven into her veins, perhaps since the moment they all confirmed readiness. The palpable reality of their mission now loomed large and undeniable.

Masoud's voice was immediate, a stark contrast to the tension that filled the room, as he answered her call. "I have Tehran on the landline," he announced, businesslike. "Are we ready?"

"We're ready," she affirmed.

"Standby."

Standby, she mused bitterly, as if she were poised to do anything else, and drifted back to Caspar's side to peer into the digital gateway that offered them a silent vigil over the scene.

"Look at this," Caspar's whisper cut through the thick anticipation, his attention riveted to the screen.

Displayed was the solitary figure of the guard, his cigarette a beacon in the night. But now, an additional form lurked perilously close, a ghostly presence on the edge of perception.

"Regular camera," Caspar decided, fingers flicking a switch with practiced ease.

The scene transformed, the digital clarity giving way to the stark reality of a dimly lit street, the guard's silhouette barely touched by the feeble glow of a distant lamp. The other, the interloper, had vanished into the shadows.

"Where is he?" Nava's voice barely rose above a breath.

"Look here ... *really* carefully," Caspar directed, his finger pinpointing a scarcely discernible anomaly on the monitor. She leaned in, her gaze sharpening, willing her eyes to pierce the darkness.

And then, a mere flicker, perhaps a raindrop's brief dalliance with light, betrayed movement. It was minuscule, easily missed, yet unmistakably human.

Jake had merged with the shadow, a mere breath away from the unsuspecting guard.

"He's *that* close," Caspar exhaled, his admiration mingling with disbelief. "And that guy has no idea he's about to be taken. Who are these guys?"

In that moment, under the glow of the monitors and the cloak of night, Nava grasped the full measure of their operation's silent, deadly precision. A dance of shadows and light, where life and death hung on the slender thread of a decision, and the Janissaries moved unseen, unfelt, until the moment of revelation.

As he refocused on the thermal lens, the shape reemerged from the veil of darkness, a phantom barely a breath away from the oblivious guard. With each step the guard took, the specter mirrored him, a silent wraith trailing through the void. It was at this juncture, with a sudden, sharp clarity, that the full weight of her impending decision crashed into her. She was on the cusp of commanding actions that would end lives, a chain reaction starting with one, then two, and cascading into an untold number within those walls. The thought unbidden, seared through her - images of wives receiving the grim news, their children's faces obscured by fear and confusion, not yet old enough to grasp the permanence of loss.

"Nava," Masoud's voice pierced the heavy air.

Her response was a strangled silence, her voice lost to the sudden tightness in her throat. Desperate for a moment to collect herself, she stumbled towards the kitchenette, the urgency of Masoud's call amplifying her disarray as she nearly collided with the camera tripod. Cabinets flew open under her frantic search, each as empty as the last - a futile quest for something as simple as a glass. By the time Masoud's voice reached her for the third time, she abandoned her search, resorting to a makeshift cup of her hands to quench her parched throat with a few droplets of water.

"I'm here," she managed, her voice steadier than she felt.

"Tehran is calling it off," Masoud's words came as an unexpected blow. "For now, at least."

The cancellation, rather than offering relief, sparked a fury within her. The hours of tension, the meticulous planning, all seemingly for naught - a mission aborted on the brink of execution.

"Why?" The word was a sharp lance, betraying her frustration.

"They want to give Haddad a chance to negotiate the exchange," he explained, the rationale doing little to quell her irritation. "They believe it's the safer route."

"And the Janissaries?" The question hung in the air, a tether to the practicalities they were entwined with.

"We're keeping them on standby," he confirmed. "Meet me at eight. My house."

Chapter
Twenty

At least staying awake the entire night for something that ended up not happening gave her an excuse to go home and sleep, which Nava planned to do after she met with Masoud at his house. She was so worn out that she wasn't sure if the caffeine in her favorite mint tea could perk her up. Knowing she'd need it just to get through this meeting, she sat outside the café and smoked cigarettes until it opened, got her piping hot cup, and walked to Masoud's.

She sat in that large, comfortable chair across from his desk with a heavy sigh of exhaustion. This was one of those days she could fall asleep in the chair – if only she wasn't so upset with him.

"Where were you yesterday?" she asked him.

He looked up from lighting his pipe with bulging eyes and blinked hard. His eyes widened in surprise, a flicker of indignation crossing his features as if the boundaries of their professional rapport had been momentarily breached.

"Excuse me?" he asked like a parent that just heard a demand from an impudent child.

She looked away and took a calming breath.

"I'm sorry," she said. "It was a... a long night."

Her boss's eyes softened, and he seemed to relax his tense shoulders.

"I had to go somewhere," he said. "I thought I figured something out, and I had to see if I was right."

"What was it?"

"I can't say," he said and raised his palm to her gently before she could say anything. "Not yet. But I will."

"Okay," she replied and tipped her head back against the chair.

He began looking through some papers on his desk when she heard her phone ring. Muscle memory sent her hand to her jacket's inside pocket, but it was the wrong phone. She'd been keeping the bugged Nokia there, but her StarTAC—her embassy-issued phone—was in her front pocket, and that was the one that was ringing.

"This is still going to cost money," she heard Masoud say before she could answer it. "The helicopter alone will be thousands."

"Why didn't we go?" she asked. "They were all ready."

He glanced up at her and chuckled.

"I thought you didn't believe in these Janissary people," he said.

"I think... maybe I was wrong."

Masoud grunted and puffed on his pipe, finally looking up from his paperwork. He seemed tired—more than usual, anyway; yet his eyes were bright and alert. Her phone started ringing again, and this time she took it out. It was Caspar. The previous call had been Jake. Whatever it was would have to wait.

"Talk to me about this disk of my father's," she said.

He rested his arms on the desk and placed his pipe on its stand. "Your father and I, we worked on a lot of things in Paris," he said. "Not just assets. We had to do it all in those days."

His voice softened toward the end, his face soft and expressionless as he fell silent.

"What's on the disk, Masoud?" she asked.

"Hmm? Oh, nothing ... The MOIS oath of office ... sort of. There are a few things deliberately out of place."

"I don't understand," she told him, growing impatient.

"It's not what's on the disk, Nava," he said. "It's what it *is*. It's a key."

"Key to what?"

"There was a—" Masoud began, but he stopped talking abruptly. He was focused on something behind and to the left of her chair, by the entrance to the office.

She leaned forward in the chair and peeked around the large back, but saw nothing before the sharp report of a firearm echoed, a sound so brutally out of place that it cleaved the moment in two. Nava's training took over, her body reacting even before her mind had fully grasped the gravity of the situation. The room, once a sanctuary of strategic discourse, transformed into a stage for a deadly dance.

She dove for cover, the plush chair that had cradled her fatigue now a scant shield against the violence unleashed. Through the haze of shock and adrenaline, she glimpsed the assailant – a specter clad in the garb of death, his movements deliberate, his purpose clear. The acrid smell of gunpowder tinged the air, a metallic taste of fear on her tongue.

In a desperate bid for survival, Nava turned her attacker's momentary oversight into an opportunity. The cup of mint tea, once a comfort, became her weapon of defiance. She hurled it with all the force her panic could muster, the liquid scalding the air as it flew towards its target. Her assailant's cry, a mix of surprise and pain, was a fleeting victory in the chaos.

She surged towards the promise of escape, her every nerve alight with the primal urge to flee; but she didn't make it to the door before the world spun and darkened, a void where time and sense blurred into oblivion.

Awakening to a world of pain and confusion, Nava's first coherent thought was a grim acceptance of her end. Instead, she was met with the stark, unyielding reality of a world unchanged by her ordeal, save for the throbbing reminder of her own vulnerability pulsing at her temple. The realization that she had not met her end, but perhaps narrowly evaded it, was cold comfort as she lay with the echoes of gunfire still ringing in her ears.

"Sabi..." she heard a voice calling, somewhat distant at first, then closer—close enough to shake her shoulders and make her head hurt even more. "Sabi!"

As she forced her eyes to obey, to focus on the source of the voice, the world around her slowly ceased its spinning. The face that swam into her vision was at once a blur of colors and shapes, gradually coalescing into a visage marked by concern and familiarity. Though her mind fumbled with names and faces, a deeper, more primal part of her recognized safety in the lines of his expression, the steadiness in his eyes.

With a groan that bore the weight of her pain, she felt his support, a solid presence as he slid an arm behind her, offering his strength as she struggled to marshal her own. Her arm found a perch around his neck, a gesture as much of trust as it was of necessity, and together they forged a precarious balance as he hoisted her up.

"We gotta go," the voice said in English, and she looked at his face, so close to hers.

"Scottie..." she muttered.

"Can you walk?" he asked her. "Come on."

The unsteady rhythm of her steps, each one a battle against the weakness that threatened to claim her knees, was punctuated by his unwavering support. They moved together, a picture of resilience amidst chaos, their destination unclear but driven by an instinctual need to flee the danger. Yet, as they neared the threshold of perceived safety, a sudden realization anchored her to the spot with the weight of forgotten responsibility.

"Masoud," she uttered, the name slicing through the haze of shock like a beacon, reigniting the memory of why they were there. With renewed purpose, she fought against the direction they were headed, her movements becoming a frantic attempt to return to where it all ended. He resisted, his intentions focused on escape, but her determination was a force unto itself, compelling him to release her.

She was drawn back to the study by an invisible tether, the scene unfolding before her with stark clarity. The elegant drapery of the Palladian window, once a backdrop to so many of their discussions, now bore the scars of violence, torn and dangling in a grotesque parody of decoration. Approaching Masoud's desk, the sight of his shoes gripped her heart with a cold hand. He had reached for the curtains in his final moments, a poignant testament to the human instinct to grasp at life until the very end.

"Masoud," she whispered, a futile benediction for the departed. Closing his eyes, she performed the last rites of friendship and respect, an acknowledgment of his life and the abruptness of its end.

"Sabi!" The urgency in Scott's voice pulled her from her reverie, a reminder of the peril that still loomed. "We have to move. Now!" His words, though harsh, were a lifeline back to the present, to the need for survival.

As she turned to him, he extended a pistol towards her. The weapon was similar to her own but differed in color, a detail that nagged at her recognition. She had seen it before, a ghost of memory in the tangible form of steel and gunpowder.

"This isn't mine," she said.

"You had it in your hand when I found you," he told her.

It was the gunman's. She was sure of it. The image of the barrel, still smoking, as he held it in his hands and stood over her friend and mentor, was now clear in her mind. She dropped it, forgetting that the model often went off accidentally when struck; but luckily it bounced once before lying flat on the ground.

Scott took her by the arm and whisked her off to the team's van. "How did you find me?" she asked him as he pulled from the curb.

"Your phone," he told her. "Caspar helped us locate you when we couldn't reach you. What happened back there?"

She ran over as much of the morning as she could remember. Masoud was telling her about Paris, about the disk her father had sent, and then... *Damn it, Masoud. Why did you never lock the door?* Whomever they were, why had they killed him and left her alive?

Two police cars, lights flashing and two-tone sirens wailing, passed in the other direction at high speed.

"Where are we going?" she asked him, looking back at the police through the rear window as they careened around a corner.

"I'll explain on the way," he answered.

As the trees, buildings, and empty lots rushed by her, her mind was back at the house, with Masoud and the last conversation they had – a conversation that they would never have the chance to complete, and it struck her.

"No ... wait ... The Baker's," she said.

"What?"

"The... safe house," she said, struggling for a moment to find the words in English.

"There's no time," he said, continuing to drive north.

"Then let me out."

"What?"

"Drop me off," she said. "Now!"

"Fine, fine ... Just tell me where to go."

Somewhere along the way, she thought to check her StarTAC cell phone. There were numerous missed calls – from Caspar, from Jake, from the embassy, and from unknown numbers.

Nava's instincts momentarily faltered as the van pulled up to the curb, a rush of urgency propelling her towards the exit. Yet, her rigorous training asserted itself, compelling her to pause and scan her surroundings with a practiced eye. The tension spiked as a car eased into position behind them, its occupants casting sharp, predatory gazes in their direction, clearly signaling trouble.

Scott's voice, steady and calm, broke through the rising panic. "Go up," he instructed, his attention fixed on the rearview mirror, a silent promise of protection in his tone. "I got you covered. Just hurry."

Acknowledging him with a brisk nod, she gathered herself for a moment, closed her eyes to center her focus, then darted from the van with the swift precision of a shadow fleeing light. Behind her, the cacophony of confrontation erupted—shouts muffled by the distance and the sharp clap of a door slamming shut—yet she propelled herself forward, her entire being narrowed to the singular goal of reaching the safety of the building.

Ascending the stairs two at a time, she reached her destination in mere moments, her heart pounding a fierce rhythm against her ribs. Pausing at the top, she cast a cautious glance down the stairwell; relief washed over her as it confirmed her solitude. With the disk secured once more, she retraced her steps, urgency lending speed to her descent.

Approaching the van, the scene that unfolded was one of stark violence. The door hung open as she had left it, a silent testament to her hasty exit. Scott, now a spectral figure, vanished from sight, his earlier posture of readiness marked by the heavy silhouette of a submachine gun—his promise of protection made manifest.

The aftermath was brutally clear: the car that had loomed with menacing intent was now a battered shell, its body marred by bullet holes, the windshield a spiderweb of destruction. The tableau was grim; one assailant lay motionless on the grass, a final grasp on his weapon linking him forever to his last breath. His companion, trapped within the confines of the car, offered a silent, wide-eyed stare that spoke volumes of the encounter's swift and deadly conclusion.

"Thank you," she said to Scott after they got going again.

"You don't have to thank me," he told her. "I'm 'the help,' remember?"

"Yes... I'm..." she stammered, seeking the words for an apology.

"Nah! I'm just fucking with you," he said with a little laugh. "See, the 'help' would have left your ass back in that house, because the 'help' had his contract canceled."

"What?!"

"Hold on," he told her, and pulled a hard left turn at high speed, the force of which pressed her body against the door of the van.

"Why are we in such a hurry?" she asked him. "Where are we going?"

"To save your hostage," he answered, then added a quiet "hopefully" as if it were a little prayer.

Her phone rang. Caspar was calling.

"Where have you been?" he asked her as soon as she answered. The young man's voice was taut with anxiety.

"I..." she started, but she wasn't sure how to explain, or even if she should. "What's going on? Where are you?"

"The station is closing the observation point down," he told her. "The whole thing is off."

"As of when?"

"About fifteen minutes ago," he told her. "The Gulag is locked down tight. They're getting ready to move the hostage."

"Where?"

"Fucking al Qaeda," he said, using the English curse word. "I tried to call and tell you. Hooman called and told us to pack up. He said it was coming straight from Masoud. We hadn't even taken the camera down when someone called Haddad and told him his brother was dead."

"Who called him?"

Scott took another tight turn at speed, but this time she barely noticed.

"I don't know," Caspar answered. "It wasn't on the cell phone we gave them. I think it was a landline ... anyway, a few minutes later, Haddad called an al Qaeda guy and told him where to come to get her."

As Caspar spoke, Scott pulled over and came to a stop on a street somewhere in the Tariq El-Jdideh neighborhood. He unbuckled his seatbelt, reached behind his seat, and retrieved a tactical vest.

"When I couldn't get hold of you," Caspar continued as Scott put on the vest and adjusted it. "I tried Masoud, but he wasn't answering, either; so, I called the Janissaries. I didn't know what else to do."

"You did the right thing," she told him, and Scott gave her a little smile and a thumbs-up. "I hope..." she added.

"What happened to you?" Caspar asked her. "Where's Masoud?"

"He's—" she stopped herself.

"Look, just tell me what to do," Caspar said.

"Just... break it down like they said," she said. "And go home."

"You got it, boss," he said. "Hey! Whatever's going on, be careful."
She hung up and turned to Scott. "Where are we?" she asked.

"Don't you recognize it? See up there?"

He pointed out the upper left corner of the windshield to an un-remarkable beige apartment building six stories high.

"That's the Al-Qaeda safe house your Syrian friend told us about," he said. "Up there is the offramp from Jamal Nasser. That's where they'll probably be coming from."

Nava stared up at it, seeing nothing but a window; but she did recall Rafiq bringing them there the night before last. She knew little of Al-Qaeda; only that they seemed brutal, hated Iranians and Shiites in general as well as Americans, Israelis, Jews, Christian "Crusaders" ... Basically everyone but themselves. It was that sort of tribalism that had torn Lebanon apart.

"Achilles, this is Ajax," she heard Scott say and looked over to see him adjusting a headset and laryngophone. "Radio check, over."

Her cell phone rang. It was her uncle with the Internal Security Forces Directorate.

"Uncle, I'm glad you called," she said.

"Nava, where are you?"

"*Mashallah*, uncle ... I have so much to tell you. I—"

"Is this your embassy phone?" he asked. "Don't say anything over it."

"What? Why?"

"Your boss was shot to death," he told her. "We recovered an Iran-ian-made PC-9 at the scene. We're checking it for fingerprints now."

She remained silent, and that most likely told him all he needed to know.

"Nava, are we going to find your fingerprints on it?"

Now she had to answer. Still, she hesitated. "Yes," she said. "I was with him when some men came in. I only saw the one that shot Masoud, but there must have been another. I was knocked out."

He was quiet, and she could hear police chattering with one another in the background.

"We're still canvassing," he told her. "But, right now, the only thing anyone saw was you leaving the house with a Western-looking male."

Nava cursed under her breath.

Scott called out over the radio, "Athena two mics out. Standing by, over."

"What was that?" her uncle asked. "Is there someone with you?"

"Yes, it's ... It's a long story, uncle."

"Someone from your embassy is on their way here," her uncle told her. "Listen to me, Nava. In a few hours, every officer at the airport and every border crossing is going to have your real name, picture, and all your aliases. If you can leave Lebanon, do it. Do it *now*."

The line went dead.

Chapter
Twenty-One

T hey sat in silence, her mind racing through the possibilities, feeling helpless against the forces that had set all of this in motion.

"Sabi," Scott called, his gaze fixed through the windshield towards the highway. "They're coming."

Erica arrived first on the motorcycle Scott had used to pick her up days earlier, pulling in front of the van to face the intersection. A rust-colored Renault sedan stopped at the intersection was abruptly halted by Erica's maneuver, the driver's horn blaring until Erica fired through the windshield, silencing it.

The moment seemed suspended in time—Erica, poised on her bike, mere meters from the car, her arm extended, firing two shots. The surreal nightmare seemed framed by the time from the shots that killed Masoud to Erica's gunfire.

Jake and Christian appeared seemingly out of nowhere, reaching the Renault before Scott parked behind it. Dressed in black, with suppressed MP5s as extensions of their forms, they dispatched neat holes in the car's windows.

"Open the door," Scott instructed, nodding towards the van's side door.

Nava, snapping back to reality, slid the door open. The sound of a bullet striking the van's roof startled her, a stark reminder of their perilous situation.

As Jake dragged a body from the Renault, more gunfire erupted. Nava spotted muzzle flashes from an apartment window—Scott had pointed out the building earlier.

"Up there!" she screamed in Arabic, though her choice of language seemed irrelevant to Jake's composed response. Despite the bullets, his movements were fluid, a testament to his skill and calm.

A louder gunshot than the others shattered the apartment window, momentarily silencing the incoming fire. Jake then extracted a bound woman from the Renault. Her hair was mussed—an odd detail that caught Nava's eye amidst the chaos. They quickly moved her into the van, with Nava assisting, just as the van lurched forward, throwing them off balance. A sharp turn threw Nava against the van's side, followed by a loud explosion, suggesting a near miss from a rocket-propelled grenade or similar weapon.

"Relax," Christian's voice was a calm anchor in the chaos as he deftly removed the plastic cuffs from the woman's wrists. "That was ours."

The van's sudden swerve pressed Nava hard against its wall again.

The woman, caught in a storm of shock and terror, looked to Christian for reassurance.

"You're okay," he told her.

Despite his comforting words, the reality of safety must ave felt distant. The woman's wide eyes, stretched to their limits, mirrored a raw fear that gripped Nava unexpectedly. Her fingers clamped around Christian's hand with a strength born of desperation, eliciting a gentle plea from him to relax her grip.

Nava felt a twinge of guilt witnessing the woman's fear. Despite the invisible lines drawn by conflict, the immediate human connection blurred the boundaries, stirring a deep empathy within her. She fought to compartmentalize these feelings, focusing instead on the task at hand. She anchored herself by holding onto the back of the passenger seat where Jake had positioned himself, the van speeding past graffiti-laden walls.

"Where are we going?" Nava's question pierced the heavy silence, seeking clarity amid the unfolding uncertainty.

Jake pointed towards a distant structure cutting a formidable silhouette against the cityscape—the Camille Chamoun Stadium loomed as their unlikely destination.

"Black Wasp, Achilles," Jake communicated into his laryngophone, his voice steady, relaying their next move with precise confidence.

She didn't know what to expect when they pulled up to the stadium, but she was surprised to find they drove straight through the service entrance and down the ramp past an unattended security checkpoint, then emerged onto the field. They must have paid the groundskeeper, she thought.

Even before Scott shut the engine off, Nava could hear the distinct sound of a helicopter approaching. When the van doors opened, the sound was nearly deafening. She looked up and instantly recognized the shape of one of the most iconic military helicopters in the world – the Sikorski Blackhawk. It hadn't yet touched down on the pitch when Erica emerged onto the field with Ridley on the bike behind her, a sniper rifle slung on his back.

"Hey!" Jake shouted above the din of the helicopter blades, then thrust an envelope at her.

"What's this?" she asked.

"Customer satisfaction survey," he told her. "Fill it out and mail it back."

Incredulous, she peeked at the paper inside to see that it was, as he had said, a customer satisfaction survey asking her to rate her experience with Janissary Solutions based on several factors.

"Is this a joke?" she asked him.

"Does it look like a joke?" he asked in return, his visage unchanging.

She looked past him at the others loading into the helicopter. Besides Jake, only Scott was lingering behind. She pushed the survey back into his hands and leaned closer to him to ensure she could be heard.

"I need to get out of Lebanon," she told Jake, but he shook his head.

"Not my problem," he told her, pushing the survey back to her. "We did what we said we would do, agreed?"

He was right, she thought, and dropped her gaze to the survey in her hands; but at this point, she had limited options. As the helicopter's blades whipped the air into a frenzy, Nava watched the team prepare to depart, leaving her grounded with a survey in hand and a pressing need to disappear.

Nava quickly evaluated her dwindling options. The relentless buzzing of her phone served as a stark reminder of the urgency to vanish within the labyrinth of her own city. Despite her deep-rooted connections and intimate knowledge of Beirut's hidden sanctuaries, the path forward was shrouded in uncertainty. The morning's events loomed over her, a puzzle she was ill-equipped to solve while evading the very establishment she once served.

"I'm sorry about your boss," Scott told her as he passed by.

She grabbed him by the arm and locked eyes with him but found herself speechless. Something in her eyes must have communicated her desperation, though, because he nodded.

"Okay," he said, and took a thermite grenade from his vest. "This is why we can't have nice things," he told her, pulled the pin, tossed it in the van, and motioned for her to follow him.

She ran with him to the waiting helicopter, hunching over slightly when she saw him do the same, and felt a plume of balmy air wash over her before they arrived at the side door, where she saw that only half of the seats were occupied. Ridley was manning a large, multi-barreled gun mounted on the helicopter's side. The fat hose attached to it made it look like something from a science fiction movie.

From his seat in the middle facing the rear of the helicopter, Jake leaned over and put up a hand.

"She stays here," he said, barely audible above the high-pitched whine of the engines.

Scott got inside and began talking in Jake's ear while Nava waited anxiously, watching for the slightest change of expression on the team leader's face indicating a change of heart and trying to look as desperate as possible when he cast his cold green eyes upon her. Before he could either relent or shake his head, however, Erica interrupted with a tap on Jake's shoulder. She pointed out the door to something in the direction of the entrance they had used.

Nava looked back to see a dark car and white pickup truck pull onto the field and swerve around the burning van and motorcycle. Scott pulled her inside the helicopter, seated her beside the woman, and buckled her seatbelt.

"Light 'em up!" she heard Jake shout, and the sense of motion hit her as the Blackhawk lifted off.

Scott sat beside her and gave her a pair of earplugs as the barrels of Ridley's futuristic gun began turning and spitting fire. In a matter of seconds, the truck was riddled with countless bullet holes, then exploded before its two occupants could escape. Three men scattered from the car in all directions, carrying what looked to her like AK-47 assault rifles, and Ridley continued peppering the area. Before they set off toward the sea, she made out one familiar face among those on the ground who were watching them fly away.

It was Yasin Haddad.

Chapter
Twenty-Two

For all the calls she missed, Nava had only one voicemail. It was her garage. Her car was ready.

"You need to chuck that phone," Christian told her.

The Blackhawk had flown them to an airstrip hangar nestled somewhere within Turkey's vast landscape. The Turkish authorities were conspicuously absent, a detail for which she was silently grateful. The hangar, devoid of life save for the Janissaries and herself, echoed with the quiet post-operation lull. Aside from a scattering of fuel blivits, makeshift seating arrangements, and their neatly organized gear, the space was stark. The team's leader, engaged in a distant conversation via a satellite dish setup just outside, punctuated the silence with intermittent bursts of frustrated curses.

In this unexpected pause, Nava found herself grappling with the whirlwind of events that had upended her life in just a few short hours. As the sun dipped low, casting long shadows from the western mountains, she was enveloped in reflection. Iran and Lebanon, once the backdrops of her life, were now realms she dared not enter – not until she could untangle the web of accusations ensnaring her. The murder of Masoud loomed large, a painful beacon urging her to unravel the mystery of her predicament and the forces aligned against her.

"What's the point of getting rid of it?" she asked Christian in return. "Your boss is probably sending me right back."

"He won't," Scott told her. "He's just venting."

"He hates it when things don't go exactly as he expects them to go," Christian expounded.

The sound of a door shutting echoed through the space, and Nava turned to see the former hostage emerging from the restroom. She was still in the same pair of ill-fitting pants and sweatshirt that Hezbollah had given her when she was being held captive.

"Doctor Lynch," Christian called to her. "How're we feeling?"

"I've been better," she said, adjusting the round spectacles on her face.

"I'll bet," he said, opening a first aid kit. "Sit down. Let's take a look at that cut."

Nava hadn't even noticed the gash on her head until now, though she wondered how she could have missed it. It was no longer bleeding, but it was a substantial cut that ran from her hairline down nearly to her right eyebrow. Christian put on a pair of latex gloves and Nava handed her a bottle of water. "Thank you," Lynch said and took a few sips. "You're not with them, are you?"

It was less a question than a statement.

"No," Nava answered. "I'm Sabi, Jordanian *Mukhabarat*."

They shook hands and Lynch winced as Christian dabbed her wound with antiseptic.

"Doesn't look like it needs stitches," he said. "This happened when we pulled you out of the car?"

"I'm not sure," she said. "I think it was when your friend broke the window. All I remember was he lifted my hood, took the gag off and asked 'you Litch?'"

Christian chortled.

"I have no idea why, but I said, 'No, *Lynch.*' He said something like 'whatever' and pulled me out."

They all laughed, even Lynch. It was the first moment of levity Nava had felt since that morning, but it was over quickly.

"A word, *ma'am*?" Jake said into Nava's ear, and she followed him outside. There, she saw the lights of a small plane approaching in the purplish dusk sky.

"Taking you wasn't part of our contract," he said.

"I know, Jake. I ..."

"So why should I take you to Vienna?"

She didn't have a reason. Nor did she have a passport, barely enough cash to buy lunch for herself, a credit card that would probably be canceled by her bank in Iran ... and the disk. She pulled it from her pocket and held it in front of him.

"What's that?" he asked, not sounding particularly intrigued.

"It's money," she said. "A lot of money."

Jake's eyes narrowed. He took the disk from her, read the label, and handed it back. "What else you got?" he asked.

"What do you mean?" she demanded. "What else do you need?"

She heard the whine of jet engines on the tarmac nearby. The plane she saw earlier, a small private jet, was taxiing toward them.

"Look, I doubt you have enough in that account for our retainer," he said.

"Which is?"

"Two million dollars, U.S." he answered. "Even if you did, your Ministry is still our client. It's a conflict of interest."

She didn't know how much was in it, but her expression must have communicated to Jake that she shared his doubts. He shook his head and walked past her. "I'm sorry," was all he said.

She could have easily fallen apart right there, watch them leave for Europe while she waited for only God-knew-who to pick her up and bring her back to Tehran ... or put a bullet in her head. But in the flurry of gloomy thoughts was a sliver of hope that consisted of Scott's voice, saying *the* help *would have left you...*

Nava turned and followed Jake.

"Your team helped me when they didn't have to," she said. "Are you telling me they did that without your permission?"

"We didn't know what was going on," he said over his shoulder. "If I knew—"

"You would have helped me, anyway," she said and caught him by the arm. He whirled around unexpectedly, and she nearly stumbled into him before catching herself and taking a step back.

"We're not a charity," he told her. "And you made it clear back in Beirut what you thought of us. So unless you can give us more business than Tehran, we have nothing more to discuss."

The jet pulled up and dropped the airstair to the tarmac. On the side was a corporate logo: "Khan Global Charters" with a jet swooshing around the letters KGC. Lynch and the Janissaries were filing out of the hangar to catch their ride.

Jake again turned his back to her and continued walking to the jet.

"I didn't kill my station chief," she said.

"Wouldn't care if you did," he said without breaking stride.

"But someone did," she continued. "And I want to make sure that someone pays. You're right, I don't know how much is in this account. Maybe nothing, but I'm asking for your help. *Asking...* as a friend."

He shook his head slightly. She could feel the opportunity slipping through her fingers, and she was desperate to grasp it. She needed help. She needed *their* help.

"Nava," she said, and his pace slowed. "My name. My *real* name. It's Nava Sarsi."

He stopped and turned around, and she could imagine how she looked. Tired, frightened, and grieving.

"I'm twenty-nine," she continued, on the verge of tears. "I'm divorced. Childless. And this morning, the man I trusted most in the world was killed right in front of me."

She saw something in that small pause between her words and his answer—a softening in his eyes she hadn't seen before.

"We'll take you to that bank in Zurich," he said.

The relief she felt was so overwhelming that she had to fight the urge to jump into his arms and smother him with kisses. Instead, she bit her lower lip, suppressing everything more than a smile, and said, "Thank you."

As soon as his back was turned, she allowed herself a fist pump. After all the setbacks she'd suffered over the last twenty-four hours, at least the longest day of her life was ending with a victory, however small.

Chapter
Twenty-Three

Nava's deep slumber was a testament to her sheer exhaustion, both physical and mental, marking a rare occasion of profound rest amidst turmoil. The journey from Turkey, a blur of fatigue, was made somewhat bearable by the smooth ride in the spacious confines of a well-maintained SUV. Her eyelids grew heavy with sleep even before they reached their destination in Vienna, the city's nocturnal embrace welcoming them around 1:00 a.m.

The neighborhood that welcomed them was imbued with a quaint urban charm, its streets lined with buildings that whispered tales of the past. The townhouse they entered was no different from its neighbors at a glance, bearing the architectural scars of post-war Europe. Yet, stepping inside, Nava found herself transported into a world that contrasted sharply with the exterior's historical facade.

The interior of the Janissary team's house seemed designed with a keen eye for contemporary aesthetics. The foyer opened into a spacious living area, where sleek lines and minimalist design principles reigned supreme. Natural light flooded in through large, floor-to-ceiling windows during the day, illuminating an open-plan space that seamlessly integrated living, dining, and kitchen areas. The furniture, while sparse, was carefully selected for both form and function. In the kitchen, a large, central island served as both a preparation area and a casual dining spot, fostering an atmosphere of communal living among the team members.

Beyond the common areas, each bedroom was outfitted with comfortable, ergonomic furniture and ample storage solutions. The bathrooms featured rain showers and heated floors, reminding Nava of spas. It was clear to her that the Janissaries themselves probably had little to do with planning and building their own living space. They were well cared for.

Exhaustion had blanketed Nava so completely upon her arrival that the details shared about the absent team member, whose hospitality she inadvertently borrowed, had slipped through her mind like sand through fingers. The shower she used to wash away the grime of her tumultuous journey, the t-shirt she appropriated as makeshift pajamas, and the bed where she sought refuge in sleep—all belonged to a stranger within the team, a name she could not recall.

More than twelve hours of deep, undisturbed sleep later, her sanctuary was breached not by a loud intrusion but by the subtle, persistent sound of someone clearing his throat. Disoriented, Nava's eyes fluttered open to find a figure seated a few feet away, observing her with an unobtrusive yet undeniable presence.

The surprise of his proximity jolted her awake with such force that she nearly vaulted from the bed in alarm. In a hasty attempt to create distance and assert some semblance of control, Nava shot upright, pressing her back against the headboard with a swift motion. However, her rapid movement proved too hasty, and she misjudged the space behind her. Her head met the wall with a thud that echoed her shock and confusion, adding a physical pang to the disarray of her awakening.

"*Akh!*" she cursed and rubbed the back of her head.

"Sorry! Sorry!" the guy at the end of the bed said, holding up an open palm. "I didn't mean to ..."

"No, it's fine," she said. "I'm sorry. You just ... Who are you?"

Something was wrong with his right eye. She could see it immediately, even in the dimly lit room. There were fresh scars all around it – on his forehead, his cheek, and his nose.

"Normally, I'd say it would be customary for a person found sleeping in another's bed to share their name first," he said.

"It's Nava."

"I'm Coda," he told her.

"Coda? Is that a name?"

"It is *also* a name," he replied, a little annoyance creeping into his tone.

He took a deep breath and glanced around his bedroom as he exhaled, stopping his head in a position where the wounded eye wasn't visible to her.

"I was named for a Led Zeppelin Album," he said. "Look, I don't mean to be rude, but I really need my room for a while."

"Sure," she said and looked around for her clothes. Her jeans were hanging over a chair near him.

"Do you mind?" she asked to get his attention.

Coda turned his head slightly, clearly doing his best to keep his right eye hidden from her. After tossing her the pants, he turned his back to her completely as she put them on.

"Dressed?" he asked her after she zipped up.

"Yes," she said, but he didn't turn around. He stood there in awkward silence for what seemed a long time before taking something from his front pocket.

"I need you to tell me something," he told her. "And I need you to be honest, no matter the answer. Okay?"

Nava gulped and braced herself for a difficult question. She could think of a dozen he could ask her to which she'd have no good answers, and which might cause Jake to withdraw his pledge to help her get to Zurich. She felt as if she was back in school, watching the teacher hand out a quiz for which she was not at all prepared.

When he switched on the light and turned toward her, his right eye was covered with a black patch, like a pirate from a movie or book.

"Which looks better to you?" he asked her. "Patch?"

He peeled the patch off his head and looked back up at her.

"Or no patch?"

She refrained from breathing a sigh of relief, but she couldn't hold back a smile from appearing on her lips. In the light, she could more clearly see the extent of his disfigurement. It wasn't nearly as bad as she imagined it might be, but still very apparent. She felt badly for him. He looked older even though he was obviously the same age as the rest of his team. The scares might heal with time, she thought; but looking at him, she wondered if he might have always been this glum.

"Let me see it again," she said, and he placed the patch back over his eye.

"Do you know who Moshe Dayan is?" he asked her.

"I know who he was, yes," she said. "He's been dead for a long time. Why?"

"Someone told me I look like him."

Of course, they did, she thought. The famous Israeli general had worn an eye patch most of his life and was rumored to have loathed it, despite the fact it had much to do with his recognizability.

"You're much better looking," she told him. "With the patch or without."

He smiled a little, though he didn't seem genuinely flattered. Perhaps he didn't even believe her.

"Maybe wear the patch for now," she told him. "Until it heals a bit more."

"Thank you."

She nodded and went to leave.

"There's a bag of women's clothing in the living room," he told her. "I guess they're for you."

"For me?"

"Erica left a note," he told her, stepping over to his nightstand and emptying his pockets onto it. "Said you might need it."

He lifted his shirt and took a black Beretta 9mm automatic from behind him, removed the magazine, cleared the chamber, and left it on his nightstand like any other accessory he'd been carrying.

"I take it she filled in for me on the contract," he said, but her attention was on the gun.

She'd never fired a gun off the practice range; nor had she ever seen anyone shot before her eyes before Masoud. She'd seen death, of course – more than enough for ten lifetimes; but it had always been in the aftermath of violence. Now she'd been in its midst several times on a bloody and chaotic day in which she'd seen and heard hundreds of gunshots, some of which may have even been meant for her. Only two, however, haunted her now. They played themselves over in her mind on the way here from Turkey, like a film on a loop; beginning with Masoud standing up, and ending with him clutching the bloody curtains hanging in front of his beautiful window.

"Nava?"

"Yes? Oh, yes... Sorry," she stammered, shaking her head in a vain effort to clear it of Masoud's final moments. "Where is Erica now?" she asked.

"Not sure," Coda answered. "But you'll probably see her at Khan's tonight."

"Khan's?"

"Khan's Café Américain ," he said. "We go there all the time." He walked into his bathroom and flipped on the light. "Hey. Welcome to exile," he said and shut the door behind him.

Having experienced a variety of European bars during her high school and college years, Nava found Khan's Café Américain strikingly unique. Unlike a nostalgic homage to the famed *Casablanca* setting, this establishment was pragmatically situated a short distance from the shared modern headquarters of Janissary Solutions and Khan Enterprises. Coda elaborated on the strategic location choice, contrasting it with the conspicuousness of a secluded office complex. He argued that such a remote facility, despite its attempts at discretion, would inevitably attract local curiosity and speculation. Instead, their urban setting blended seamlessly into the cityscape, embodying the Janissaries' method of operating hidden in plain sight.

Security at Khan's was unexpectedly tight for a nightlife venue, featuring a bouncer and a metal detector through which, curiously, only Coda bypassed without scrutiny. The exterior belied its interior, which at first glance mirrored a standard dance club. However, Coda told her, the establishment's dynamic ambiance transformed nightly, adopting various themes to offer patrons a total immersion experience. That evening, the atmosphere echoed a Western saloon, complete with sawdust, peanut shells underfoot, and a crowd adorned in cowboy attire dancing to lively country tunes. The clientele, predominantly young blonde Russian women, oscillated between nightclub chic and

Western wear. Many donned cowboy boots and hats, adding a peculiar yet captivating atmosphere.

Coda's demeanor brightened unmistakably with the arrival of Jake and Scott. Their reunion was marked by genuine warmth and laughter, suggesting a deep bond that transcended their professional affiliations. Seated together, they indulged in beers and shared stories, with Coda recounting his hospital stay and humorously lamenting the his new prosthetic eye 'itched,' much to the amusement of the others, who playfully dismissed his gripes.

"They didn't just let you out today, did they?" Scott asked him.

"A couple of weeks ago," Coda answered.

"Where did you go?" Jake asked.

"Home."

"What did you do?"

"Mostly think about blowing my brains out," Coda said; and the fact that he said it without a hint of facetiousness in his voice didn't stop Jake and Scott from bursting out with laughter and slapping him on the back. Coda eventually joined in the laughter; but his expression, tone, and body language told Nava that he hadn't been joking.

"Anyway," Coda said, "Khan, of all people, came and got me."

"Khan," Jake said as if the name itself were ridiculous. "What the hell did he want?"

"Muscle," Coda told him. "Some deal. It's what he told me, anyway."

"Where did you end up?" Scott asked.

"Sudan ... But I wasn't muscle. Not really, anyway. I mean, how could I be? My depth perception is shot to hell. I can barely hit a target. I was just ... *there*, with my thumb up my ass while he talked to this Arab guy and some fucking cokehead apparatchik called Bout."

"Can I ask?" Nava interjected, and they all looked at her. "Why did you put your thumb in your bottom?"

It gave them a good laugh, though she didn't understand why until Coda said it was a "figure of speech" that meant doing nothing meaningful.

"What did he want you for, then?" Jake asked him.

"He wants me to come work for him," Coda said. "Be his little protégé."

"Holy shit," Scott muttered.

"What did you tell him?" Jake asked.

"Nothing ... yet," Coda said.

An uneasy quiet hung in the air as they sipped their drinks and ruminated. Something was going unsaid – she could feel it. She just didn't know what it was until Jake broke the silence.

"You should do it," Jake told him.

"You think?" Coda asked.

"Why not?" Scott interjected "The guy's obscenely rich. That could be you."

"I think he just feels sorry for me."

"You feel sorry for yourself," Jake said.

"Oh, fuck you!" Coda shot back.

"He wants you because you're smart," Jake said a little sternly.

Scott nodded in agreement, and the silence settled on them once more. This time, however, it was lighter; and she saw Coda's face brighten ever so slightly.

"Na zdorovye!" one of the Russian blondes at the bar said loudly.

A half dozen similar-looking women held up shot glasses filled to the brim with vodka and repeated the toast. They threw back their glasses, slammed them down on the bar, and began their best imitation of rebel yells.

"Who are they?" Nava asked as she watched them laughing and making fun of one another.

"The Russian trim?" Scott asked. "They're harmless."

"Spies," Jake grumbled.

Scott blew a raspberry and snickered at the idea.

"We don't really know," Coda said. "They just started showing up one day. But Jake's right... Some are probably trolling for intel."

As if summoned just as they began to talk about them, a sultry Russian girl in a sparkly silver dress approached their table, her smokey eyes fixed on Jake.

"Here's one of them now," Jake said. "Natasha... *moy milyy kotenok.*"

"Jake," she greeted him, her deep voice like a cat's purr, her accent thick. "You never call."

"*Pojaluista, koshechka,*" he answered. "No service where I was."

"*Vy ljetz,*" she said as she bent over with her back arched and legs straight, as if her waist were a hinge, and put her hands on his thighs. Their faces within inches of each other, she grinned and said "Little liar."

"No really," he said, beginning to dig into his right pocket. "Why don't you get us a bottle and I'll tell you all about it."

He offered her some bills and she accepted them before running her finger along the contour of Jake's nose down to his lower lip, which she playfully pulled down a little before letting it plop back into place.

"*Zaderzytes,*" she said softly to him, standing erect and slinking her way back to the bar.

It made Nava feel like she was intruding on some intimate moment, but neither Jake nor Natasha seemed to care. It was almost as if they were play acting with one another.

"She seems nice," she said to Jake.

"Here's the deal," Jake told her once Natasha was out of earshot. "Tomorrow morning, we're taking you to see our Regional Director, Paul Sikorski. Everyone calls him Ski."

"What should I say to him?"

"Hell if I know," Jake answered. "Just try not to piss him off."

"That's going to be tough," Coda warned her. "He's pretty much permanently pissed as it is."

"Don't listen to them," Scott said. "You'll be fine. Ski's a big teddy bear."

"Really?"

"No," Scott admitted. "He's a prick. But worrying about it won't help, so just try to have fun."

"Anyway, it's best if you get out of Vienna soon," Jake told her. "This is the first place people are going to look for you."

Natasha soon returned with a bottle of vodka, a tray full of shot glasses, and an inebriated friend named Anya, who sat next to Coda.

Nava hadn't listened to much country music before. She couldn't understand the words, but what she could make out wasn't uplifting.

> Oh, but I'll be alright, as long as there's light from a
> neon moon.
> Oh, if you lose your one and only, there's always room
> here for the lonely...

"What does mean, 'one and only,' huh?" Anya asked.

"It's just a song, darlin'," Jake answered her, twirling his half-full shot glass on the table.

"Hey! You dance with me!" Anya said, poking Coda with her elbow.

Coda shook his head.

"Come on! Dance!" she said, poking him harder.

"I'm not much for dancing," Coda told her. "I mean, I got this..."

He stood up and launched into his best cabbage patch. He moved both fists counterclockwise, in sync with his gyrating hips, all while biting his lower lip. The Russian girls clapped to the rhythm of the dance and cheered him on while Nava burst out in laughter.

"You know, I actually think that's the first time I've seen you laugh," Scott said to her.

"Really?" she asked as she regained her composure.

He nodded.

"Maybe if you were funny..." she said.

"Oh! Wicked!" Scott said, and she started laughing again. He stood up and adjusted his pants. "All right... That's it. We're dancing."

"Now, Scottie can *dance*," Coda told her. "He went to Juilliard."

It sounded so unbelievable that Nava wasn't sure if he was joking. If he was, no one gave it away.

"You did?" she asked.

"I was an acting major," Scott told her, holding his hands out to her. "I don't know any more about dancing than you."

"Really?"

"Actually, I probably know a lot more," Scott admitted. "But just ... come on."

"I don't think I want to," she said.

"Why not?"

She raised her eyebrows and scoffed at the question.

"No one is dancing," she said, gesturing to the empty dance floor. "And you're this... trained dancer and I'm..."

"You don't need any training to dance," Scott said dismissively. "You just feel the music and move to it." They listened to the melancholy music that filled the club for a few seconds before he said, "Okay, not this. I'll be right back."

She watched as Scott went over to the bar and tried to get the bartender's attention. Jake and Natasha were speaking to one another in Russian, looking as if they might begin kissing at any moment; but Anya seemed more interested in the vodka than Coda.

"You weren't joking about wanting to die, were you?" Nava asked Coda.

He gave a little laugh and held his glass out to Anya, who managed to touch her glass to his but not without spilling most of its contents. Coda drank about half of it and wiped his mouth.

"You don't know us," he told Nava. "It was bad enough that we were raised on the notion that we were going to fight to save freedom itself, only to be thrown away like trash. This life was all I had. No, it was *who I was*. Now, what am I? I hear a lot of people say that family is everything. For us, *this* is family."

Coda made a sweeping motion and paused, spinning the half-empty shot glass on the table as he ruminated.

"There's a poem," he said. "I don't know all of it, but it goes something like, '*The moment we cease to hold each other, the moment we break faith with one another, the sea engulfs us, and the light goes out.*' Right now, it feels like that's exactly what's happening to me."

The sentiment was clear, even if the context wasn't. She didn't know exactly what Coda had been through, but she knew it must've been extremely arduous. The feelings he was describing, though, sounded much like what many veterans of the Iran-Iraq war described. Unimaginable fear and panic in the chaos of battle were allayed only by the presence of the ones they fought beside.

"Since this happened," Coda said, pointing to his false eye, "I've been drifting away from everyone. I've been going under."

Coda finished his vodka and Anya dutifully poured him another with all the concentration she could muster, probably spilling more on the table than she got into the glass.

"I suppose you'll tell me to turn to God," he said.

Nava answered with a wry laugh as the country music faded.

"Don't worry," she told him. "I don't have any sermons to give you. But I think I know how you feel."

"Yeah?"

She hesitated, thinking that if she'd been drinking, maybe it would be easier to tell him about her struggle with infertility. Instead, she toiled to come up with a way to tell him without telling him.

"I just... I know what it is to feel damaged, or... broken."

Coda looked at her with his one good eye, which now seemed softer than it had been. She couldn't see herself, but her expression must have convinced him of her sincerity. He choked up a bit, which evidently surprised himself enough to make him laugh a little as he brushed away a tear.

"Well, um... Thanks for listening," he said.

"Hey! I listen," Anya objected.

"Oh yeah?" Coda asked, turning himself around to see her.

"*Ty v depressii*," she answered him, and Coda chuckled.

"What?" Nava asked him.

"She said I'm depressing."

"You *are*," Nava heard Scott say from behind her.

"Fuck off," Coda shot back. "Take this girl and go dance."

"Wait ... Listen to this," Scott said, looking up. The first electronic chords of a pop song brought a broad smile to his lips. "Oh yeah!" he said. "You can't *help* but dance to Erasure! Come on! Give me a little respect!"

He took Nava by the hands, his enthusiasm contagious as he almost lifted her from her chair. Before they even reached the dance floor, his body was already in rhythm with the music, a preview of the joy to come. Initially, Nava stood mesmerized by his uninhibited movements: arms reaching skyward, hips swaying freely, and feet moving with a precision that seemed innate. His face radiated pure delight. Caught between laughter and awe, she began to sway, awkwardly attempting to match his rhythm and clap along with the beat. The dance floor soon became a whirlpool of energy, attracting flaxen-haired Russian women who emulated Scott's infectious energy, each moving with a blend of grace, humor, and vitality. She caught glimpses of Jake and Natasha intertwined in dance, their laughter mingling with the music, while Anya coaxed a reluctant Coda into the fray, his quirky moves unexpectedly charming their audience.

Still, Nava found herself worried about Coda—this man she just met and with whom she seemed to have little in common other than their shared experience of emotional hardship. Through the lens of this night, she understood that the camaraderie she witnessed was more than mere friendship; it was a lifeline. These individuals, bound by circumstance and forged in adversity, found solace and joy in each other's company, despite the shadows that trailed them. Watching Scott engage Coda in a playful dance-off, coaxing smiles and laughter from him, Nava recognized Scott's role as more than the lighthearted boy he appeared to be. He was a beacon of hope, a steadfast presence pulling Coda back from the brink. In this moment of shared laughter and dance, she realized the profound potential of their unlikely fellowship.

Chapter
Twenty-Four

"**J**esus Fucking Christ!" were the first words that thundered through the conference room as Paul "Ski" Sikorski, the towering Director of European Operations for Janissary Solutions, made his entrance. His presence was as commanding as his physique; a man who, despite the years, carried the build of a seasoned weightlifter, his sheer size amplifying the intensity of his ire.

Nava, escorted by Scott and Jake to the Janissary Solutions' high-rise, had navigated the building's anonymity with a mix of curiosity and dread. The reception process—a photo, a bright red visitor's badge, and a silent journey to the 24th floor—felt surreal, culminating in the stark, utilitarian conference room that now played host to Ski's tempest.

The room, with its spartan decor and the aroma of coffee mingling with tension, seemed to shrink under Ski's gaze. Nava, nursing her mint tea, found herself an unwilling participant in a drama that unfolded with Ski's every word. His suit, though impeccably tailored, seemed at odds with the volatility of his demeanor, a contradiction made all the more apparent as he launched into a tirade at Jake, the team leader.

"You lost control of the situation, team leader!" he yelled at Jake.

"She's a client," Jake answered calmly, and she recalled his preternatural calm under fire in Beirut. "I did what I thought was—"

"She's a fucking *Iranian*, team leader!" Ski interrupted, his massive neck bulging and his face turning redder. "Besides, MOIS is the client, not her! You had no fucking business bringing her here, especially after you fucking learned that the Iranians wanted her back."

Nava's heart sank as the room's atmosphere thickened with tension.

"Who cares what the Iranians want?" Scott challenged him.

"Oh, who fucking cares what... Jack fucking McBain cares what the Iranians want, Scottie!" Ski retorted. "Iran is an entire market that could open for us. We needed to knock this one the fuck out of the park. That's why I sent you fucking jackasses to Beirut."

"I thought you sent us because Mo's team was busy on another contract," Jake retorted.

As he was speaking, Ridley casually strolled in and went right for the coffee, never taking note of Ski's glare except to smile back at him.

"Hey Ridley," Ski called to him. "Thanks for showing up today."

"No problem," he said as he poured himself some coffee.

"Fucking... fuck," Ski muttered, apparently at a loss for non-curse words. To Nava's horror, he turned to her next and asked, "You! What's *your* story?"

"Me? Um, I—" she stammered, but he quickly cut her off.

"Fuck!" he said, "I don't even wanna fucking know right now. Just ... Drink your tea."

"Okay," she answered meekly, and sipped.

Ski began pacing and muttering something about ingratitude, stopped to bury his face in his hands and sigh only to shake his head and resume his pacing. When he was done, his rage seemed to have reduced from a roiling boil to a gentle simmer.

"Tell me your plan, team leader," he said. "If you've even fucking got one."

"We're just taking her to a bank in Zurich," Jake replied.

"That's already problematic," Ski told him. "Fucking Swiss don't like us fucking around on their turf."

"Who does?" Scott countered.

"We're just taking her to a bank," Jake told him. "After that, we'll just see."

"What do *you* think, Ridley?" Ski asked.

She looked back to see Ridley casually leaning on the coffee service table, one hand in his pocket and the other holding his mug.

"Hey, I'm just happy to be here, man," he said.

"Fucking prick," Ski grumbled. "You look like a hard-on waiting to be stroked."

"I have no idea what that means."

"Are you still fucking around with married women?"

Ridley's gaze flicked upward before a tortured smile appeared on his face.

"You know I don't have to tell you a fucking thing about anything like that anymore," he said. "Don't you, Ski?"

Ski shook his head and turned his attention back to Jake.

"The good news is the fucking Iranians agreed to pay us in full," he said, then pointed at Nava. "But they want her back."

"What does Jack say?" Scott asked.

"He hasn't said anything yet," Ski answered. "But right now, we don't have a reason to tell them no, do we?"

Jake glanced at Nava and she sunk down in her chair, wanting to disappear.

"The Iranians are sending someone here to talk to Jack," Ski told them.

"When?"

"Tomorrow."

The room fell silent, save for Ridley slurping his coffee. Ski held his arms akimbo and hung his head with a heavy sigh.

"Okay," he said and scratched the back of his head. "I'm going to let you run with this, team leader; but you're on a very short fucking leash. I'll call the Swiss ... let them know you're coming."

Nava felt as if she'd been holding her breath and hadn't been aware of it. They wouldn't be turning her in. At least not yet.

Chapter
Twenty-Five

The journey from Vienna to Zurich unfolded over nearly seven hours, a scenic tapestry of lush meadows, picturesque hamlets, and a blend of ancient and contemporary urban landscapes that included the historic Salzburg and the diminutive principality of Liechtenstein. Nava chose to sit apart from the Janissaries, seizing the solitude to reflect and recuperate.

Her situation felt precarious at best. Without access to the account, her options were severely limited. Bereft of funds, devoid of contacts in Iran or Lebanon she could safely communicate with, her only immediate support was a group of mercenaries who might soon part ways with her. Her predicament was dire. Yet, no matter how far her thoughts wandered, exploring the events of the past week, they invariably circled back to the harrowing scene in Masoud's study, the moment of his death forever etched in her memory. She surmised that whatever clandestine operations her boss and father were involved in, operations that had somehow resulted in her possession of the disk, were directly linked to Masoud's murder and the conspiracy framing her.

As they neared Zurich, still a couple of hours shy of Stadelhofen Station, Jake approached her, breaking her reverie. He extended a cellular phone to her.

"Ski wants to talk to you," he told her.

She felt a pang of fear in her chest, but she reasoned that if they decided to hand her over to the Iranians, they wouldn't bother talking to her about it.

"Your people are fucking pissed," he told her. "But you probably knew that."

"What did they say?"

"They demanded we hand you over to them," he said, and she felt her heart sink again. "But you're lucky Jack McBain doesn't care too much for Iranians pressing him with demands."

She held her hand to her chest and closed her eyes, regained her composure, and asked what McBain's response was. Ski told her that, as far as the Iranians knew, the Janissaries had brought her to Vienna at her request. By the time Janissary Operations could reach Team 12 about Iran's request to detain Nava and hand her over to Iranian authorities, they had already parted ways.

"So they think I'm still somewhere in Vienna," she said.

"I wouldn't assume anything, if I were you," Ski answered. "Anyway, Jack wants to keep their business. We were going to pull Jake's team back, but here's the twist: the fucking Swiss twist. They want to meet with you."

She lifted her eyebrows and pointed at her own chest.

"With me?"

"Jake and you, yeah."

"How do they even know who I am?"

"Probably because I fucking told them," Ski answered. "The Swiss are prickly motherfuckers. We try to be as upfront with them as possible. By the way, there's an Interpol notice out on you."

"*Mashallah ...*" she groaned and ran her hand over her face.

"Relax," Ski told her. "It's standard to ignore notices from Iran. Fuckers always want them to arrest dissidents and journalists and shit. When can you be ready to meet with them?"

"I haven't agreed to it yet," she said, and she heard him grunt on the other end of the line.

"Well, you're essentially a fugitive without money or resources," he said. "You're headed to their country on our dime; so, if they want to fucking talk, I advise you to talk. If you don't, they're just going to pick you up anyway and bring you in, and they'll probably be in a much fucking worse mood for it."

Despite her instinct to steer clear of Western intelligence agencies, she knew he was right. She resisted the temptation to rebut Ski's harsh directives, to assert some semblance of control over her fate, as she reminded herself of the precariousness of her position. A reluctant nod was all she could muster, an acknowledgment of her reliance on the Janissaries' grudging hospitality and Ski's pragmatic advice.

"Did they say what they wanted?" she asked him.

She heard him sigh and say, "Probably a contract of some sort. Considering their entire service is about the size of a fucking McDonald's, my guess is something small. How's the day after tomorrow?"

"Okay, fine."

"Fan-fucking-tastic," was his joyless reply, making her laugh a little. "We'll see what comes of it. Could be good for both of us, yeah?"

"Sure."

"Look, we're going to have to keep a little distance until then," he said. "We don't think your people will be able to find you that quickly, but we can't afford to be seen as helping you. Get it?"

"I understand," she told him.

"Oh, and hey – you must have made an impression on Coda," he said. "He's offered you a line of credit at Khan Enterprises. Up to a hundred thousand dollars. Anything you need, just call him and ask."

"You just said that you couldn't help."

"They're a separate company," Ski said. "I'll give you his number."

The unexpected offer of a line of credit from Coda brought a momentary lift to Nava's spirits. It was a small beacon of support in the overwhelming darkness of her situation. A hesitant smile touched her lips, a rare moment of warmth in the cold calculus of survival and espionage.

After the call, Jake told her the cell phone was for her to keep, courtesy of Khan Electronic Industries.

"Erica and Chin have been sitting on the bank written on your disk for the better part of two days," he said. "Plenty of Saudis and Emiratis, but no one they thought could be Iranian."

"You think it's safe, then?"

"I didn't say that," he told her. "By the way, I'm sorry about before. You know, for the ..." and he ululated quietly.

She couldn't help but chuckle at it, ridiculous as it was. "Don't worry about it," she said.

Jake paused, tracing the rim of his coffee cup with a finger, his gaze fixed on something only he could see.

"It's just ... I know what its like to be treated that way," he said. "It sucks."

"People were racist to you in the States?"

"Hell yes," he said. "Europe—they're even worse, but the States is still bad. I mean, I remember back when we were in training, when we were waiting around, our instructors would ask us to sing a song. Scottie ... he always had one ready to go. Sometimes they wanted someone else, though. One time, they told me to sing *La Cucaracha*."

"What is that?"

"That's what I asked," he said. "It's a Mexican song. I'm Puerto Rican. I mean, I've never even been there, but ... I'm not Mexican, anyway. They didn't care. I had to do two hundred push-ups, two hundred squats, and two hundred pull-ups; and they told me I'd have to do that every time they asked me to sing *La Cucaracha* and I didn't know it."

"What did you do?"

"I learned *La Cucaracha*," he said. "Fast."

"How is the song?"

He sang a bit for her, "*La cucaracha, la cucaracha, ya no puede caminar porque no tiene, porque le falta marihuana que fumar.*" After finishing, he explained, "It's about a cockroach smoking pot. Now, Scottie brings this musical horn thing with us everywhere and installs it in the cars we get to play that stupid song."

They laughed together, and for the first time, his eyes didn't seem like two cold, hard emeralds looking right through her; but instead looked *at* her and *saw* her. As stern and serious as he appeared, just that little expression of curiosity seemed to somehow touch him. It reminded her of seeing the mask of charm slip from Ridley's face and seeing something tortured underneath. Now the mature professionalism slipped, and she saw something quite different. She just wasn't quite sure yet what it was.

"The program you went through ... I heard it was really difficult," she said.

175

He responded with a quiet scoff, the way an adult might when a precocious child asked an impertinent question.

"Is this a government program?" she asked.

"It was," he said. "They ended it ... ended *us*."

"Tell me something about it," she said, hoping that mask would slip again enough for her to see what was underneath.

Nava didn't know how much influence Jake wielded over what his team did. She only knew that they were here with her because she asked him for help and he gave it, despite whatever indifference or conflicting business interests his higher-ups harbored. She didn't know how much longer she'd need his help or when he would stop lending it to go off on some other contract, but she had to know if she could at least trust him.

"I had a lot of trouble with these things we did, called box drills," he said. "The thing they did was put a hood over our head, spun us around, and when they lifted it, there would be one or two people there with like knives or guns or whatever, and we'd have to use our training to take them down. I always knew what to do every time, but when the hood went up, I would just ... freeze. Like I was paralyzed, you know? Then they would attack me, and I'd just curl up."

"Curl up in the box?" she asked.

He squished his eyebrows together and asked, "What?"

"You ... you said box drills."

"Oh ..."

He laughed and said, "It was just a name the SEALs used. There wasn't any box. Or maybe the hood was the box at some point ... I don't know."

"Oh. So, what did you do?"

He shrugged and shook his head. Nava heard the train's horn sound, and a moment later they were plunged into the darkness of a tunnel.

"One day, I guess it just clicked for me," he said as the tunnel lights streaked across Jake's face one after another, casting his features in a rapid, flickering dance of shadow and light. "They lifted that hood up, two guys were there and I just ... did what I was trained to do. It's weird. I really liked that phase until then. It was the only time in my life before college when I was really ... *happy*. Then after ..."

He paused, shaking his head slightly.

"I don't know," he said, lifted a closed, hand, and opened his fingers as if releasing some invisible little bird.

"You weren't happy anymore?" she asked.

"I ... guess I really didn't feel much of anything," he said, as they emerged from the tunnel. "It wasn't hard. It was *grueling*, and it went on for years. I lost friends, gained a few scars... In the end, I just wanted to feel like our country needed us. I mean, they told us it did. That was what it was all about, right? I was willing to go through all of it and do what they trained me to do for the rest of my life; but I wanted to do it for the United States. I *hate* doing this for money."

He wrinkled his nose as he spat the last word from his mouth.

"You know what I mean?" Jake asked, but he didn't wait for an answer. "Using the skills that we suffered to gain for money. Something about it just seems ..."

He frowned and shook his head, looking out the window again, searching for the word.

"Profane," she said softly.

The word just popped into her head as the natural end to his sentence, and she wasn't sure why that was, but it seemed right. Jake seemed to agree, turning his head sharply to her when her utterance reached his ear, and he nodded.

"Yes," he agreed, sounding genuinely surprised that it had been the word he was looking for, and that she had known it.

She had a fleeting notion that it might have been a breakthrough in their relationship, but her hope quickly faded. He seemed more alarmed that she was able to finish his thought as if he'd told her too much already, even if he'd barely told her any real information. He stared blankly out the window as the train went onward, clicking and clacking and gently rocking them back and forth in their chairs; and the mask slowly slid back into place.

Chapter
Twenty-Six

N ava stepped into Ergensbank's grand marble foyer, its columns towering around her, less than an hour before the bank was due to close. A sense of solitude enveloped her, a stark contrast to the absence of the Janissaries who were compelled to maintain a distance. The mystery of what her father had stored here loomed large, her resolve firm to be the first to uncover it, away from prying eyes.

She was met by a teller whose dark features softened into a welcome. The sight of the disk in Nava's hand, however, shifted the teller's demeanor almost instantly. What was once a cordial smile morphed into a complex expression that Nava struggled to decipher. It wasn't merely surprise that flickered across the teller's face but something less benign—a mix of irritation, perhaps even a trace of indignation. Without a word, the teller ushered Nava into a cubicle, leaving her to the company of an empty chair and her own swirling thoughts.

The window behind the vacant seat offered a view, albeit through a much narrower lens than the expansive Palladian window of Masoud's study. Yet, the delicate white curtains that framed it evoked a poignant reminder of past conversations held in the warmth of Masoud's presence. Her mind unwillingly replayed their last encounter, the serene moment shattered by the abrupt violence that claimed his life, leaving a silence that echoed louder than the memory of gunfire.

"Miss Hakimi?"

She jerked her head and jumped in her chair away from the voice. No masked gunman was there. Only a banker in a dull gray suit with blonde hair so shiny and slick that it might as well have been plastic.

"Sorry," he said. "Thomas Muller."

He shook her hand and took a seat as she tried to clear her head and refocus.

He said, "I understand you're here to access an account."

"I am," she replied. "Do you need to see my passport? I'm afraid I left it at the hotel."

"I understand you have the access disk."

She handed it to him.

"Perfect," he said and began signing onto the computer on the desk. "Unfortunately, you won't be able to withdraw or transfer funds without a passport, but access to the safe deposit box does not require identification. Possession of the disk, or more precisely, the file it contains, is all that's required."

"How does that work?"

"Ah, well we put the file through what is called a one-way algorithm," he said, inserting the disk in the drive. "Honestly, it is a lot of math that not even bankers can understand, but the point is it produces a specific set of characters based on what is in the actual file. That acts as a cryptographic key that gives you access to the accounts. If the file is altered in any way – an extra space at the end, even – the characters will not be the same, and it will not grant you access ... Which, I see here already will not be a problem. It is a bit late to access the safe deposit box, but we could still give you a few minutes if you like."

"I would appreciate it," she said.

"Certainly. And would you like a printed statement for the account?"

"Please."

He excused himself to retrieve the printed statement and shortly returned with the young lady who had greeted Nava and shown her to the cubicle.

"Here is your statement, and Isha will escort you to the vault," he said, handing her an envelope. "Please note we close in thirty minutes."

She followed the woman downstairs, where they passed armed guards that nodded politely after checking the woman's identification.

"Isha," she said, and the young woman turned her head to her. "Such a pretty name."

"Thank you," she said with a forced smile.

"Do you mind if I ask its origin?"

"Kashmiri," she answered.

Aside from the steel doorway they passed through, and iron bars on the other side, it was just walls full of small safes, a table, and some chairs. While the lady located her box, Nava peeked at the statement and saw the balance: CHF 21,206,815.61.

"What's the exchange rate to the dollar?" she asked the woman.

"A Swiss franc is about two-thirds of an American dollar," the woman said.

She did the math in her head ... *Roughly 16 million USD.*

The safe indicated by the young woman stood out immediately; it was the only one equipped with a floppy disk drive. Once alone, Nava inserted the disk. A light beside the drive glowed green, and the safe door nudged open slightly, inviting her to retrieve its contents.

Hesitation took hold as she took a step back, eyeing the safe with a mix of curiosity and dread. The unknown contents marked a pivotal moment, crossing into new, uncertain territory.

Anger tensed Nava's body—fists clenched, jaw tight. She seethed over the betrayal from her compatriots, Masoud's death, her father's web of secrets, and the burden now thrust upon her. Despite attempts to quell the storm within, her frustration remained unyielded, forcing her to press on amidst the turmoil.

Inside the safe lay a single binder, brimming with documents. A cursory glance revealed transactions and invoices, primarily from Khan Research Laboratories. The mention of Khan evoked memories of the bugged phones used against Yasin Haddad, yet this connection diverged sharply. These documents tied back to Pakistan, spotlighting Abdul Qadeer Khan, a renowned nuclear scientist, with certain dealings linked to the Iranian Atomic Energy Agency among other unrelated activities. As Nava absorbed the information, Isha's voice pierced the silence, warning of the bank's imminent closure in ten minutes. Hurriedly, Nava skimmed through the documents, resecured the safe, and, clutching the account statement, made her exit.

Chapter Twenty-Seven

Nestled in the dim light of a pub, Nava sat with a half-eaten burger and fries before her, enjoying a cigarette, lost in thought. The weight of sixteen million dollars lingered on her mind, a hefty sum that promised a fresh start, a new identity, perhaps in Canada or even America. As a former MOIS operative, she understood all too well the Iranian regime's focus—quelling dissent, silencing voices of opposition. Journalists, activists, dissidents: these were the targets, the ones Tehran sought to suppress with unwavering determination.

Yet, fleeing meant embracing exile, a permanent severance from the lands she cherished. Iran and Lebanon were woven into her very essence, and the thought of never returning carved a void within her. The losses were already too great—her mother, her husband, Masoud, her mentor—each absence a haunting echo of what was. Coda's words in Vienna, though not remembered verbatim, resonated with her; loyalty had yielded only betrayal and loss, leaving her adrift, questioning the very foundations she had stood upon.

Determined, Nava resolved to seek justice for Masoud, to unravel the mystery of his death and vindicate herself. To do so, she acknowledged the necessity of assistance, the kind of support only one source could provide. With resolution hardening in her gaze, she retrieved the phone Jake had entrusted to her and dialed Coda's number, stepping into the unknown with a resolve to reclaim her place and honor in the tangled webs of Tehran and Beirut Station.

Nava first noticed her followers outside the mobile phone shop, a clear sign she hadn't shaken them since departing the bank. Among them, two men stood out distinctly, their attire not quite fitting the late summer heat—jeans and button-down shirts, a choice too heavy for the season. Both in their thirties, one bore the mark of a clean shave, while the other sported a meticulously groomed full beard. Their Western dress did little to conceal their Middle Eastern origin, though Nava couldn't be sure of their nationality. Were they Iranian, perhaps?

After purchasing a calling card, Nava exited swiftly, only to be shadowed anew aboard the tram. This latest pursuer, with his darker skin and gold-rimmed spectacles, boarded shortly after her, his appearance making him a beacon among the ordinary. Navigating through a sea of daily commuters engrossed in their newspapers and tourists eagerly consulting guidebooks, Nava made her way to the rear. Glancing back, she noted his strategic positioning in the car's heart, maintaining a deliberate distance.

Choosing not to head directly for Zurich Hauptbahnhof, Nava instead vanished into the bustling throngs of the city. She adopted the guise of an average local: purchasing a nondescript baseball cap, a plain t-shirt, and a hair tie from a nearby vendor. Transformed in the restroom of a packed pub, her hair now restrained in a casual ponytail and her face shadowed by the cap's brim, she emerged into the throng with a new visage.

Her eyes swept the bar's interior, a space now tinged with the thrill of the hunt. There, among the patrons, her keen gaze identified two figures weaving through the crowd, their movements betraying their intent. They were searching, searching for the Nava who had just vanished into the ether.

Nava flagged down a passing waitress.

"Excuse me," she said. "Do you speak English?"

"Yes, I do."

"There's a man inside who's really bothering me," Nava confided, earning a sympathetic smile from the waitress. "Is there a way to exit without going back through there?"

The waitress looked around cautiously before gesturing for Nava to follow her. "I'm not really supposed to let customers use this exit, but..."

"Thank you so much."

The waitress unlocked a door, temporarily disabling an alarm, and allowed Nava to slip out into the alley. Grateful, Nava handed her a few francs and hurried off towards Zurich Hauptbahnhof.

There, she found what she needed – a bank of public telephones right by one of the train platforms. She stood sideways to get a view of the entrance from the main terminal and used her calling card.

"*Allo*?"

"It's Nava," she replied.

After a brief pause, she heard Hooman say, "*Khoda ro shokr, Nava* ... Are you okay?"

"I didn't kill him, Hooman," she said. "You know—"

"Nava," he said, his voice calm and reassuring. "Whatever's going on, we'll make it right. Just tell me what you need. Do you need money?"

"I need to speak with Caspar," she answered him.

"Caspar ... The technician?"

"We were working together before all this," she said. "I think he may be able to help."

"Right, right. Just give me a number he can reach you."

"I have his cellular number," she said. "Could you just call and tell him it's okay to help me?"

She waited a solid fifteen minutes, feigning interest in the paperback books displayed at a nearby newsstand, but the tails didn't reemerge. Then, she called Caspar.

"Boss?" he answered, his voice low.

"It's me," she said, and his barrage of questions followed swiftly. What happened to Masoud? Why does everyone think you killed him? Are you okay? Where are you?

"I didn't kill him," she clarified. "I need your help to find out who did."

She held her breath. Caspar was reliable, yet she couldn't be certain what the embassy officials had told him or whom he trusted. If he refused to help, she'd be back to square one.

"What do you need?" he finally asked, prompting her to breathe again. "Wait... First, there's something you should know. Remember when I overheard Haddad on the phone, being told his brother was dead?"

"Yes."

"Well, he's fucking not," Caspar revealed, emphasizing with the English curse. "After Haddad handed the hostage over to al-Qaeda, the Israeli, Isaac, called and told him that his brother is still alive. They even allowed a brief call for proof of life. Then, Haddad chased after the al-Qaeda people to try and retrieve the American hostage."

She yearned for a moment to digest this information, but time was pressing, and the calling card had limited minutes.

"Listen," she urged. "Do you still have the numbers from Haddad's cell phone?"

"Of course. Which ones do you need?"

The first number on her list was the one that she guessed caused Caspar the most consternation to give; but she asked for his trust, and he gave it to her. That she'd so rarely given other that sort of trust was not lost on her.

"Yes?" the voice on the phone answered flatly. No greeting, no identification. Barely more than a grunt.

"Is this Isaac?" she asked in English.

"Who's this?" the voice demanded.

"Nava Sarsi."

Silence. Just when she was sure the connection had been lost, the voice came back.

"What do you want?" it asked, not sounding particularly given to accommodation.

"You know something I need to know," she told him. "I have something you'll want."

More silence. It was maddening, but she kept her patience.

"Your location?" he asked.

"Zurich."

"*Club Spiel,*" he said. "Tomorrow night at eleven."

Chapter
Twenty-Eight

On the train journey to Zurich, Nava had tentatively broached the subject of arming herself with Jake. His refusal was immediate. "Why not?" she had pressed, only to be met with a look that bordered on incredulous.

"Um, because guns are dangerous," Jake had explained, as if stating the obvious. "And we don't trust you yet."

The reply rankled her. "Don't trust—What was it you said about being friends?"

"We're friends," he conceded. "But we're not good friends. Not yet."

Nava bristled at the distinction, finding it both petty and frustrating. "What's the difference?" she demanded, seeking clarity.

"A friend will help you move," he quipped. "A good friend will help you move a body."

The dark humor caught her off guard, a bizarre attempt at lightening the mood that left her momentarily speechless. His laugh, a stifled, muffled sound as though he were trying to suppress it entirely, only added to her bemusement. She watched, still puzzled, as he vanished through the connecting door between train cars.

Back in her room, Nava opted for a low profile, keeping the lights off and the "Do Not Disturb" sign in place to suggest an unoccupied room. She hadn't even had a chance to unwind with a shower when an unexpected knock at the door seized her attention. Instinctively, she reached for the only semblance of protection she had managed to acquire—a hunting knife.

In the tense silence that followed, she found herself silently rebuking Jake's earlier caution with a mockingly deep tone, "Um, because guns are dangerous." She couldn't suppress a roll of her eyes, nor the muttered curse that escaped her lips, as she braced herself to face whoever was on the other side of the door.

She took a cautious step toward the door, listening for the sound of muffled voices on the other side. The words were unintelligible, but she hoped to catch a familiar voice. Abruptly, the voices ceased, and she halted mid-step. Holding her breath, her body tensed, her grip on the knife handle tightened until her knuckles whitened.

The next sound startled her from behind. She whipped her head towards the bed at the loud ring of the cell phone Jake had given her. Realizing whoever was outside must have heard it too, she glanced at the caller ID on the little green-yellow screen. It was Scott, likely outside with Christian and Erica.

She opened the door and they all piled into her room, dressed rather smartly.

"Where are you going?" she asked them.

"You mean 'where are *we* going,'" Scott said. "Don't tell me you're turning in."

"Someone picked me up after I left the bank," she told them. "They followed me for hours. I lost them, but it took a while."

"So what?" Scott asked with a dismissive shrug. "There's this great jazz club not far from here. Our treat. You can take in some tunes and smoke until your lungs turn black."

Her gaze shifted among them, bewildered by their nonchalance despite Ski's warnings about being seen with her.

"Really?" she asked them. "What if someone spots me?"

"I doubt any Iranian agents are hanging out there," Scott said.

"Plus, a blond wig and some colored contacts go a long way," Erica added.

"You have those?"

"Come on," she said, taking Nava's hand. "I'll hook you up."

Embracing the night at the club, Nava discovered a joy she hadn't realized was missing from her life. Laughter flowed easily as she indulged in the company's absurd humor, her feet tapped rhythmically, and her head bobbed to the pulsating music. A particularly captivating drum solo swept her away, erasing her vigilance against potential threats as she immersed herself fully in the moment, feeling almost ordinary again. She reveled in the camaraderie, smoking and absorbing Scott's passionate discourses on jazz, while observing the unmistakable bond between Christian and Erica, hinting at a depth beyond mere friendship.

For the first time in what felt like an eternity, Nava experienced genuine happiness, a stark contrast to the shadow of Masoud's tragic end that had loomed over her. Amidst the melodies and shared laughter, she briefly grappled with a sense of guilt for allowing herself this respite. Yet, as the night progressed and the music enveloped her, such concerns faded, leaving only the pure, unadulterated joy of the moment.

Between sets, Christian curiously inquired about the knife he had noticed in her room. Nava explained Jake's refusal to arm her, sharing the amusing yet telling exchange they had aboard the train.

"Then he made this weird noise," she told them. "Almost like ..." and she did her best to imitate the strange noise she'd heard from him. All three immediately broke into laughter. "What was that?!" she asked them, grabbing Scott's arm. "You've heard it too?"

"We all have," Christian told her. "It's the Jake Laugh."

He did his own imitation of it, then Erica gave it a try, then all three of them together. They had her in tears.

"He's done that forever," Christian said. "But ... *But* ..." he added, his index finger in the air. "In fairness, we all have weird habits and stuff that we—"

"He's a total freak," Erica interjected, making them laugh more. "I love Jake. We all do. Total freak."

Nava leaned over the table a little, and they all leaned in to hear her when she began speaking in a lower tone. "When we were in Beirut," she said, "when you guys were fighting those Al-Qaeda, he was like ... completely calm. Like he was meditating or something."

"Yup," Erica said, shaking her head and picking up her drink. "Fucking Jake."

"If anyone was ever a natural at all the shit we do," Scott said, "it's Jake."

"He struggled," Christian said as the musicians took their seats for the next set. "Less than the rest of us, in most things, maybe; but he did. We know he did."

Erica and Scott seemed to quietly acknowledge the truth of it.

"You know, I don't even know your last names," Nava said.

"That's because we don't have them," Scott told her. "Not really. We change them a lot."

"Huh ..."

Strangely enough, Nava somehow expected some sort of answer like that. The more she learned about them, the more she thought of them as almost entirely invented in a way that normal people were not. They had a past, of course ... but no real roots; at least, not in the way she thought of them.

"Okay, I have to ask ..." Erica said. "Just knowing you a little better now, at least enough to know you're not a religious fanatic. Why did you choose to do what you did for a living?"

"I know what Americans must think of Iran," she said. "And I don't always agree with everything my government does. My guess is most of my American counterparts don't always agree with everything their government does, either."

"No," Christian agreed. "And America is far from perfect, but Iran is different; and by that, I mean its government is different. America is capable of change."

"So is Iran's," she countered. "Look what's happening now, with Khatami ..."

Christian shook his head.

"What's the difference?" she asked, a little annoyed at his certainty.

"Look, it's just my opinion," he said.

"No ... Tell me. Please."

He played coy, sipping his drink; but she waited patiently. "In America, the people decide which laws they want to follow," he said. "The whole purpose of Iran's government is that it's built on divine laws that can't be changed. Reform challenges the premise of everything, and the system crumbles. It's why authoritarian systems like Iran's are failing."

"You don't think Khatami will succeed?"

"If the people had their way, maybe he would," he said. "But Khatami isn't the highest authority. He's just the highest elected. If what he wants challenges the system, he simply won't be allowed to succeed."

Erica gently elbowed him in the ribs.

"Don't listen to him," she said.

"Just an opinion," Christian said again.

"No," Nava told him. "I appreciate the honesty."

And she did, however difficult it was to hear.

They took a leisurely route back to the hotel, walking down Bahnhofstrasse and window shopping among the throngs of tourists doing the same.

"Did you always love music?" she asked Scott.

"I think so, yeah ... As far as I remember, anyway," he told her. "My mom ... she was a dancer in New York. Broadway shows. There were always artistic types around our place. I guess I just caught the bug."

"It sounds like you were happy," she said.

"I was ... I think. I was young, you know?"

"What happened?"

The smile vanished from his face, and Nava could feel this wasn't something he felt entirely at ease talking about with her, or possibly with anyone at all. "She was killed," he said.

"Oh ... Scott, I'm ... so sorry."

She took his hand, first to comfort him; but neither let go after the moment passed. Though exciting, it felt so natural that she found it alarming as well.

"It was just me and her," he explained. "I didn't know any other family, and no one came for me. Anyway, as those of us in the program got older, we started to get more time off and more money, so I went home a lot. I don't know why, but ..."

"Because it reminded you of her," she said.

He grinned and said, "Yeah ... probably; but I kept going back. I took in everything I could – musicals, plays, concerts, art ... I loved it. One day, I'm really hoping to get back to that world, you know? Do something of my own. What about you? How did you end up at Oxford?"

"My family left Beirut when I was young," she told him. "We lived in Tehran for a few years, but then my father's job moved us to Paris."

"Paris? Great city."

"It was different for me," she explained. "Even though I could speak decent French, I was a foreigner, a Muslim ..."

"High school?"

"Yes."

"So ... on top of being a teenager ..."

He whistled.

"It was pretty awful," she agreed. "But then my mom got sick."

"You were close?"

"Very," she said. "I took it very hard. So did my father. Masoud was the only—"

"Masoud, your station chief?"

"He worked with my father in Paris," she said. "He really helped me through it."

"Ah!", he said, and she saw a flash of realization cross his face. "That explains it."

"Explains what?"

"Why you can't just disappear."

She shook her head.

"Whoever did this made a mistake," she said. "They don't get to win. Not while I'm alive."

She saw then, in the way he looked at her at that moment, something different in his eyes – something more than just the attraction she felt from him before. Whatever it was, it made her smile so much that her cheeks began to hurt.

As the elevator ascended, the tension between Nava and Scott was palpable, their shared silence a prelude to the unspoken words hanging heavily in the air. Their rooms, coincidentally on the same floor, meant their night together didn't end with a simple farewell as the elevator doors glided open.

Nava's heart was a tumultuous sea, waves of anticipation crashing against the shores of uncertainty. Scott's voice, recounting the evening's joy, reached her ears, but her mind was ensnared by the rapid beating of her own heart.

"I had a really good time, Scott," she said when they arrived at her door. "Believe me, I did. But this isn't real life ... for either of us."

"Sure, it is," he retorted, the happiness on his face undiminished.

"No, it's ... It's just a moment," she told him.

"What's life?" he asked her. "It's just a series of moments."

"I'm sorry," she said, turned around, and used her keycard on the lock.

The knot in her stomach, far from receding, only grew as the green light blinked and the lock slid back. This was wrong ... She needed to be honest with him, even if that meant he might lose interest in her. If that was the case, it was better to find out right away. She hadn't taken a second step across the threshold, however, before she turned around again.

"I can't have children," she blurted out, making Scott stop and spin around in the corridor.

He was only a step or two away, and he was quickly back with her at the door. She found herself breathing through her mouth a little heavily as if saying those words had taken an effort equivalent to running a hundred meters.

"That's why my husband left me," she said, eyes downcast to avoid seeing his reaction.

"What a douchebag," he said.

Not quite believing her ears, she picked her head up and saw him gazing down at her with soft glossy eyes.

"Yes ... He *is* a douchebag," she said breathily as he drew closer to her.

Their kiss was an impromptu confession, a moment of vulnerability and desire intermingling. The taste of the night's indulgences mattered little; what mattered was the connection, the mutual yearning; but as much as she yearned for more, Nava knew this was all it could be for now—a perfect, fleeting moment. But somehow, that was enough.

Chapter
Twenty-Nine

T he jet poised on the tarmac of Speck-Fehraltorf Airport, with its sleek twin-engine Dassault design, stirred a sense of unease within her. It was precisely the kind of aircraft she envisioned in scenarios where, under Tehran's orders, she might be spirited away, blindfolded and bound. These fears had niggled at her since Coda's call about the arranged car service, half-expecting an ambush by IRGC Qods Force operatives. Yet, the reality that greeted her bore no trace of the imagined danger. Coda was immediately identifiable, his eye patch in place over his prosthetic eye as she had once advised—a detail that offered an odd comfort. Accompanying him was another man, possibly of Indian descent, who appeared older and deeply absorbed in his notes, his pen dancing across a leather-bound journal on the jet's foldout table.

Coda saw her and smiled broadly as if she were an old friend.

"Hey," he said, getting up from his seat.

"Hey yourself," she said, and she was pleasantly surprised that he hugged her. Janissaries were not generally the warmest people. Initially, Coda had been the same; but she sensed something beginning to change in him.

"Thank you for the car service," she said.

"I heard you needed a passport," he said, squinting with his one good eye. "I think there's one behind your ear ..." He reached behind her head, and the hand he brought back held a Lebanese passport.

She smiled wryly and took it from him. "I think the expression in America is cheese," she said.

"Cheesy," the Indian man said without looking up, still scribbling notes in a journal of some kind.

"Sorry," Coda said, motioning to the Indian man. "This is Rohan Khan."

"Khan Enterprises," she said.

"Correct," Khan said, closing his journal.

"You know the hooptee you gave us in Beirut that a door fell off while a client was in it?" Coda asked Khan. "This is her."

"That was Scottie's fault," Khan objected. "Nevertheless, my apologies, Ms. Sarsi."

As they shook hands, she noted Khan's air of success. His suit, watch, cufflinks, and shoes—all meticulously chosen—projected an image of wealth and sophistication.

"He's the guy that told me I can look like Moshe Dayan," Coda told her.

Khan held up his index finger to Coda and said, "Hey, women *loved* that guy."

"It must be the patch," Nava said.

"It must be," Coda agreed, his tone ripe with sarcasm.

She peeked inside the passport to make sure they got the name she wanted correct. It was an excellent forgery – probably better than she could have expected from MOIS – and it occurred to her that it may be genuine. Given the level of corruption in Lebanon, getting one was probably not difficult.

"You deliver all of these personally?" she asked, holding it up.

"We're on our way to Paris on business," Coda told her. "Thought we'd swing by."

"Mr. Khan," Nava said, looking up at him. "Any relation to Abdul Qadeer Khan?"

Khan didn't seem one to betray many emotions with facial expressions, but she could tell that he was at least a little taken aback when he heard the name.

"You know A.Q. Khan?" he asked her.

"Khan Research Laboratories."

"Is that what he's calling it?" Khan snickered and shook his head. "No relation," he said. "I assure you."

"You on your own now?" Coda asked her.

She frowned and nodded.

"Sorry."

"Personally, I think it's a mistake," Khan told her. "Jack's not going to keep those contracts, anyway."

"Why do you think that?" she asked.

"A country like Iran eventually asks us to do things we won't do," he said, and retook his very comfortable-looking seat. "Directly attack American interests, for instance. They'll find someone that will, though; and cheaper."

"You won't do anything that harms America?"

"Hmph. We all have our ... lingering loyalties, don't we?" Khan said.

Coda then gave her the other two things she requested—two thousand Swiss Francs and a Glock 9mm automatic with three full magazines—before he walked her down the tarmac.

"Are you okay?" he asked her.

"As okay as I can be," she answered. "Are *you* okay?"

"I think I will be," he said and looked at the horizon. "It's hard when you realize that, no matter what you do, you can never go back to the way things were."

The effect his words had on her took her completely by surprise. He was talking about himself, she knew; but she felt he could just as easily be talking about her. No matter what she did, she had to face the possibility she couldn't go back to her old life.

"Yeah, it's hard," Coda mused. "But hey ... I'm headed to Paris in a private jet."

"You'll just have to make the most of it," she said, managing to force a smile.

Armed with her new passport, Nava arrived at the bank around noon to move cash into new accounts that she could access easier, then went down to the vault to take a closer look at the papers in the safe deposit box. The dossier documented in excruciating detail how A.Q. Khan was selling tubes and centrifugal designs, among other things, for uranium enrichment to North Korea, Libya, and Iran. Precisely crafted equipment, technical expertise, warhead designs ... even skilled labor; everything needed for a budding nuclear weapons program except the uranium.

It was all right there in that box – everything her father and Masoud had managed to collect on A.Q. Khan's network. For more than a decade, the two of them had been meeting the Pakistani scientist two to three times per year, usually in Switzerland. Their job was primarily to procure whatever equipment and knowledge Iran's nuclear scientists needed. Nothing came cheap. At the same time, they were collecting all the information they could about A.Q. Khan, his clients, and the middlemen they used. When the entire enterprise was mapped out, it amounted to a sprawling proliferation ring that was generating enormous profits for A.Q. Khan and his partners.

Nava firmly believed that Iran had every right to pursue nuclear capability if that was what its leaders decided, despite her personal feeling that it was unwise. Nevertheless, the entire thing sickened her that Iran was acting like a thief in the night. It put her country, imperfect as it was, in the same category as two others run by megalomaniacal dictators that believed in nothing but themselves.

However, as an intelligence officer, she was particularly intrigued by her father's suspicion that there was a fourth customer that only A.Q. Khan knew about. Given that the file was nearly up to date, her father must have continued to work with A.Q. Khan even in retirement. The amount of material Khan Laboratories made or acquired added up to much more than what it was using in Pakistan and sending to its clients. It was enough, according to Masoud and her father, for a complete additional uranium enrichment program.

The papers also solved another mystery. Shortly after each payment to Khan Laboratories, about ten percent of that amount would be deposited into the account now under her control from a company in Dubai. Over the years, these kickbacks amounted to a slush fund of millions of dollars.

Her review complete, she remained in the vault sitting in an uncomfortable chair with both hands on her stomach. She found the entire situation repugnant, from the scientist whose ego and greed helped put lethal weapons in the hands of the least responsible leaders in the world, to the corruption of both her father and her mentor. She needed something to give Mossad in return for the information she wanted. The problem was that most of the secrets in this dossier, if viewed in full, were damning for Iran. She took copious notes of those parts she believed she could trade in good conscience, though she was beginning to wonder why she was being cautious on behalf of a country that wanted her in jail or dead.

If it was what she thought it was, Nava had to admit that it was both brilliant and a bit funny. *Club Spiel* was, according to her hotel concierge, one of Zurich's top nightclubs. It was known for playing downtempo, techno, and synth music; serving beverages that seeme to glow under the lights; and having the latest synthesized party drugs available. It was the name, however, that she found amusing – literally, "Club Spy." Was there any better way for a Mossad front to operate in plain sight?

She chose a black dress that was just long enough to conceal her automatic inside her left thigh, though it would be exposed if she sat. In any case, she expected them to relieve her of it quickly. She got into a taxi at about 10:30 p.m., and almost immediately picked up a tail. Every few minutes of the ride, she held up her compact and checked the mirror to see them still there – square headlights, right behind her.

Breezing past the long line of well-dressed Swiss 20- and 30-some-things, she drew attention as she approached the entrance. Loud house music thumbed rhythmically in her ears while nightclub lights appeared on the floor just inside, swirled and faded. Looking back at the street, she saw her tail – a blue Citroen – drive slowly by. The beefy bouncer sported an earpiece wired, she guessed, to a receiver in his pocket or hitched to his belt. When she reached him, she looked directly into the camera mounted on the wall beside the main door.

"Name?" he barked in accented English. Before she could answer, he furrowed his brow and turned his head slightly away, holding his left hand to his ear. "I got it," he muttered into his left sleeve, and turned back to her. "Upstairs to the right."

She was instantly immersed in the club's atmosphere, which she found intoxicating without imbibing the glowing red cocktails she saw waitresses carry by on trays. There were two staircases that mirrored one another at the back of the room. Staying focused was difficult as she made her way through the writhing mass of sweaty young bodies moving rhythmically to downtempo music. A man in a black suit and an earpiece was waiting for her at the bottom of the left staircase. He signaled her to follow him up.

She followed him up the stairs and through a hefty door into a corridor. Once the door swung shut, he asked her to put her hands on the wall and proceeded to frisk her thoroughly but professionally, took her Glock, and opened another door for her.

The dimly lit room overlooked the pulsing club floor through a dark glass that, she guessed, was a two-way mirror. Her escort stayed in the corridor and closed the door behind her, leaving her with the two men inside. Both were dressed in dark business suits, but only one had the kind of earpiece she'd seen on the bouncer and the man that walked her upstairs. He held an Uzi fitted with a stock and kept his eyes firmly fixed on her. The other was much more relaxed, seated in one of two comfortable-looking swivel chairs behind a small round table that was otherwise empty save for an ashtray. His age and baldness reminded her of Masoud. If he had a mustache, she thought, he might bear a striking resemblance to her boss ... albeit without the belly.

"Please ..." he said, motioning her to the other chair.

She approached carefully, trying not to look at the armed man whose eyes were burning a hole in her, and sat. The bald man seemed amused at her apprehension, maintaining a smile and relaxed posture as he watched her.

"Are you Isaac?" she asked him.

"Call me Ari," he said. "Care for anything to drink? Mint tea, perhaps?"

The reference to her favorite beverage, which was clearly meant to give the impression that they knew much more about Nava than she did them, elicited a smirk from her.

"Just water, thank you," she said.

He nodded to the man with the Uzi, who murmured into his sleeve, then took a pack of cigarettes from his jacket's pocket and offered her one. Whatever brand it was, it was good.

"The number you called," Ari asked once both cigarettes were lit. "Did you get it from Yasin Haddad?"

"Yes."

He nodded slowly, exhaling smoke, with the ever-present smile still on his lips.

"My question is how he came to have it," she said.

"He didn't," Ari said. "At least, not always. No ... he had the number to another of our associates; one he met at the April Accords. We find it best to maintain back channels with our enemies, even in the worst of times."

He kept his smile on and studied her in silence until the man who'd escorted her upstairs brought them two small bottles of water.

"So ..." he said. "What would you ask of us, and what do you believe we need in return?"

"You know who killed Abu Faysal," she said.

He shook his head, chuckling.

"Wasn't that us?" he asked, leaning over a bit and motioning to his chest with both hands.

Nava remained sitting comfortably, her back against the rest and legs crossed, holding the cigarette in her right hand and tapping the armrest with her left index finger, patiently waiting for him to finish amusing himself.

Ari squinted at her through the smoke, leaning forward in his chair.

"You really don't know, do you?" he asked her, but she refused to respond. "You know, we thought you were coming here to ask who killed your station chief."

"Wasn't that me?" she asked, which seemed to amuse him even more than hearing himself say something similar.

"I like you," he said, pointing to her with the same hand that held his cigarette. "Even if I'll never understand why you work for those pigs in Tehran."

"Good dental insurance," she told him.

"You get *dental*?" he asked, seemingly sincere before he laughed a little again and sat back.

"What do you have?" he asked her.

"Pakistan's chief nuclear scientist is selling on the black market," she said.

"We know about A.Q. Khan," he replied flatly. "We have for years. Iran is one of his best customers."

She let the remark go.

"We've been collecting information on his operations for a decade," she told him.

Ari's smile never wavered, but his eyes narrowed, and his head cocked. He was skeptical. "What makes you think you have more information on him than we do?" he asked her.

"You know whom he sells to?"

"You," he said. "Libya, North Korea. The usual suspects, so to speak."

Now Nava smiled, and she saw that it had an inverse effect on Ari, whose face lost just a quantum of the self-satisfaction and superiority that he projected.

"There's a fourth client," she said.

Even in the dark, she could tell the blood drained from Ari's face. He ran his hand over his lips, nodding slightly while keeping his eyes fixed on her. She put out her cigarette and drank some water, letting him ruminate.

"And you know who this client is?" he asked.

"No."

He scoffed and shrugged with his hands out wide.

"Then how—"

"I have all the figures," she told him. "His network produced enough centrifuges and other equipment for an entire fourth customer."

"You have production numbers?"

"Numbers, equipment specifications, payments ..." she said. "I imagine that might go a long way with your bosses."

His face once again broke into a smile, but this time it was different. He was a gambler that saw someone put something he very much wanted in the pot. Although he may not have expected it, it was something that he could now not bear to leave the table without. He said something in Hebrew to the guard, who nodded once and said something into his microphone.

"I wish I knew who killed your station chief," he said. "For what you offer, I would give you that much; but we don't."

"Abu Faysal," she said.

"Am I to take it on faith that you will deliver on your end?" he asked her.

"I have nowhere to go," she said.

She watched as he got up from his chair and stood at the window overlooking the club floor, his arms akimbo, gazing down at the customers.

"There is this American movie," he said. *"All the President's Men.* Have you seen it?"

"I'm afraid not," she replied.

"Oh, you should. Hoffman, Redford ... These reporters, they're trying to expose a political scandal. One of them has a source inside the government that tells him to 'follow the money.'"

Nava waited for him to elaborate or explain why this was relevant. He turned his head in her direction.

"We're not certain who killed Abu Faysal," he said, and her heart felt as if it shrank by half in her chest. "But we're *nearly* sure," he added. "I just wanted to be upfront about it."

"Do you have what I need, or not?" she asked.

Ari's caginess was wearing thin. She was beginning to think she was wasting her time. Her mind had already partially moved on, beginning to formulate alternative plans to those she built around this deal happening.

The door opened, and the man who brought her in gave her a very small camera.

"We tracked a series of transactions that we think funded Abu Faysal's assassination," he told her. "Photograph the documents with this, and we'll give you what we have. Agreed?"

"Yes," she answered, and put the camera in her bag.

Before she was escorted out, she decided to take a chance and asked Ari, "Where did the money originate?"

He turned his body to face her and took a step forward. His smile was completely gone now, replaced with a somber visage.

"From MOIS," he told her.

Chapter
Thirty

In the back of a taxi, Nava stared blankly out the window at the passing city. When they first set out, she tried to spot the blue Citroen, but not seeing it had the unconscious effect of giving her mind license to be preoccupied with the new information Ari provided. She had to consider the possibility Mossad was trying to trick her, or that they simply had bad information. She had to admit that she would try to manipulate one of their people if they came to her in a similar situation. The fact that they had some doubt about their own information could be part of the act ... But something about it rang true, even if she didn't yet know why.

She heard the taxi driver cuss just before she felt herself violently jerked forward against her seatbelt. A terrible crunching sound, like a metal can being crushed, got her bracing herself against the back of the passenger seat. When it stopped, she quickly scanned herself. She wasn't injured. Neither was the driver, as far as she could see. However scary, the accident seemed minor.

"You okay?" the driver asked her, giving her a thumbs up.

She nodded, and he got out to survey the damage to his car. She followed him outside, cognizant of the passing cars, and tried to discern where she was. Her driver began talking to the other car's driver.

"Hey," she said, trying to get his attention.

When she failed, she took a step closer and tapped him on the shoulder to get him to turn around.

"Which way?" she asked him.

He pointed to her right, and the driver of the other car came into her view. His complexion and hair were dark, he had a thick mustache. *Indian, maybe ...* It was the blue Citroen. Inside were at least two, but perhaps three others. She couldn't see from her angle in this light.

"How far?" she asked, but the taxi driver was already re-engaged in an argument with the Indian-looking driver of the Citroen. She had to tap him again and repeat her question. This time, the other driver turned his eyes to her. They were searing. His hatred for her, blind and primal, was palpable. She had never experienced anything like it in Iran, Lebanon, or anywhere else; and it made her want to bolt across a lane of traffic to get away from him.

"One kilometer," her driver told her. "Maybe one and a half."

She waited for a driver to stop for her, glancing at the men in the Citroen before she was finally able to cross. The feeling of the Glock against her thigh gave her some comfort, but her adrenaline was pumping both from the accident and the evil eye she got from the Citroen's driver.

Before entering a narrow cobblestone street, she looked back to the main street and the scene of the accident one last time. The Citroen's doors were open, and she could see two men emerging from it. She quickened her step, but her heels were noisy and inhibiting. She looked for places to go that were either crowded and bright or out of the way and dark. She looked ahead to the next street, hoping to find a bar or restaurant she could go to and try to lose them. If she ran, she could make it; but the heels made it impossible, and running that far barefoot on these streets in this dress ...

There was a better option, or so she hoped. Several townhouses had separate basement apartments, the entrances to whic were mostly unlit and difficult to see from the street. Nava darted down the stairs to one that looked dark, crouched by the door, and loaded a round into the Glock's chamber. She heard people pass by, talking in German and English, laughing and shouting. She pressed herself against the wall, peering from under the stairs that led up the main house at the stairs leading down to her. Heavier footfalls reached her ears, and she flipped the gun's safety off. As they grew louder, she found herself tensing up to the point where she had to concentrate on not pulling the trigger by accident. She gulped her breaths, doing her best not to hold them.

They were close enough that she could hear them speaking in hushed tones to one another. She recognized only a few words, but it wasn't Farsi that they were speaking. It was Urdu.

When they passed the steps, she finally drew a full breath; but they stopped, and now it sounded as if they may be arguing, or at least confused. Their steps and voices grew louder. They were coming back.

She aimed the pistol at the entrance to the stairs, careful to keep it out of the light from the street above, and she pulled the hammer back to put it on a hair trigger. The sound of it locking into place hushed the voices above her, and she waited in the pitch-black silence for their faces to appear. Rather than the sound of weapons being drawn and shouts in Urdu, however, she heard the revelries of a group of young people coming from the direction in which she'd been heading before she'd made her way down here. Laughing, talking loudly, shouting ... Until they passed, and then there was absolute silence.

Slowly, cautiously, she stepped forward, letting her heel fall as softly as possible on the first stair and simultaneously lowering her gun to a low carry position. She strained her neck to look up, ready to bring the weapon up and fire at close range. Seeing the empty sidewalk, she took one more step to ensure they had gone before stepping back into the dark and switching the safety back on. The hammer clicked back into place, and she slouched back against the wall and bent her knees until her bottom touched the ground, resting her elbows on her knees and letting the gun droop between her legs.

Chapter
Thirty-One

The suspicion that Isha, the bank agent, had compromised Nava's anonymity by possibly alerting Pakistani authorities lingered heavily in Nava's mind. However, confronting Isha or her superiors about such suspicions could inadvertently expose the sensitive nature of the documents housed within the bank's secure vault. Thus, Nava opted for caution, attempting to steer clear of Isha as much as possible—a task that proved to be futile.

Once left alone in the vault, Nava meticulously sifted through the documents, selecting only those critical to her mission with Mossad, while scrupulously excluding any material unrelated to her target, the enigmatic fourth customer.

Upon her return to the bank's main lobby, escorted by Isha, Nava was greeted with unexpected warmth. "Ms. Hakimi!" exclaimed Muller, his welcome brimming with cordiality. "It's a pleasure to have you back. How may I assist you today?"

Nava, maintaining her composed demeanor, expressed a desire to enhance the liquidity of her funds by dispersing them across various accounts. "I need greater accessibility," she succinctly explained.

"Certainly," Muller responded, ushering her to take a seat opposite him. "There are several options we can explore to meet your needs efficiently."

Glancing at her watch, Nava calculated that she had barely more than an hour left before her rendezvous with Jake and their subsequent journey to Bern. Time was of the essence.

"There are additional adjustments I wish to make," she ventured further..

"And what might these changes entail?"

Nava produced the floppy disk from her possession. "Not to the accounts," she clarified, her voice steady. "To this."

In Bern, a man whose appearance was as unremarkable as it was precise—bald, with diminutive round spectacles perched on the bridge of his nose—extended a greeting with a practiced smile. He introduced himself as Helmut Schmid, a name attached to a title so ostentatiously cumbersome it bordered on the absurd: Director of Atomic Weapons Technology Counterproliferation at the Service for Analysis and Prevention. Nava couldn't help but suspect that the grandiosity of his title far exceeded the scope of his actual responsibilities.

The drive to their meeting point was punctuated by an air of forced civility, with Jake finding amusement in the bureaucratic verbosity that defined Schmid's professional identity. At Jake's behest, Schmid recited his title in German, a request met with a smile that seemed to tighten around the edges, betraying the effort it took to maintain. The title unfolded in a stream of syllables so extensive it verged on the comical, eliciting chuckles from Jake, which Schmid met with a strained chuckle of his own, his demeanor a blend of indulgence and subtle irritation.

"You must understand," he told them, "Switzerland isn't like the U.S. or Britain. We don't have the need for large intelligence agencies that collect and process data to inform policymakers and such."

"I can see that," Jake said, deliberately looking around the sparse, tiny conference room.

They were meeting at a nearly deserted office park, the facility stark and utilitarian, with only a few technicians present, threading computer cables in an otherwise silent space. Schmid's constant, measured smile suggested a professional distance, creating an atmosphere of polite detachment rather than genuine engagement.

"Mr. Espinoso ..."

"Call me Jake."

Jake took a sip of his espresso as a policeman entered the room, swiftly handed Schmid a small briefcase, and left. There was that smile again, unwavering and polite.

"We have a small problem that requires some discretion," Schmid said, and manipulated the dials of the briefcase until the lock flipped opened. "We heard of Ms. Sarsi's situation through Interpol, that you were coming to Zurich from the colorful Mr. Sikerski, and thought, well, this is a happy coincidence, yes?"

Jake sipped his espresso again instead of proffering any sort of reply. He seemed barely engaged, and definitely bored.

"What is the Swiss interest in Lebanon?" Nava asked.

"Oh, this is nothing to do with Lebanon, of course," Schmid replied. "No, no ... this has to do with your father. You see—"

"Can I ask we speak alone, Herr Schmid?" she asked and saw that Jake glanced at her.

214

No doubt he was annoyed, she thought; but she still didn't want the Janissaries to know more than they needed to know.

Schmid smiled politely once again, adjusted his glasses, and said, "I'm afraid not."

She looked at Jake, who shrugged slightly and smiled wryly at her.

"Davud Sarsi and Masoud Zana have been the primary Iranian contacts with a network based in Pakistan," Schmid told Jake. "The man at the top of this network is Mr. Abdul Qadeer Khan."

He took some papers from the briefcase and handed them to Jake. Nava glimpsed a picture of A.Q. Khan in the corner and guessed it was a profile of the man.

"This is Pakistan's chief nuclear scientist." Schmid went on. "He sells technology, plans ... even components needed to make uranium-based nuclear weapons."

"You want us to take down this network?" Jake asked, and his question elicited a polite laugh from Schmid.

"No, no," the Swiss bureaucrat replied. "As I said, we're not a global intelligence service by any means, and our counterproliferation efforts are strictly limited to issues directly related to Switzerland and our citizens."

"Okay ..."

Schmid fished through the briefcase and produced another stack of papers.

"Our primary interest in this matter concerns this man: Freiderich Tinner."

Jake and Nava looked at the picture he placed on the table of a middle-aged man.

"He's Swiss?"

"Indeed, he is," Schmid affirmed, the practiced ease in his voice belied by a subtle tightening around his eyes—a hint of discomfort perhaps at admitting a compatriot's involvement in such affairs. "Tinner studied alongside Mr. Khan during the 1960s. Their paths diverged, with Mr. Khan establishing Khan Research Laboratories in Pakistan, and Mr. Tinner, well, he ventured into less savory endeavors by 1981, contributing his expertise to centrifuge designs for uranium enrichment. A significant clientele for such technology, regrettably, includes Iran."

Schmid gestured to Nava as he spoke the last sentence, and she couldn't help but feel embarrassed.

"Okay ... how can we help you?" Jake asked him.

Schmid closed the briefcase and folded his hands together on the table.

"Eventually," he said, "this will all come out. It must. When it does, we would rather not have Swiss citizens jailed abroad or killed as a result. It would be bad for them, bad for Switzerland and our international standing."

"I don't know about that one," Jake said. "Every country has criminals."

"Yes," Schmid replied. "But they're not usually nuclear scientists."

"Right."

"We have tried to lure Herr Tinner and his son, Marco, back to Switzerland for three years without luck. Now we have lost track of them. They could be anywhere in the world."

"You want us to find them for you," Jake said.

"In part, yes," Schmid said. "We don't know the full extent of this network and all the places it operates. So, when we heard Ms. Sarsi was coming, we thought this presented us with a unique opportunity to finally locate Herr Tinner and bring him back home."

"You want him *alive*?" Jake asked, surprise in his tone.

"Of course."

BEIRUT STATION

Schmid turned his gaze to Nava. The ball was in her court, she knew. Her father had collected more information on the A.Q. Khan network than possibly anyone save a few Western intelligence services and the Mossad.

"I don't mean to try to upsell you, Herr Schmid," Jake said. "But wouldn't it be better to contract us to destroy this entire network from the top down?"

"Ha! Yes! Maybe it would," Schmid agreed. "But that would require years, yes? Perhaps tens of millions of dollars?"

"Estimates aren't my bag."

"We have neither the budget nor the interest," he said. "And if that were our objective, whatever her current problems with the Iranian government, we doubt Ms. Sarsi would use her knowledge of this network to help you destroy it. No ... as I said, our objective is limited: Friedrich and Marco Tinner behind bars, in Switzerland."

"Even for such a narrow purpose," Nava asked, "if I did know anything of this network, why would I use that knowledge to help you?"

"Because we can still freeze most of the money in your father's account," Schmid told her. "Arrest you and send you back to Lebanon. Or you may help us by continuing to work with Janissary Solutions, we can undercut this frivolous Interpol notice on you, and Fraulein Sara Hakimi may stay in Europe for as long as she wishes."

Even when making threats, Schmid kept a pleasant smile on his face. It occurred to her that he didn't know what happened to her in Lebanon, and he didn't care. She could be a completely innocent refugee, a criminal on the run, or a mass murderer. He needed what he needed, and anything beyond that was not his concern. He could let her walk out with Jake, have her arrested and sent home, or take her out back and shoot her. That smile would never leave his face.

217

Chapter
Thirty-Two

Although Nava didn't know where the contract with the Swiss would lead, if she couldn't return to her old life, perhaps this was a glimpse into what her new one might be like ... at least for a while. If it was, she would be working with Jake's team for longer than she had anticipated. The notion prompted her to try to engage him again on the train ride back to Zurich. It was a daunting task.

"Is Natasha your girlfriend?" she asked.

"No," he answered without looking up from the book he was reading, *The Clash of Civilizations and the Remaking of the World Order.* It wasn't an auspicious start, but about what she had expected.

"Erica mentioned you don't like religious people."

"I don't."

Okay...

"May I ask why?" she prompted him.

"They're all completely fucking unspooled."

He still didn't look up. Time to ask what she had wanted to ask since seeing him so calm in the middle of the firefight in Beirut.

"Are you afraid to die?" she asked him.

His head flinched backward slightly. He dog-eared the page he was reading and closed the book.

"Where is this coming from?" he asked her.

"*If* we're going to be working together for a while," she said. "I'd like to know whom I'm working with, and it seems you have a death wish."

"I don't," he answered.

She sighed heavily and ran her fingers through her hair as she gazed out the window at the darkness. God, it seemed, enjoyed putting her together with men like this. They were like isolated fortresses with no entrances. Nothing got in and nothing got out. It made her wonder what good such a fortress was – one that safeguarded nothing and no one but itself.

"My mother was the most fearful person I've ever known," she heard him say, and she turned back to him. Now it was Jake who was looking out the window. It occurred to Nava that this might be the only way he could interact with her – without the eye contact that would make sharing something personal intolerably intimate. "It's what I remember best about her," he went on. "She was afraid of people leaving her, most of all; so she tried to control everything around her, so that she didn't have to worry."

"Is fear what you felt?" she asked. "When you did the box drills? Is that what caused you to freeze?"

After a beat, he said, "Yes ... But I wasn't afraid of getting hurt. I was afraid of failing, and that's what nearly caused me to fail." He scoffed and shook his head. "Fear makes you do some crazy shit," he said. "Better not to feel it at all if there's nothing you can do about it."

But he *was* afraid. She knew he was. Not of dying, per se; but fear played a larger role in his life than he knew. She recognized the symptoms, and now that she was aware of what in Jake reminded her of her father, she felt like she had a better understanding of the root cause. They feared experiencing loss and pain, so they detached themselves. Her father detached himself from anything and anyone that could hurt him; and Jake, unable to separate himself from just one emotion, detached himself from all his own emotions... Or, at least, he'd learned to turn them down like the volume knob on a radio.

"My turn," Jake said, and she smiled.

The fact that he was now curious enough about her to ask anything was, in a slightly perverse way, flattering.

"What do you want from all this?" he asked her.

It was a good question.

"I want my life back," she said. "And I want justice for Masoud."

"You won't get either," he told her.

"How do you know?"

"Whoever did all that stuff in Lebanon, they're not going to suffer any real consequences for it," he said. "It doesn't matter what you do. They're too powerful."

"I disagree," she said. "The truth matters."

"Nava, if your boss was killed by an outsider – an Israeli, Syrian, whatever – your people wouldn't have turned on you. Whatever your differences, you'd be with them now, figuring out a way to even the score. But you woke up with a gun in your hand. That tells me someone on your own side did this, which means someone higher than them likely sanctioned it, and someone higher than that knew. You see where I'm going with this?"

She did; and deep down she knew it herself. It still turned her stomach to hear it aloud.

"I know it's hard," he went on, "to believe in something, only to find out you're at the bottom of a world full of lies. But the sooner you accept your old life is gone no matter what, the better off you'll be."

BEIRUT STATION

At the station, she got behind him in the cab line.

"I'll have my operations people book us plane tickets for the morning," Jake told her. "I'm sick of trains."

The taxi pulled up and he opened the door for her.

"You go ahead," she told him.

"Not going back to the hotel?"

"I have some business to finish," she said.

"I'll call you with the flight time," he told her, got in the car, and left.

She hadn't dressed for the posh crowd at *Club Spiel,* but Nava didn't intend on hanging around long. As soon as the bouncer saw her, he let her in. She followed the same procedure as she had the previous time, going upstairs, surrendering her Glock to the guard, and entering the room where Ari and his armed guard were waiting for her. A third man relieved her of the tiny camera they had given her and disappeared for about fifteen minutes, after which he returned and gave a thumbs-up.

Ari opened a small electronic safe and took out a stack of documents held together with a spring clip.

"The missing pieces," Ari explained, "are these transfers in Dubai. If you have a source there that we don't, you'll be able to find where the money ultimately ended up."

She folded the papers to a size where they would fit in her bag.

"I'm curious," Ari said as he walked her to the door. "Given your situation, how do you think this information can help you?"

"That depends," she answered him. "When I look into these accounts, am I going to find the truth of what happened?"

"I believe you will," he told her.

"Right now, that's all I want."

The bouncer pointed down the street when asked for a taxi stand, and she started walking that way without much thought. At the end of the block, when she still couldn't see one ahead of her, she looked back at the bouncer. The large man just held up his hand and waved her forward. It was just after eleven o'clock at night, and most of the city appeared to be asleep. Even on the broad, well-lit boulevard she was on, both vehicular and pedestrian traffic was dwindling.

She wasn't yet three blocks from the club when she was certain someone had found her. One of the two men walking behind her was the driver of the blue Citroen. She was certain of it. The eyes, even with just one good look from a distance, were unmistakable.

She picked up her pace, checking behind her regularly. Her pursuers closed the distance quickly, passing the few other pedestrians that had been between them. Soon, her frequent checks behind her tipped them off, perhaps persuading them to act immediately—exactly what she'd been trained to avoid. She barely had time to process the feeling of being pulled, stumbling, and losing her balance before being held upright. Jake stood her against the wall and peeked down the street in the direction from which she'd come.

"Who are they?" he asked her.

"Pakistanis," she answered, noticing that she was breathing hard.

He peered around the corner as she felt her heart pounding in her chest. She looked in the opposite direction down the alley, noticing the large garbage bins next to her, but not seeing any people.

"They're splitting up," Jake said in a low voice, his eyes hawkish and fixed. "Two of them are going around to box us in here."

"Then let's go!" she urged him as quietly as she could manage, pulling his arm and breathing even harder now. Her heart felt like it could explode.

"No," he said.

What? Why? What the f—she pursed her lips to ask any one of these questions, but none came out.

"We're going to kill them," he said. "Conspicuously, in case any of their friends are watching." He looked at her with cold, glassy eyes. "Listen, the deeper we get into this network, the harder they'll come at us. So, let's show them who we are. Shall we?"

Jake held up his fist, and without thinking she bumped it with her own.

He handed her his Sig Sauer P239 semi-automatic and said, "Watch my back."

She instinctively took it, momentarily forgetting she had her own weapon, and crouched by the garbage bins to cover the alley.

"Aim and squeeze," he told her.

Jake withdrew into the shadows just as two of the Pakistanis emerged onto the main boulevard, and waited for them to turn the corner. The sudden appearance of Jake, vastly different from their quarry, seemed to leave the Pakistanis shocked and indecisive. Later, doubting her heat-of-the-moment perception, she remained almost certain Jake had executed a slight bow, reminiscent of a magician before a trick. The driver with the hard eyes spotted Nava first, and his expression changed from surprise to rage in the span of less than a heartbeat. He reached inside his jacket while his partner started groping for something at the small of his back.

What unfolded next spanned mere seconds, yet seemed to stretch into slow motion, echoing the Beirut firefight. She could almost see a younger boy ... Surprisingly younger, and perhaps barely an adolescent, waiting with a black sack over his head in preternatural tranquility. His eyes were closed, but that was for the sake of his own focus, for there was no way he'd be able to see through the sack to the two men who were waiting for him, weapons in hand. Even as an unseen instructor briefly lifted the sack from his head, his eyes remained closed until the attackers made their move. Then his eyes sprang open, took in all the information he needed in an instant, and all that potential energy stored in his body became kinetic.

Jake's right hand went first to the driver's throat in an open-hand strike, crushing the man's Adam's apple. It triggered an involuntary reaction in the driver that overrode his intended movements. The driver's hand, holding a gun, came up toward his own throat. Jake effortlessly took the gun from his hand, shot the second man in the face, then brought the gun under the driver's chin and pulled the trigger.

The apparent ease of execution was more shocking than the violence itself, mesmerizing in the skill it unveiled. So captivated was Nava by the scene that she initially failed to notice the screams in Urdu echoing from the opposite direction. The first shot in her direction, however, quickly refocused her attention.

She turned her head around again and quickly spotted two men running toward them, with weapons drawn. It was the second half of the Pakistani team, which had been sent around the block to cut off their escape.

"Aim and squeeze," Jake told her again, now crouching behind her.

She lined up the sights and fired two shots in quick succession. One of the Pakistanis dropped. The other scrambled for cover in a door frame and fired at her again. A bullet whizzed by so close that she heard its hum like a buzzing bee. She fired again, missed, and the Pakistani left the cover of the doorway to advance on her while steadily firing. It made her keep her head down until she finally heard a metallic click. She peeked her head up to see the Pakistani man pressing himself against the wall, changing magazines. She sprang to her feet, took a step back, and fired several shots. Just as the Pakistani's magazine locked into place, he stopped and looked down. The bolt locked on Nava's own weapon, but she didn't need more ammunition. The Pakistani looked up at her, having seen the two holes in his chest, and crumpled to the pavement.

When it was all over, Nava sat on the ground, back against the wall, shaking. Jake must have taken the gun from her hand, though she didn't recall him doing it. He said something, she was barely aware of him. Every car that passed, the few people who dared to peer over in their direction before scampering away ... all caught her attention. She was acutely aware of anything that could present any other danger.

"It's the adrenaline," she heard him say.

"What?"

"Come on, get up," he said, grasping her arm.

He helped her to her feet, and they started walking.

Before the adrenaline started to wear off, they were back at the hotel.

"Shit ... I have to call that Schmid guy and tell him what happened, just in case," he said, searched his pockets for his card, and took it out.

"Why were you following me?" she asked him.

"Scottie wanted me to make sure nothing happened to you," he told her, dialing Schmid's number on his phone.

"Not because you still don't trust me?" she asked.

"I gave you my gun, didn't I?" he countered.

"Oh ...Right. I was going to tell you ..."

She took the Glock out of her purse and showed it to him. His eyes opened wide, and his eyebrows rose. She thought he might explode at her for withholding it from him, but when the surprise wore off, he just smiled wryly and shrugged.

"Figures ..." he mumbled, and did his signature bizarre closed mouth laugh before Schmid answered and they started talking.

She waited until he was done with Schmid, then confessed that it was the first time she killed anyone.

"Well ... at least it wasn't in cold blood," he said.

She waited for him to ask how she felt, not knowing how she would answer; but he didn't, and she got up to leave.

"The Pakistanis..." he said. "How did they find you?"

It was a good question. She initially thought they might have staked out the club, but the Mossad would probably have spotted them. They also didn't ambush her immediately as she exited. They waited until she was a few blocks away. Had the Israelis given her up? But why would they?

"I'm not sure," was the best answer she could give.

"Think about it," he said, stepping toward the bathroom.

"I will," she promised.

"See you in the morning."

But she couldn't leave just yet.

"Jake," she called to him before he could shut the bathroom door. "Maybe there is a reason you went through everything you did... even those horrible box drills."

"Yeah?" he asked, sounding only about half interested.

"I think it saved my life," she said. "I know it's not the reason you intended, but … It's something, anyway. Something other than money. Thank you."

"Yeah, well… don't get all schmaltzy on me," he told her. "I'm probably going to bill you for it."

Nava smiled as he closed the door; but just before it shut, in the sliver of space between the door and the frame, she believed she saw a smile come to his lips as well.

Chapter
Thirty-Three

It was risky, but Nava had to get away from the hotel and Jake to call Hooman while she had the chance. The train station was the only place she knew with a bank of pay phones.

"Nava," he answered after several rings. "Khadem's bugging every phone in the embassy trying to find you. So far, I've managed to keep him away from our station, but I don't know how much longer I can hold him off."

"Where are you now?"

"Safe house in Jezzine," he told her. "Waiting for my source."

"Can you help find out about some bank account activity in Dubai?" she asked.

"Dubai? For what? What did you find?"

"I'm not sure, but ... I think Yasin Haddad killed Abu Faysal," she told him.

"Good God ..."

"I think he even used our money to do it, somehow," she added.

Hooman sighed heavily on the other end of the line.

"I really miss Masoud," he said.

She didn't need to tell him that she shared his sentiment.

"With the IRGC looking over our shoulder, this is going to be tough," he said. "But I have an idea."

"Okay ..."

"We're not the only ones with good sources in Dubai," he said. "Do you have any contacts in Syrian intelligence?"

"Seriously?" was Rafiq's answer, and even if she knew the reason for his intransigence, it still annoyed her. "You lied to me about the hostage, about the contractor you were with, about Haddad ... Why, of all people on Earth, would you come to *me* for a favor?"

"Because you're the only one I can trust on this," she replied.

Dead silence.

"I don't even know how to respond to that," he said impassively.

"Raf—"

"If the shoe were on the other foot, Sabi, would you do this?"

She was, to a certain extent, trained to lie; but it was far easier when she was lying to protect her mission and not herself. Her silence evidently spoke volumes.

"I didn't think so," he said, and sighed heavily. "Look, you left a mess here, anyway. Half of Lebanon now seems to think that not only did we kill Abu Faysal, but we also killed some Hezbollah militia and an Iranian intelligence officer to cover it up."

"Then we might be able to help one another," she told him, and explained how the information she had gathered could implicate someone else in Abu Faysal's assassination. "If you can't do it," she said, "I understand. Maybe you could at least give me a number—someone in Dubai that I can call to look into these accounts."

More silence, this time followed by curse words.

"Where did you even get this information?"

She winced at the prospect of lying again, but there was no way she could tell him it came from Mossad. As he was likely to hang up and never take another call from her, Nava chose a different option.

"I can't tell you that yet," she said.

She heard him scoff. "Is it reliable, at least?" he asked her.

"I believe it is, yes," she answered.

Another long silence.

"Well ... If it does point the finger for Abu Faysal's death at someone other than us, maybe it'll be worth it. I can't promise anything, but ... give me a couple of days."

Nava pumped her fist, barely able to keep from shouting in joy. Before she could open her mouth to thank him, however, someone caught her eye. He was on a train platform facing the row of pay phones. A slight man in a brown trench coat with mostly gray hair and dark, sullen eyes stared at her with something approximating regret.

It was her father.

Chapter
Thirty-Four

D avud Sarsi raised his right hand, signaling a halt with an all too familiar slow blink that spoke volumes of his irritation. It was a gesture so characteristic of him that Nava could pick him out in a crowd of thousands. He had, undoubtedly, caused her yet another problem, probably for his own benefit. And yet, he seemed preemptively irked at the prospect of being challenged by his daughter, as if her grievances were unwarranted interruptions to his plans.

"Before you begin, Nava, I—"

"Enough," she cut him off sharply, grabbing his arm to hasten their exit from the crowded station.

"I'm on my own," he attempted to assure her, but she wasn't in the mood for his explanations.

Only when they had found seats on the tram, blending into the nondescript flow of public transport, did she allow herself a moment to possibly hear him out. Their choice to converse in Farsi might attract some curious looks, yet Nava's bubbling fury made her dismissive of such concerns.

"I can explain everything," he assured her.

"I don't think so, *baba*," she said. "But go ahead."

He sighed deeply, a sound of frustration that did little to elicit her sympathy. Rather than offering the promised explanation, he opted for silence, folding his arms defensively and retreating into a sullen demeanor. Nava couldn't help but scoff at the sight. It struck her how the man before her, a figure from whom she once sought approval and guidance, now seemed no more mature than a petulant child.

"Why don't you start with the disk?" she asked.

He turned his head sharply toward her and asked, "Is everything where it was?"

"All your files and your money are still there," she said, and when he seemed relieved, she added, "Most of it, anyway."

He turned his head again, but she preempted his question by telling him to talk.

"It's for your protection as much as mine and Masoud's," he said.

"Masoud was murdered," she interjected. "Shot twice right in front of me. I was almost killed tonight by the people you've been dealing with."

"What?" he asked, sounding genuinely surprised and a bit angry.

"Talk," she told him.

Turning away, staring blankly ahead into the void, Davud's voice softened, laden with a nostalgia tinged with regret. "You've been in the field for years," he started, "but you've never truly known Tehran. Not the way I have. Back when you were a child, we transitioned from revolutionaries to rulers. You can't fathom the sacrifices, the dangers of those days. The infighting was relentless. Those of us loyal to Khomeini managed to navigate those tumultuous times, but we also witnessed the fallout for those who didn't. Khomeini's age was a ticking time bomb; his death could unravel everything we'd built. There were fears of purges after his death. Aligning with A.Q. Khan for nuclear capabilities wasn't just strategic—it was our lifeline against the instability that threatened to engulf us after he was gone."

"The money was in case you needed to flee from Iran?"

"The government was tossing enormous sums at this project," he said. "They still are! They don't know how much any of that stuff costs because no one's ever done anything like this before. We added ten percent on top of every purchase we made. We knew we might not be able to travel with our real names, so we set up the access protocols the way we did."

"And the files? Was that part of your contingency plan?"

"Part of our assignment was to collect information about A.Q. Khan and his network," Davud said. "Everything we have in that file we also sent to Tehran. We just kept copies. We never trusted the Pakistanis. Those files were insurance that they would never cross us or try to kill us for what we knew."

Every time the tram stopped, Nava made mental notes of who was getting on and off. As she listened to her father, she maintained her awareness of who was in earshot. She never noticed any other passenger's gaze lingering on them too long, or anyone around her listening just a little too intently. Regardless, she insisted on switching trams before heading back to the hotel, which had a bar and café on the top floor open for another hour. When they found a quiet corner and got their tea, she asked him the question that had been on her mind for days.

"Why did you send me the disk?"

"Even after I retired, the Ministry kept me on as the primary contact with A.Q. Khan," he said. "Everything was as it was before ... Until the IRGC began getting into the intelligence game. The Supreme Leader, he ... enjoys playing the power broker and pitting various parts of the government against one another. When President Khatami was elected, I think it scared him. Suddenly, an extremely popular president appeared out of nowhere with a mandate to make reforms; and if there's one thing powerful people are notoriously afraid of, it's change. The Supreme Leader is expanding the IRGC's intelligence unit and looking to take the nuclear acquisition program away from MOIS... away from the president, who might bargain it away to improve relations with the West."

"The IRGC was poking around your program, and you got spooked," Nava said.

"They're poking around everything of significance, Nava," he told her. "Acquiring authorities like this is how you acquire power. President Khatami has no authority over the IRGC. If they take it over, he won't be able to stop this if he wanted. The same thing goes for the war in Lebanon. It's all political maneuvering, trying to box Khatami in until they can put someone more conservative in office."

Nava leaned back, the weight of her father's words pulling her down. He remained impassive, his actions as mundane as stirring his tea, yet each sound seemed amplified in the quiet, resonating with a dissonant clarity. She reflected on a time when his mere presence didn't grate on her, a time when his rare approval and attention were her world. Her mother, in contrast, had been a beacon of warmth and affection, a stark departure from the man before her. Their union, unarranged and built on mutual attraction, puzzled Nava now as she pondered what traits her father once possessed that endeared him to her mother. Those traits, whatever they were, seemed extinguished, leaving behind a man shadowed by resignation and sorrow.

"Alright," she said, and he finally stopped his incessant stirring to put the spoon on his saucer and take a sip. "Is this what got Masoud killed?"

"Of course not!" her father answered, dismissing the idea with a wave of his hand. "We kept it hidden too well to—"

She stopped him with a snort, and said, "Not nearly as well as you think *baba*."

He gave her a startled and irritated look as he sent a wide-eyed glance her way across the table. Was it because she had the temerity to suggest their little scheme got one of them killed, that she interrupted him, or that she told him his secret account and box at the bank weren't as secret as he thought? She didn't have the energy to care.

"Who knows?" he demanded in a harsh whisper.

"The Swiss," she answered. "The Pakistanis; and now the Janissaries."

"Who?"

"They're a company the Ministry hired to ... you know, it's not important."

He sat back in his seat with a sigh and shook his head staring blankly out the window at the city lights.

"I went to the bank as soon as I got here," he said and produced a floppy disk from his jacket. "With this ..."

"It didn't work," she said.

She had envisioned this moment: his bafflement, the inversion of their lifelong power dynamics. She might have unleashed a tirade on his self-centeredness, critiqued his failure as a paternal figure, lamented how that void influenced her failed marriage, and mourned the mutual loss of her mother. Yet, facing him now, she felt neither affection nor animosity, but a profound sense of pity. It was as if she had finally seen him clearly for the first time, her lifelong perception of his grandeur now dispelled, revealing a man far less formidable and more fallible than she had been led to believe. This disillusionment transformed her resentment into empathy, recognizing the fragility behind the façade he had maintained to command her respect and obedience.

"I changed the file," she told him.

As she confronted her father, Nava felt a torrent of emotions swirling within her. She had anticipated a moment of triumph, perhaps even a touch of satisfaction in seeing him powerless, his usual dominance and control stripped away. Yet, as she stood there, witnessing his frustration and anger, no sense of victory emerged. Instead, she was struck by a profound realization of his utter desolation. Here was a man, her father, who had sacrificed everything for a cause that had eventually betrayed him, leaving him empty and alone. It dawned on her that his life had come full circle, ending up as hollow as it had started, his dreams of revolution reduced to mere ashes.

"Don't worry," she assured him with a calmness that surprised even herself. Her voice was steady, almost compassionate, despite the chasm that had grown between them. "I won't take more than I need; but I do need it. Maybe in a few years, you'll get a disk in the mail. Until then..." Her voice trailed off, leaving a silence that was heavy with unspoken thoughts and emotions.

His grip on her arm was a desperate plea, a raw display of emotion she had rarely seen from him. "For God's sake, Nava ... I am your father!" His words, laced with frustration and anger, could not mask the underlying fear of losing whatever was left of their bond.

Nava's laugh was devoid of humor, a reflex to the absurdity of the situation. "I told you I was almost killed tonight," she reminded him, her voice tinged with disappointment and a trace of bitterness. "Did you even ask about it? You never even said that you were happy I was alive after what happened in Lebanon. All you care about is your money and your secrets."

His defensive posture and his attempts to justify his actions only served to widen the gap between them. "Go ahead then," he challenged, his pride wounded, yet his eyes revealing a vulnerability she had never seen before. "Say what you want to say, Nava."

"Goodbye, baba," she said, her voice barely above a whisper. Walking away, she felt a weight lifting off her shoulders. This was not just a departure from her father, but a liberation from years of unmet expectations and unreciprocated love. She was no longer the daughter seeking approval from a man who could never give her what she needed. She was free.

Chapter
Thirty-Five

K han's Café Américain shimmered like a scene straight out of a 1970s discotheque fantasy, complete with the vibrant energy of a John Travolta classic. The ambiance was electric, bathed in the glow of multicolored lights cascading from the central disco ball. Russian girls, decked in skintight tops and flared jeans, their hair voluminously styled, moved rhythmically to the era's iconic beats. The entire venue pulsed with life, encapsulated in the retro allure of a bygone era.

"Seventies night," Jake muttered as they stepped inside, his voice barely piercing Nava's bubble of excitement.

Her eyes darted through the crowd, scanning past patrons lost in the nostalgia of "Give It Up" by KC and the Sunshine Band. The anticipation of reuniting with Scott had painted a persistent smile on her face during their flight from Zurich to Vienna.

Now, her heartbeat quickened with every step they took deeper into the heart of the café.

"There," Jake nudged, pointing out their companions amidst the lively throng.

Nava spotted Erica and Christian first, but it was Scott who captured her gaze, transforming her anticipation into a tangible thrill. The emotional barriers that once seemed insurmountable now appeared trivial. The urge to rush to him was overwhelming...

"Hey, babe!" Scott's warm greeting cut through the din, his smile mirroring the joy in Nava's heart.

With a newfound boldness spurred by her recent epiphanies, Nava didn't hold back. The encounter with her father had stripped away layers of reservation, leaving her feeling uninhibited and empowered. Her kiss, fervent and revealing, caught Scott by surprise, igniting a spark between them that was impossible to ignore. They danced, lost in each other, until mutual desire was evident in their eyes.

Guided by a magnetic pull, she led him out of Khan's, their hurried departure charged with a promise of intimacy. The journey to his bedroom felt agonizingly slow, every second a test of her resolve not to give in to the passion that threatened to overflow in the backseat of the cab.

The fervor between them was undeniable, their clothing discarded in a whirlwind of urgency, and though their initial union was brief, the pause that followed was nonexistent. Scott's readiness for a second encounter was almost immediate, imbuing their connection with a depth and passion that Nava had never known. Her previous experiences, particularly with Farzin, paled in comparison to the fervency with which Scott engaged, prioritizing her satisfaction as much as his own. It was a revelation, affirming not just his skill as a lover but his considerateness and generosity. Even in the aftermath, as they lay entwined, he indulged her desire to smoke a cigarette indoors, an act of leniency that spoke volumes.

As Scott shifted beside her, the movement exposed the intricate tattoo adorning his left shoulder blade—a majestic eagle in mid-hunt, talons outstretched towards its quarry. Encircling the powerful image were the Latin phrases "INVENIAM VIAM" arching above and "AUT FACIAM" etched below

"I like it," she said, her voice soft as her fingertip gently traced the inked contours on his skin.

"That? Oh ... we all have one."

"Everyone at your company?"

"No, no ... Just Janissaries."

He turned his body to face her. They were still new enough to one another that their hands wandered, exploring every curve of a new lover's body with delicate caresses.

"What's the difference?"

"Only the people who went through the Program are Janissaries," he told her.

"How old were you when it all began?"

"Eight."

The stark simplicity of his admission momentarily stilled her. His smile, tender and reassuring, bridged the gap her shock had created.

"The first few years, all we really did was go to school," he told her. "It was just in Russian and other languages. There were all kinds of doctors. Lots of tests..."

"That must have been hard," she said, caressing his cheek.

"I think ... I had it easier than most kids," he said. "Looking back now, I think the difference was that I had someone who loved me."

"Your mom."

"Right ... Like, the others thought I never stressed about things. That I was always laid back and happy and stuff. I did stress. I just ... thought that no matter what, I would be alright. Guys like Jake and Coda–they thought that if they failed, it meant they were worthless; but I never felt that way."

"I understand how they must have felt," she told him. "I think I felt the same way. Like I failed as a daughter, then as a wife."

"What made you change your mind? Was it me?"

They both smiled and she flicked him playfully on the nose.

"No ..." she said. "Not completely; but you were part of it."

"Happy to help."

"Shut up," she said, pushed him onto his back, locking her lips to his. "So are you afraid of anything?" she asked him as she rested her head on his chest.

"A lot of things," he answered, stroking her long black hair. "Losing more brothers, mostly."

"Don't you worry about never getting to go back to America and doing what you love?" she asked him and lifted her head to face him. "That you're going to do this the rest of your life?"

He smiled mischievously and said, "Oh, I'd be perfectly happy doing *this* the rest of my life."

She smiled as he laughed at his own joke.

"You know what I mean," she said.

"Sometimes," he said. "But... our lives have been so hard that I just try to appreciate what I have now. I'm alive. I'm well fed, warm and dry. And now there's you."

"Now there's me," she said, climbing on top of him and bringing her lips to his.

"That's the smile of a girl that got laid last night," Nava heard Erica say a bit too loudly as she took a seat in the small café a few blocks from the Janissary team's home. She poured Nava a cup from a French Press and they clinked their cups together, causing a little spill that made them laugh.

"Scottie's the best," Erica told her. "Seriously."

"Would you tell me otherwise?" Nava asked her, fixing her coffee with sugar and cream.

"Yeah," Erica laughed. "If it was Ridley, I'd tell you to run–fast."

"Really? I wasn't going to say anything, but I got a weird feeling from him."

"It's like, of all my brothers ... they're technically all very dangerous people."

"I've noticed."

"But I'm one of them, and I know they'd never hurt me ... Except Ridley. Him, I'm just not sure."

The admission hung heavily between them as they sipped their coffee in contemplative silence. Erica, ever the epitome of effortless cool, lounged in the booth with an air of detached elegance, her bare feet resting on the seat, sunglasses perched atop her head in the sunlit café.

"What if it were Jake?" Nava asked, making Erica roll her eyes.

"I'd tell you not to waste your time," she said. "No woman could ever love Jake as much as he loves himself."

They shared a little laugh, after which Nava asked her, "Why did you join the Program?"

Erica smiled, showing some of her perfect white teeth. Picking up her coffee, she answered, "You wouldn't ask if you knew where we came from."

"Where did you come from?"

"We were abused, neglected, exploited..."

"I don't mean to make you uncomfortable," Nava told her.

"You're not," Erica assured her, but Nava knew better.

"It's just, whenever I ask about you, you tell me about the Janissaries in general," Nava said. "Never specifically about what you've been through."

She watched Erica mull that over, running her fingers through her blonde hair absentmindedly. After a minute, she lifted her sunglasses onto her head, sat upright on the bench, and the smile faded from her face. Her gaze shifted from looking up and to the right, to Nava's face, down to her cup, and back again as she spoke, never lingering in one location very long.

"I hated being vulnerable," Erica told her, her tone deeper and more somber than before, even when she'd been speaking of Ridley. "That's what I remember most. When you're young, people can just take what they want from you. The Program didn't take anything. Yeah, I didn't have birthday parties and shit ... But they took care of me. And they just wanted me to learn what they taught me. That was it."

"You must have known this training was making you very dangerous people." Nava said.

Without missing a beat, Erica shook her head and said, "We didn't even know what it was until we were almost done with Phase Three. Sorry, that's high school. Ours was just ... different. Anyway, we could always choose to leave, right up until we finished college. By that time, most of us were so used to it, leaving seemed ... absurd. You know?"

Nava nodded, though she knew she didn't understand – not fully.

"Can I ask how you and Christian ...?" Nava began, letting her infer the rest.

Mentioning their relationship seemed to lighten her mood. She kicked her feet up again and leaned back against the wall.

"Chin ... that's what we call him," she explained. "He's ... different. He's smart. I mean, we're all smart, I guess ... But he's *smart* smart. Like, eidetic memory, Mensa-level smart."

"Really?"

"Yeah ..."

"Why is he doing this?" Nava asked, and instantly regretted her question. "Sorry, I didn't mean to suggest ..." she began a fumbled apology, but Erica just had a little laugh at her little faux pas.

"It's alright," she said. "He never knew his parents. Grew up in a group home until McBain found him when he was starting a new class."

"Class?"

"Yeah ... Like, McBain, Ski, Khan – they were in the first class of Janissaries, in the fifties and stuff. We were the second class."

"The Program is that old?"

"Kinda," Erica replied, bouncing her head slightly from side to side. "They only did one class and got disbanded in the seventies. When they started the Program back up in the early eighties, Jack and Khan recruited and oversaw the training of our class."

"A lot of history behind this," Nava said.

Erica briefly raised her eyebrows and took a sip of coffee.

"Anyway ... The Program is all Christian knew before he went to Harvard," Erica went on. "It was hard for him to stay, especially after the government disbanded us again and Jack took us private."

"What made him stay?"

Erica sighed and said, "The same as everyone, I guess. So that we could stay together."

Nava sat back in her chair, thinking about how close the bonds between these people must be. No wonder they called each other "brother" and "sister." They were far more than a company – at least, those who'd been through this "Program" were. They were, for all intents and purposes, a family. They gave up a country they loved for one another. They'd fight for one another ... do anything for one another. She felt envious of them for the first time since meeting them in Beirut.

The waitress came and they ordered some pastries. By the time they received their order, Christian had joined them.

"It's official," he told them. "Coda's gone to work for Khan."

"Can I ask what happened to Coda's eye?" Nava asked them.

"Oh ... he was looking through a rifle scope," Christian answered. "Bullet came through this way."

He held his left hand to his right eye, fingers curled with his thumb and index finger forming a circle – a rough approximation of a scope. With his right hand, he used his index finger to simulate a bullet coming in through the side of the scope.

Nava put her hand to her mouth as she pictured an exploding scope sending shards of glass into Coda's eye. That image in her head was perhaps worse than the actual incident looked in real time.

"Yeah ..." Christian muttered and sipped his coffee.

As Erica started speculating about the prospect of ever returning to lead her team or becoming Coda's permanent replacement on Team 12, Nava thought of Coda. She recalled that night in the bar when he admitted that his passing reference to suicide had been, in fact, a serious consideration after he realized the extent of his injuries would stop him from "operating." She realized now what it was that put him there. It wasn't, as he said, the prospect of not doing what he's been trained to do most of his life. It was the fear of his injuries becoming a rift between him and those he loved, and never experiencing that kind of feeling again.

When Scott arrived and sat next to her, she felt happy – joyful, even – just being with him. The feeling that she was doomed to live the rest of her life alone, which had been so pervasive since the day Farzin told her he was leaving her, was too fresh to have vanished; but she could sense that she was beginning to heal. Even if this unexpected relationship ended, which her rational analytic mind decided was probably due to several factors, she knew there was life beyond what she had planned and expected. Life was full of possibilities, including love.

Nava excused herself, went outside, and used her phone card to call Rafiq.

"Any luck?" she asked him.

"Some," he told her. "After Haddad authorized the transfer of two million USD to the shell company in Dubai, it went to several companies registered in the Cayman Islands, Belgium, Seychelles, and a few other places ... It gets kind of difficult after that, but our source is pretty sure it all went to subsidiaries of a company in Vienna called Janissary Solutions."

Nava had never fainted, but the shock was enough to make her heart race and send a rush of blood to her head. She looked back at the café, but her vision seemed to fail her. The world was blurry, soft with no edges. One color ran into the other, like paints caught in a whirlwind. She felt the strength in her legs dwindle as her skin tingled. Rafiq was going on about how more than half the money had been returned going through many of the same routes, but she couldn't really take in what he was saying. She heard herself muttering that she had to go, and registered Rafiq's annoyance with her for not answering any of the questions he was asking.

At first, she wanted to wait until the heaviness in her stomach passed; but it didn't. Scott came out of the café to check on her. His nearly ubiquitous smile was gone the moment he saw her face. She wanted to hit him, kick him, spit at him ... most of all, she wanted the emotional release of a hard sob. She did none of those, but the look in her eyes must have told him enough to be nervous. He approached slowly, cautiously, with his eyes wide open.

"What's up?" he asked her.

She looked at him with sore eyes. Her mouth dropped open, and her chin was trembling so much that she thought she might not be able to speak before bursting into tears.

"Did you kill Abu Faysal?" she asked, feeling the dryness in her throat.

He glanced around quickly, which only made her angrier. Why would he care if anyone was listening, when he could see how keeping this from her had made her feel?

"DID YOU KILL—" she began, annunciating each word, before he tried to shush her.

Scott tried to put his arms around her, but she stepped back and held her hand out.

"Nava, we don't discuss other contracts," he said. The calmness in his answer did nothing to quell the feeling of betrayal.

"Fuck you," she said. "Did you—"

"Yes!" he answered, nearly shouting, then glanced around again. "Okay. Yeah, we did. It's the kind of shit we do, Nava. You know this. Come on."

"Did you kill Masoud?" she asked.

"What? No!" he answered.

Christian and Erica came out from the café, but they kept their distance.

"Why should I believe you?" she asked Scott, her eyes darting from him to Christian and Erica and back again.

"I won't lie to you, Nava," Scott told her.

"Just withhold the truth," she shot back.

"Nava, clients couldn't trust us if—"

"That's all I am, aren't I?" she asked before he could finish. "A client. I might be the target of your next contract."

"You know you're more than that by now," he told her, but she was apoplectic.

"What am I, then? I'm not one of *you*. I could never be."

Scott didn't offer any rebuttal, not that it would have mattered. Still, she wanted *something* from him. He was one of only two men with whom she'd ever shared a bed, and she felt like it had to mean something ... Exactly what, she didn't know; but she wasn't getting it.

"I'll get my things and be out," she said. "Don't follow me."

"How soon can you get me to Beirut?" she asked Coda as soon as he picked up the phone.

"It depends on how much you want to pay," was his answer.

It was Thursday morning. The best day to go back would be the next day. He told her it wouldn't be a problem, and she called Rafiq to arrange a meeting.

Jake, who happened to be at the house looking and smelling like he had just returned from some sort of intense exercise, seemed curious about what had happened, annoyed that Scott had told her, and largely indifferent to her as long as she would give him access to the files on the A.Q. Khan network.

"Don't get yourself killed," he told her as she was carrying her bag to the door.

"What do you care?" she shot back.

"I don't want anything happening to my intel," he told her.

She opened her bag, dug the computer disk out, and tossed it to him.

"Here," she said. "Consider it payment for Zurich."

Chapter
Thirty-Six

Eighteen hours had passed when she found herself in a Zodiac— a sleek, black inflatable boat powered by an outboard motor, discreetly released from a Singapore-flagged container vessel off Lebanon's coast. She beached the craft far north of Beirut's bustling cityscape, secured her backpack, and armed herself with her Glock, tucking it securely at the small of her back. Standing alone on the shore, she watched the men skillfully navigate the gentle waves back to the open sea. As the engine roared to life and they vanished into the nocturnal abyss, she hoped this marked her final dealings with Janissary Solutions and Khan Enterprises.

In that moment, cloaked in solitude and the familiar air of her homeland, she wrestled with a sense of belonging and autonomy. Despite her insistence on independence and the comfort of home, doubt lingered, blurring the lines of truth in her declarations.

It was a Friday, a day when the devout in Beirut would gather for Ṣalāt al-Jumu'ah, leaving the streets quieter than usual. Rafiq met her just after midday, at a time when the city's rhythm slowed and those who might recognize her were otherwise occupied. He guided her from the sanctuary of her preferred café to the Syrian Embassy, nestled among the diplomatic quarter on the city's eastern fringe, a stone's throw from the Lebanese governmental edifices. The embassy was predictably serene, its halls mostly deserted save for the essential staff, a common sight on Fridays. Yet, as she crossed its threshold, an unmistakable nervous flutter besieged her stomach, a silent testament to the complexities of her return.

"You're armed?" he asked her when they arrived at the guard station inside.

Nava surrendered her weapon to the guard for a claim ticket and a flimsy plastic red visitor's card on a metal bead lanyard. She placed her backpack on the x-ray machine belt, emptied her pockets into a little plastic dish and walked through the metal detector.

"Nice phone," Rafiq said before she put it back into her pocket on the other side.

"They gave it to me," she told him.

"Janissary Solutions?"

"Yes."

They took an elevator down to the basement level, where his small windowless office was located.

"I'm sorry I couldn't tell you everything when I saw you last," she told him.

"Couldn't? Or wouldn't?" he asked her, taking a seat behind his desk and reclining back slightly in his squeaky chair.

He took a pack of cigarettes from a drawer and offered her one, which she gratefully accepted.

"So, these ... Janissaries killed Abu Faysal," he said, pushing the ashtray on his desk to within reaching distance for her.

"For Yasin Haddad," she said.

"You're sure?"

"The only way to be sure is to hear it from Haddad himself," she said.

"Well ... we might be able to arrange that," Rafiq said, opened a drawer and took out a stack of papers held together by a spring clip. He tossed them on the desk in front of her.

The report, written in Arabic, was from a Syrian Mukhabarat office in Damascus. It listed the payments made from several accounts, but she only recognized a few of them as being linked to Dubai shell businesses run by MOIS and Lebanese Hezbollah.

"Before we go any further, I need to know exactly where those account and transaction numbers came from," she heard Rafiq say. His voice cut through the stillness, his words measured, his tone bearing the weight of unspoken gravitas. Nava, roused from the depths of the report before her, caught the rhythm of his fingers tapping a silent Morse code on the desktop, his gaze upon her tinged with a shadow of suspicion.

In the moments before, she had endeavored to foresee his reaction, to navigate the myriad possibilities that the revelation might engender. Rafiq, in her estimation, was the epitome of pragmatism, a man who, she believed, held truth in high regard, no matter how unpalatable it might prove. His was a mind that could grasp the necessity of certain alliances in the face of dire circumstances. Yet, she was acutely aware of the dichotomy within him, a product of his upbringing—a deep-seated animosity towards the "Zionist enemy." The notion of a ceasefire, a begrudging tolerance, was one thing; to actively engage in cooperation, even when such actions promised substantial gain, quite another. This was the tightrope she found herself walking, each step a calculation, a gamble on the unpredictable terrain of loyalty and ideology.

"Mossad," she said, keeping her tone and expression flat.

Rafiq's head jerked back a little and he arched one eyebrow.

"Okay ..." he said, sat upright in his chair, rested his elbows on his desk and tented his hands. "I take it you don't have a source in Mossad."

She shook her head.

"May I ask what you gave in return?"

"Information on the A.Q. Khan network out of Pakistan," she told him.

He nodded, put his hands flat on the desk, and looked away from her.

"Well ... Obviously I can't say this in my report," he said, and looked up at her with a wry smile on his face. "The ironic thing is, neither of us could have figured this out without the other's assets; but I don't think Damascus would be keen on swapping intelligence with the Mossad any time soon."

"No," she agreed. "Look, Rafiq ... I went to Mossad because at the meeting in Jezzine I heard one of them say something that suggested they knew what happened to Abu Faysal when they met with Haddad. They were my only lead."

She told him about her father and Masoud's involvement with the A.Q. Khan network and what she had offered the Israelis in return for their help. She also told him about meeting her father in Zurich and all that he'd said to her. He took it all in like a cerebral professor, interested but without much emotion. He was difficult to read.

"So, what do you think will be gained speaking with Yasin Haddad at this point?" Rafiq asked her when she was done.

"The morning Masoud was killed, Haddad got a call from someone," Nava told him. "We don't know who it was, but they told him that the Israelis killed his brother."

Rafiq raised his eyebrows and asked, "He believed it?"

"He believed it so much that he gave his hostage up to al Qaeda for disposal," she said. "When he found out he was alive, he tried to get her back."

"Okay," he said and took a pause, biting his lower lip.

"So what's our play?" she asked before she could get any more anxious than she already was.

"Our ambassadors meet every Monday," he said. "Hooman has concluded that Israel killed Abu Faysal and the IRGC is pushing for an all-out offensive in the south. Ambassador Gul has reservations about attacking the Israelis, which probably means Tehran has reservations as well. The evidence against them is scant; but he also believes that Israel's antiwar movement has grown stronger. He thinks that an offensive could weaken the doves in Israel and strengthen Ariel Sharon and the other hardliners."

He paused and stroked his mustache pensively. Her memories of Masoud doing the same thing countless times behind that big desk at his house in front of the big paladin window came to the front of her mind. She may have thought at the time that his presence was just a constant that she could count on – a source of wisdom, insight, and at times warmth and comfort. Despite all his flaws, he'd been kind and fair. She missed him.

"Masoud told me that Haddad may be working with hardline conservatives in Tehran," she said. "Trying to cause conflict with the United States to weaken President Khatami and limit whatever engagement with the West he has planned."

"Very plausible," Rafiq conceded. "Also, a very dangerous game to play for the hardliners."

"Why?" she asked.

"If Khatami discovers this, the tension between the hardliners and liberals in Tehran could boil over and turn into outright hostilities," he said. "Worst case, civil war."

The words seemed to cast a somber pall over them. The office was quiet enough for Nava to hear the electric hum of the fluorescent lights.

"Okay," Rafiq finally said, breaking the silence. "Let's talk to Yasin Haddad."

Chapter
Thirty-Seven

As night descended, Nava observed the third missed call from Scott on her phone. She ached to hear his voice again, to engage in the easy banter, to laugh at his invariably silly jokes, and to keep sharing snippets of her life with him. Yet, the sting of betrayal lingered, sharp and unwelcome. While her mind could grapple with and even accept the reasons behind his omissions, her heart struggled to reconcile with the sense of betrayal that clouded her emotions. Still, in the silence of her non-response, Scott's persistent attempts to reach out offered a strange comfort. Scott, ever so carefree and untroubled by the world's weight, was genuinely concerned for her well-being, a thought that, despite everything, warmed a corner of her heart.

"What's that smile for?" Rafiq asked her, looking at her in her rearview mirror.

"Keep your eyes on the road," she said from the rear seat.

She tested the tiny Dictaphone they bought at the only open electronics store they could find.

"You don't even need it, you know," Rafiq told her. "This car is wired. Everything we say will be transmitted back to my embassy and recorded."

They were only a few kilometers from Jezzine. Nava lit a cigarette and rolled down her window, letting the early evening breeze wash over her face, taking in the scent of the air. It was good to be home, even though she knew it wasn't for good.

"Why is Haddad out here, in the Israeli-controlled zone?" she asked Rafiq. "Is he meeting with them again?"

"No! No!" Rafiq laughed. "I think that was a one-time thing. At least, I hope it was."

"Doesn't he still have to get his brother back from them?"

"Oh, he got him back the other day."

"What? How?"

"Your Janissaries shot up the Al-Qaeda cell pretty badly," Rafiq said. "But there were still a few of them left at Janta. Haddad put bags over their heads and traded them for his brother."

Nava could only shake her head and take another drag from her cigarette. Blowing the smoke out the window.

"Things change fast here, don't they?" she said and heard Rafiq chuckle at her remark. "What is he here for then, if not to meet with Mossad?"

"He's got a girl he meets in a hotel up near the waterfall," he said, and Nava couldn't help but break into laughter. "What's so funny?" he asked her.

"Nothing," she said. "Men are just predictable."

Rafiq grunted in agreement and said, "Life would be a lot harder for people like us if we weren't."

An hour into their wait, Nava's confidence started to wane. Despite two attempts to reach Haddad, leaving a voicemail on their second try, they were met with nothing but unsettling silence. To occupy herself and quell the growing uncertainty, she ran another check on the concealed recorder nestled beneath her clothing, ensuring every word exchanged in the front seat was captured with crystal clarity.

"I don't think he's in there," she said from the back seat, looking through a monocular.

"He's there," Rafiq said with easy confidence, as he lit a cigarette.

"How can you be so sure?"

"I told you I have surveillance set up on the suspected Mossad cell," he said. "It's not far from here. We record everything up and down this street. That's how we knew you and Masoud came here."

"I never came here with Masoud," she said.

"I mean that's how we saw him when he came here," Rafiq said.

"When?" she asked. "When was he here?"

"Like ... Two days after you, I think," he said.

"Two days ... Are you saying he was here the day before he was killed?"

"Sounds right," Rafiq replied, but that kind of imprecision wouldn't do. Not for this.

"Rafiq ..."

"Look," he said, motioning out the windshield.

Nava adjusted the monocular to her right eye, her left eye shut, as two figures stepped out of the hotel's entrance. One of them was Marwan, Haddad's trusted lieutenant, instantly recognizable even at this distance. They paused, casting cautious glances up and down the street, their movements betraying a sense of vigilance against unseen threats.

Rafiq's phone vibrated, the screen coming to life with an incoming call. "It's him," he announced. "Niqab."

Nava slipped on a niqab, pairing it with her hijab to leave only a narrow slit for her eyes. Through the monocular, she observed Marwan and his companion standing sentinel at the hotel entrance, their attention divided in a silent, coordinated sweep of their surroundings.

As Rafiq concluded his instructions over the phone, Marwan's gaze seemed to probe the parked cars along their street, searching. The car's headlights blinked once under Rafiq's command—a silent beacon in the dim evening. Marwan responded with a subtle nod, a silent acknowledgment, before stepping aside as Haddad stepped into the open, his presence commanding even from afar.

With a quiet click, Nava readied her Glock, an action that didn't go unnoticed by Rafiq. His eyebrows rose in a mix of alarm and curiosity at the gesture.

"You think that's necessary?" he queried, his voice laced with a hint of concern.

"I hope not," she replied, her focus unyielding as she tracked Haddad's approach through the lens. The tension was palpable, a silent testament to the stakes of their mission.

As Rafiq muttered a string of expletives and flicked his cigarette out the window, Nava silently activated the Dictaphone, ensuring their conversation would be recorded. A final puff of smoke escaped into the air as he closed the window, sealing the cabin from the outside world.

Assuming the guise of a bored spouse, Nava feigned disinterest, her gaze fixed on the world passing by her window. Yet, her attention was keenly focused forward, using her peripheral vision to monitor Haddad's approach. Her heart rate spiked as she observed him draw near, stopping just short of the vehicle to peer inside. Her grip on her hidden Glock tightened instinctively, a silent acknowledgment of the tension filling the car. Rafiq, maintaining his composure, gestured casually to Haddad, inviting him closer with a subtle wave. Obliging, Haddad took the final steps towards them, narrowing the gap between suspicion and confrontation.

"*Salamo Alayk,*" Rafiq greeted him when Haddad opened the door.

The Hezbollah leader quickly got in, closed the door and answered, "*Wa Alaykum as-salam.*"

"I hope you don't mind my wife being here," Rafiq said in English, motioning to the back seat. "We just came from services. She doesn't speak English, so..."

"It's fine," Haddad answered, then gestured to Rafiq's lap and asked, "What is that?"

"Something I'm working on," Rafiq answered, and Haddad nodded.

"What do you need?" he asked.

"I'm a spy," Rafiq answered him. "I need what I always need. Information."

Haddad sighed and dropped his head.

"What sort of information?" he asked.

"Eck ... You know how it is," Rafiq said with a roll of his head. "Damascus wants all kinds of shit we can't possibly know."

"Right."

"Everyone's all up in arms over there about this Abu Faysal business still," Rafiq went on. "Now with the Iranians losing their station chief, they're asking if any of this is them, or is it infighting ..."

"Where would they get that idea?" Haddad asked sharply.

"I have no clue," Rafiq laughed. "Hell, they even want to know about the Al-Qaeda cell that got shot up."

"I told you all I know about them," Haddad said. "They're not a factor here any longer."

"Not here," Rafiq countered. "Not in Beirut; but they're bound to be pissed."

"So let them be pissed," Haddad answered. "They're all bark, no bite."

"They managed to get that American," Rafiq returned. "If they can do that ... Who knows?"

"Don't worry about that," Haddad said.

"Why shouldn't I?"

"Al-Qaeda didn't grab that American," he said. "They don't have the resources or the expertise for something like that."

"You know something about it that I don't know?"

"No," Haddad snapped. "Just ... rumors."

"Shit ... It wouldn't be the first time I passed on rumors as intelligence," Rafiq said. "Tell me."

Haddad snorted, scratched the back of his neck, and said, "I don't know, Rafiq. Anything else I can do for you?"

"Just give me something, Yasin," Rafiq pleaded, but Nava could see Haddad readying to leave.

"Sorry," Haddad told him, and popped his door open.

"Close the door," Nava said, causing Haddad to freeze with one foot on the ground and jerk his head around with a quizzical look on his face. Marwan approached slowly, his right hand concealed behind his back, slightly bent over to see inside the vehicle.

"Yasin?" he called to his commander.

"Tell him to back off," Nava told him.

This time after she spoke, a look of recognition dawned on his face.

"Sabi..." he said her assumed name in a tone a decibel or two above a whisper.

"Tell him," she said, glancing at Marwan. "I'll put one in your back, Yasin. You know I will."

Haddad stared at her, seeming intent on calling her bluff. Marwan took a step closer, and she saw the weapon in his right hand partially concealed behind his leg.

"It's fine," Haddad said. "Give me a few minutes."

Marwan nodded and stepped away. Haddad brought his foot back in and closed the door.

"You killed Abu Faysal," Nava said.

"Is that a question?" Haddad asked her.

"No," Nava told him, keeping tabs on Marwan and the other guard that came from the hotel. "I know it. "You used *our* money to do it."

"And made it look as if we did it," Rafiq said, took the folder from his lap and dropped it on Haddad's.

From the backseat, Nava could only see Haddad's profile; but she didn't have any trouble reading his reaction. He'd looked shocked and disoriented when presented with the folder, but in the half minute or so it took him to flip through the papers inside, the smug self-assurance had returned to his face.

"Why?" Nava asked. "No matter what you thought of him, he was your colleague."

"Well, in one way, it's quite simple," Haddad answered, tossing the folder back into Rafiq's lap. "The problem with having two military commanders is that, when the fighting stops, each of them spends nearly all their time trying to figure out how to get rid of the other."

"So, this is a power play," Nava said.

"I only did what needed to be done," he told her. "But the IRGC needed a little convincing before giving me the green light."

Nava felt an adrenaline rush when Haddad admitted to working with the IRGC. It gave her instant hope that she would be able to expose this entire rotten cabal, be vindicated for her efforts, be welcomed back to her ministry, and watch as the reformers in Khatami's government were strengthened and emboldened. Anything seemed feasible ... until she reminded herself that nothing would bring Masoud back. With that came the realization that there were only so many wrongs she could right, and even those things she felt she could change might not be.

"Abu Faysal was a dreamer," Haddad continued. "He thought that Lebanon was weak because we were divided. Maronite, Catholic, Sunni, Shiite, Druze ... Distinctions he thought we had to put aside, or we would always be prey to outside powers like Syria and Israel. He all the occupiers out so that Lebanese could make their own decisions about their future, but he didn't see where that would leave the Shiites; outnumbered and vulnerable ... *again*."

Haddad paused, looking almost sad, Nava thought. She could see that Haddad sympathized with that idea, even if he thought it naïve – the kind of dream that more than a decade of war had hardened Haddad's heart against.

"Was that why the IRGC sanctioned Abu Faysal's assassination?" she asked.

"The IRGC wants this war to go on as long as possible," Haddad replied. "As long as there's an occupation, they can justify arming us; and as long as we're armed, we guarantee them influence here."

"They don't want Israel to leave?"

"Israel is *going* to leave," Haddad said. "Tomorrow, five years from now ... It's just a matter of time. The closer we get to that, the more it will show that we don't all agree on how this war should end. Abu Faysal believed we should disarm and become like any other political party. He never realized that the ultimate purpose of violence is *power*. He would have torn Hezbollah apart trying to get it to disarm."

"Nasrallah knew what you were going to do?" Rafiq asked him.

"No," Haddad said. "He only knew about the American. He couldn't know about Abu Faysal. If he had, he would have lost the confidence of the council; but he must have realized by now that it had to be done."

"You used the Janissaries to keep your hands clean," Nava said.

"As did you, to get the American," Haddad answered.

"Why do you think we used them?"

"You saw me on that football pitch," he said. "Guess what flew right into my face as you were flying off? The same fucking customer satisfaction survey they gave me." Haddad laughed mirthlessly and shook his head. "I never should have released them from the retainer," he said. "But you were all over me about the money, and Al-Qaeda wasn't paying fast enough."

She wanted to ask him about the call he received that made him think his brother had died in Israeli captivity, but it would give away her bugging operation. Instead, she asked, "Why did you give the hostage to Al-Qaeda in the first place?"

"Why don't you tell me how you knew that I gave her to Al-Qaeda?"

"Because I'm the one holding the gun, Yasin," she replied, making Rafiq chuckle.

Haddad scoffed, hung his head, and shook it.

"I got a call," he said. "From someone I trusted."

"Who?"

"Why do you want to know?" he asked.

"I want to meet them," she said. "In person. Alone."

Haddad turned as much as he was able in his seat to face her.

"That can be arranged," he told her, and held up the folder with the incriminating money transfer statements. "Provided this goes away."

Chapter
Thirty-Eight

They listened to the entire tape twice and specific parts of it several more times before they arrived in the coastal city of Sidon. The streets in this mostly Sunni city were nearly empty this late at night, minimizing the chances that anyone would notice her entering the Syrian safe house near Hajj Baha'a El-Dine Hariri's mosque.

Rafiq turned the engine off and let out a sigh of exhaustion, resting his head in the palm of his hand.

"You know, chances are that nothing we did today will make a bit of difference," he told her.

"Maybe," she said with a nod. "But if this stands any chance of keeping the ceasefire in place, I have to try."

Rafiq seemed disappointed, though Nava wasn't sure why. Perhaps it was because she wasn't receptive to his advice; but she'd come this far.

"What happened with the Janissaries, anyway?" he asked.

"Nothing," she said, looking away from him.

"Obviously, *something* did."

She opened the door and said, "Good night, Rafiq." But she sensed something was not quite right. She hesitated with one foot on the pavement and looked back to him. "I'm sorry I didn't trust you," she said.

Rafiq laughed a little and said, "Don't worry about it. I wouldn't trust me, either."

She moved to get out of the car.

What happened next was a blur. She felt a scorching fire-like pain in her right arm that traveled up to her shoulder. The right side of her face was pressed against the pavement, held down by something incredibly heavy, feeling as if it would crush her skull. She could hear shouting in her ear in some language she didn't know. Her arms were pinned to the small of her back and both of her forearms burned, feeling as if they'd been slashed open near her wrists.

She remained like that, her mind quickly catching up to what was happening to her. She had just begun to register that she'd been captured by men in black military-style boots (that was all she could see of them), and that they were speaking Russian, before she felt a sharp pain on the left side of her neck and everything went black.

───────────

Before she could open her eyes, she could hear a conversation happening nearby. Her world was blurry and out of focus. She didn't even know the day or time.

"*Mamani* ..." she said, though she wasn't even sure if she were saying it aloud. "*Ma ... Mamani* ..." This time, she was sure her lips were moving, and the sound wasn't just in her head. Her mother must have heard her.

She heard shoes scuffling on a bare floor and the voices of men. Her mother seemed far away – much too far away to help her now. Who was there, and what were they saying, anyhow?

Russian ...

She opened her eyes, but all she saw was a field of black dotted by tiny spots of light. The men were shouting now – shouting to one another. She saw movement through the tiny holes and realized she was wearing a hood. Some unseen force yanked it off her head, exposing her eyes to the harsh light.

"*Sobh bekheyr*," she heard as her eyes slowly adjusted.

Nava was bound to a wooden chair, her hands and arms completely immobilized and fastened behind her back. There were several men in the room dressed in military-style camouflage uniforms and black watch caps. Some were lean and young, others older and larger in build. All were armed with assault rifles slung on their backs and sidearms. Dark green filled her field of vision, and she picked her drowsy head up to see Major Khadem smiling down at her.

"Nava, Nava, Nava ..." he tsked, gently lifting her chin further upward. "We could have done great things together for Iran. For Lebanon, too."

He dragged a chair along the floor and sat in front of her with his legs crossed, looking smug and comfortable.

"You know what your problem is?" he asked her, and she was still too foggy to render a response – witty or otherwise. She was too foggy even to feel any kind of fear for herself; but she did feel sadness, even if she wasn't sure what the source of that sadness was.

Nava realized then that it was no longer the drugs in her system that kept her chin falling back toward her chest and her eyes falling to the floor It was the shame brought on by realizing she had failed. She had failed the Ministry of Intelligence and Security, failed the president, failed Masoud.

Khadem offered an entirely different explanation.

"You're a loner," he said. "A self-righteous loner. You're not wholly part of anything because you can't give yourself fully to anything. Are you Iranian, or Lebanese? Muslim? Westerner? Where is your loyalty, Nava?"

"Iran," she muttered.

"Hmm ... No. No, no, no ... See, if that were true, you would have done what I'd asked you to do and concluded that the enemy of our country had broken its agreement. Instead, you ran into its arms the first chance you got."

She looked up at him to see the smile gone from his lips, replaced by a hard scowl.

"The Pakistanis told us what happened in Zurich," he said.

He stepped behind her chair and slowly spun her around to face a table, where the contents of her bag and pockets were all neatly placed in evenly spaced rows, along with the file Rafiq had carried with him to their meeting with Haddad. It was then that she knew they were in a place she'd been dozens of times before. They were in the safe house named the Baker's.

Khadem picked up the file and her cigarette lighter, ignited the corner, and dropped it into a metal trashcan at his feet.

"All you've managed to do is give the Syrians some blackmail material over Hezbollah's new military leader," he said as he took the tape from the Dictaphone and tossed it into the fire.

He half-sat on the table, crossed his arms, and looked down at her.

"So ... where does that leave us?" he asked. "More precisely, where does that leave you? See, when I ask myself that, I think about what's best for Iran."

"You mean what's best for the IRGC," she spat back.

"For the Revolution," he returned.

"Whether or not it's a lie."

"Anything in the service of the Revolution cannot be a lie," he told her forcefully. "God and the Revolution are the Truth ... always. They say you're a traitor. A murderer. A Zionist spy that conspired to cover up an assassination, cast dispersions on Hezbollah's most respected military leader, and even indict the IRGC and, by extension, the Supreme Leader himself. A bitter, vengeful woman that lashed out at the people and the country that showed her nothing but love."

Khadem looked up at the Russians and said, "I took a page from your book. I outsourced. These gentlemen are former *Spetsnaz*. The Russian Business Network – that's what they call themselves now. They're the ones that tracked you and Rafiq."

Nava asked herself how, and she reasoned that the cell phone that Jake had handed her was the prime suspect. She searched the table for it, but it was the one thing she was sure she had with her when she was captured that wasn't there.

"It's probably superfluous having them here," Khadem said. "But I wasn't sure if you'd come with your Western mercenaries, these so-called Janissaries. So ... there's a cell waiting for you in Evin Prison, and these gentlemen will make sure you get there safely. Had you ever been stationed in Tehran, you'd be familiar with Evin and the kind of specialists we have there. You'll tell them what you told the Israelis, of course. You'll tell them everything you've done, everywhere you went, everyone you spoke with ... You'll even make some of it up, I'm sure. Everyone does, just to make the pain stop. Oh, and, uh ... being a woman, I'm sure you'll get some extra attention at night as well."

He slid the hood back over her head.

BEIRUT STATION

"If I were you," he said, "I'd tell them everything they want to hear straight away. Because they have all the time in the world to question you, over and over again; and if your story changes in the slightest, they'll make it even worse for you. Starting now and for the rest of your life, you can count on two things only. You will never leave Evin. *Never.* And no one is coming for you."

Chapter
Thirty-Nine

H eld captive by Russian mercenaries at the Baker's, she spent the night and the following day in a state of introspection, her thoughts oscillating between her perceived failures and the harsh realities of her imminent fate. Khadem's parting words echoed in her mind, a painful reminder not just for their biting accuracy, but also for evoking a cascade of critiques she had endured from the men in her life, both overt and subtle.

As the convoy of three sleek black SUVs carried her away the next morning, unhooded and ungagged in a silent acknowledgment of her defeated state, she found herself overwhelmed by a flood of emotions. Among these, the memory of Scott emerged with clarity, stirring a profound sense of loss. He had shared his innermost thoughts and fears with her, embracing her complexities without reservation. Yet, the slightest breach of trust had triggered her deepest insecurities, reviving old habits of skepticism and isolation. Gazing out at the passing landscape, the familiarity of her homeland now tinted with the somber hues of farewell, she harbored no regrets about her return, driven by a sense of duty and resolve.

"*Posmotrite na etu mashinu!*" the Russian to her left said, pointing out the window and laughing.

His amusement triggered a chain reaction, prompting the others to crane their necks, eager to catch a glimpse of the cause of the laughter. As they spotted the object of interest, their chuckles filled the space, their jokes weaving through the air in Russian. Nava, lost in her own sorrow, paid them little mind, her tears a silent testament to her internal turmoil.

But then, amidst the cacophony of laughter, a distinct sound pierced her haze of grief—a car horn, playing a melody that tugged at the edges of her memory. Seventeen notes, each one sparking a flicker of recognition, urging her to match the melody with its words.

Lifting her gaze, Nava peered through the window in the direction the Russians found so amusing. There, speeding past their convoy, was a car so beaten and neglected it seemed a relic from another era. And in that moment, the source of the melody crystallized in her mind. She couldn't grasp the entire song, the language foreign to her lips, but the opening lines resonated clear and familiar.

La cucaracha, la cucaracha ...

The airfield they took her to had obviously been out of use for many years. It was small, with a single runway and a single taxiway, and one operational hangar. There were also the remains of what had probably been a terminal, and in the tall grass that overtook every unpaved space were hulks of mostly single-engine propeller aircraft, all of which looked like they had been picked clean for any usable components.

The RBN mercenaries pulled their vehicles to a stop at the hangar opening and piled out, lit up cigarettes or leaned against the vehicles and talked to one another. The man she assumed to be their leader, a thick-necked man with a weather-lined face, came to check on her.

"You need piss? Huh? Shit?" he asked her.

She shook her head.

He gave an order in Russian and a younger mercenary bound her ankles together with plastic flex cuffs.

"We wait," he said, making a motion of an aircraft landing with his hands, complete with sound effects.

She nodded, and he lit up a cigarette.

"May I?" she asked, holding her index and middle fingers to her lips. He obliged and gave her one.

She looked around as far as she could see, trying to determine the best place to go should she get the opportunity. The hangar had a small office and a restroom, but there was nowhere to go from there. There was an exit door to the rear of the hangar and the large opening at the front. With her ankles bound, though, both might as well be on the other side of the moon.

"Kto-nibud' yeshche eto vidit?" she heard one of the mercenaries who was looking out on the airplane boneyard ask, drawing the attention of some of the others.

Holding his cigarette between his lips, the Russian held up his assault rifle and peered through the scope to get a better look at whatever he had spotted. Nava heard a soft pop, followed by a dull thud; and the Russian's back seemed to explode before he fell, dead.

Before the blood spread from the corpse, his comrades sprang into action. Their commander shouted orders at the others while crouching next to Nava and hiding behind the SUV door. They took up positions behind the other SUVs or by the hangar entrance, using the thin metal body for concealment. On the order of the leader, one of them started a vehicle and tried to move it to a better fighting position.

A few others got behind it, using it as cover to maneuver. Nava heard the crackle of glass breaking, and the SUV kept rolling out of the hangar and out of her field of vision, leaving the men scrambling for another cover. One was shot through the back as he tried to run back to the hangar.

The staccato sounds of heavy automatic gunfire erupted, interspersed by shouts in Russian as the RBN mercenaries moved out into the field and engaged their unseen attackers. The commander shouted orders to three of them that stayed behind and took up positions behind the remaining SUVs. Nava was in the rear seat with the open door facing the front of the hangar, completely exposed. She tried to get to the floor of the vehicle, but the commander yanked her out and sat her down by the right rear wheel, facing the back of the hangar.

"*Ya vizhu samolet!*" she heard one of the mercenaries in the hangar shout twice.

The commander peeked around the SUV, looking out and up. He cut her ankles free.

"We run," he told her and went back to watching the sky.

He stayed that way for a few minutes as the sounds of gunfire and explosions from the airplane boneyard intensified. His expression began to change to a frown, then to anger as he said, "*Nyet! Nyet!*" over and over.

The other soldiers were shouting excitedly, and he was shouting back when the rear door of the hanger opened. He pointed and shouted, and they opened fire at the doorway. Aiming through their sights and scopes, they probably missed the canister that spun and rolled on the floor toward them. Nava had barely seen it, but something told her to shut her eyes tight and cover her ears.

Even so, the device rendered her nearly blind and deaf; but her eyes recovered a little quicker. She saw Ridley and Scott enter in a crouch,

273

firing at the three RBN mercenaries behind the other SUV, but they didn't immediately see their commander, who had evidently been partially blinded but could still see well enough to aim his weapon and fire in their general direction. Nava threw herself at him with every ounce of energy she had.

It was enough to throw him off, and his shots missed the Janissaries. She saw a flash of light when he struck her in the face with his left elbow, landing the blow on her nose and making her eyes well up. She fell to the concrete floor of the hangar on her side, holding her nose in pain. The shooting stopped, and she opened her eyes and saw the commander of the Russian mercenaries staring back at her, a neat round black hole in his forehead.

"It's broken," she said as Scott carefully moved her nose from side to side. "Just say it."

Thankfully, one of the SUVs only had a few bullet holes in it, making it far more appealing than the derelict vehicle in which the Janissaries had arrived. They were driving it down the coastal highway. Somewhere along this route, they told her, were small boats waiting to ferry them to a larger boat somewhere off the coast, then on to Cyprus.

"Sorry to tell you, it's not broken," he told her. "I know it hurts like hell."

"How would you know?"

"That fucker hit me square in the schnozz once," he said, motioning to Christian in the passenger seat, who looked back and gave her a wink.

"Good training," he said, and Scott echoed the remark.

Scott handed her the cold pack to reapply to her nose and continued treating the cuts on the side of her face, which she wasn't even aware she had, with antiseptic.

"How did you find me?" she asked him.

"Some dude named Rafiq took your phone when you got snatched," Scott told her.

"I thought he sold me out," she said, a little embarrassed.

She took his hand gently away from her face, lowered the cold pack and looked him in the eyes.

"I'm sorry," she said.

"Forget it," he told her with a dismissive shake of his head. "It's nothing. For what it's worth, I'm sorry I didn't tell you about Abu Faysal."

The two-vehicle convoy pulled off the highway at a construction site for a new beach resort in Jiyeh, where the security guard opened the gate for them to pass through. They came to a stop on the sand, where two zodiac boats waited for them. Next to them were five young women armed with assault rifles, one of whom was Erica. Jake opened her door from outside and looked at her impassively through dark sunglasses.

He cocked his head, the very faintest of smiles on his lips, and asked "You good?"

"Yes, thank you," she replied.

He stepped aside and jerked his head.

"Let's go. I want to make it back in time for salsa night at KCA," he said, did a little dance step as he walked toward the boats.

"Why did you come for me?" she asked as they followed him. "I gave you what you needed for the Swiss contract."

He turned, continuing to walk backward toward the boats as he said, "Maybe I'll need you to help move a body."

He flashed a toothy smile and turned around to walk forward again, and she heard that bizarre, closed mouth laugh of his. This time, however, it made her laugh.

Chapter Forty

Three months later, Nava returned to Lebanon for what she knew would be the last time in a while... perhaps ever. While still in Vienna, she contacted Rafiq and learned that he had delivered the recording of their conversation with Haddad and a copy of the evidence regarding Abu Faysal's assassination directly to the Syrian ambassador, who allowed Ambassador Gul to see and hear both before they were destroyed as promised. President Khatami reportedly brought it to the attention of the supreme leader, who claimed he was positively shocked at the IRGC's transgressions.

Then again, we investigated the issue thoroughly, and it was just a few rogue agents. Neither the supreme leader nor any general officer of the Islamic Revolutionary Guard Corps would ever commit such a gross overstep.... and on and on.

"Khadem was recalled to Iran," Rafiq told her over the phone.

"What do you think they'll do to him," she asked.

She heard Rafiq scoff and say, "Probably give him a medal. The game goes on."

"It can go on without me," she replied and heard him laugh on the other end of the line.

"Well, if you're still interested, Haddad is keeping his end of the deal," he told her. "You finally got that meeting you wanted."

Nava's return to Lebanon carried a solemn purpose, the first of which was a visit to Masoud's house. As they approached, it was evident from the exterior's neat appearance that efforts had been made to cleanse and mend the scars the building had suffered. Though it stood unoccupied, a silent testament to the life and struggles that once filled its rooms, Nava refrained from stepping inside. Respecting boundaries unseen but deeply felt, she placed a pouch of Masoud's preferred tobacco on the steps—a modest tribute to the man who had impacted her so profoundly. Mounting the motorcycle once again, she took a moment to collect her thoughts, her eyes closing gently as she offered a prayer into the quiet air around them.

"O Allah, grant him Your forgiveness," she whispered into the wind, her words a tender plea for peace. "O Allah, bestow upon him Your strength."

With her homage paid, they turned their journey towards Jezzine, carrying with them the weight of memories and the hope for closure.

In the shadowy confines of a sparsely furnished apartment, where the only adornments were two wooden chairs and a nondescript table, she awaited the unfolding of events with a patience born of necessity. This austere room, positioned strategically near the rendezvous point of

Haddad and his clandestine lover, also lay within the same unassuming edifice that Rafiq had casually mentioned might conceal a Mossad cell. This was one of the places Masoud visited in his last hours on earth, engaged in matters of such gravity that her own calls had fallen by the wayside, unanswered.

With a silenced pistol resting discreetly in her lap, she endured the passing hours, her only companions the relentless ticking of a clock and the relentless chew of nicotine gum. Coffee, her erstwhile ally against the encroaching weight of sleep, now betrayed her with an unwanted gift of edginess. At one juncture, a creeping paranoia that she might have been compromised—spotted either entering this barren hideaway or observed through the scant windows—nearly compelled her to abandon her vigil. Yet, she resolved to persist a while longer, convincing herself of the virtue in patience until the cloak of night could offer its cover.

The telltale clink of keys outside the door, a sound both mundane and momentous, confirmed the wisdom of her waiting. She rose, the weapon now a hidden extension of her own form, concealed behind the sinew of her leg as the lock whispered its surrender to the key. The door swung inward, revealing a figure carrying a grocery bag, his features obscured under the brim of a hat.

For a fleeting moment, he remained unaware of her presence, a ghost in his periphery. It was only with the door's closure and his subsequent turn that their worlds collided, his eyes widening at her silhouette framed against the dim light, a specter of his past or perhaps his conscience made manifest.

"Nava!" Hooman greeted her, breathing a sigh of relief. "*Alhamdulillah*, you're alive! I thought Khadem—"

"Expecting INFERNO?" Nava cut in sharply, her tone laced with suspicion.

279

Hooman shifted uncomfortably, his gaze darting briefly to the door as if expecting someone—or something—to burst through at any moment. "He should be here soon," he replied, the words barely concealing his underlying nervousness.

"I was in Zurich," Nava pressed on, her stance firm and unyielding. "I needed Mossad's help. I traded Pakistani secrets for the information I needed. But then, the Pakistanis tried to kill me. How did they find me, Hooman? The only explanation is that the Israelis betrayed me. Why would Mossad risk losing a valuable asset unless they were protecting someone else? Someone more valuable."

As the accusation hung in the air, Hooman's complexion turned ashen. His eyes widened, betraying a deep-seated fear, and his lips parted slightly, but no words came out. He seemed trapped, cornered by the truth of her words.

"I know there's no INFERNO," Nava continued, her gaze piercing. "What I want to know is whether you were just embezzling funds, or if you were betraying us all along. Trading secrets with Mossad."

"Let me explain," Hooman pleaded, a hint of desperation creeping into his voice as he took a tentative step toward her.

Nava instinctively sidestepped, maintaining a deliberate distance between them, a physical manifestation of the chasm that now lay between their trust. "Do you have a cigarette?" he asked, almost as an afterthought, a feeble attempt to bridge the gap.

"Quit," she responded curtly, her eyes never leaving his.

Hooman glanced down at the groceries he still carried, an implicit request for a momentary truce. "At least let me put these down," he said, moving towards the table, his movements betraying a sense of defeat.

"INFERNO was real, at least... I thought he was," Hooman confessed, the words heavy with the weight of his realization. "He was a fucking dangle, Nava." The bitterness with which he uttered the last word was palpable, a laugh devoid of any humor.

"I didn't see it until it was too late," he admitted, his voice barely above a whisper.

"Masoud found out," Nava stated, her voice steady, seeking confirmation.

"Khadem found out," Hooman corrected her, his voice laced with resignation. "But we reached an understanding." His next words were heavy with implication. "He wanted a conflict with the U.S., or at least, with Israel."

"And that's why you called Haddad that morning, telling him his brother was dead," Nava concluded, her voice a mix of accusation and sorrow.

"I had no choice," Hooman said, and dropped the bag of groceries.

He spun, reaching for his weapon; but Nava, with months of meticulous preparation etched into her muscle memory, was faster. The cold precision of her training took over as she lifted her weapon, her eyes narrowing, focusing through the sights. She fired two suppressed shots, the bullets finding their mark before Hooman's own gun had fully turned in her direction. His body hit the floor with a resonant thud.

Approaching with cautious steps, Nava ensured there would be no reprisals. A swift kick sent Hooman's pistol skittering across the floor, an echo in the stillness. She fired again, twice, a grim punctuation to his fate, each bullet a closing note to their entwined narratives. His body jerked with the impact, then went still.

Remaining vigilant, she crouched beside him, her weapon still an extension of her wary stance. With a deliberate motion, she removed the hat from his head, unveiling the remnants of their shared history. There, barely visible against his skin, was the mark left by the scalding tea from that fateful morning in Masoud's office—a mark as indelible as the memories it conjured.

Rising, Nava cast a final glance at the man who had orchestrated so much pain, his body now still in the growing pool of his own making. It was a stark departure from the vibrant life of Masoud, whom Hooman had so callously betrayed. Without another word, she turned her back on the scene, leaving Hooman to the silence and the shadows, a lone figure in the aftermath of his choices.

"Did you do what you needed to do?" Scott asked her when he picked her up by the waterfall.

"I did what needed to be done," she answered.

They both took a moment, admiring the view from the top of the waterfall. To the right were tree-covered hills; forests that appeared to have been there for a thousand years. To the left were newly constructed homes built at the very edge of a precipice.

"Beautiful country," he said. "Tragic history."

"Better a tragic history than a tragic future," she said. "Despite everything that happened, this place could tear itself apart just as easily as the armies that occupy it. Maybe all I did was buy it time."

"Maybe that's all we ever do," Scott told her. "I mean, in the long run, we're all dead anyway, right?"

She smiled and kissed him before putting her helmet on and mounting the back of the motorcycle.

"Hold on tight," he told her.

"Don't worry," she assured him. "I will."

BEIRUT STATION

THE END

Printed in Great Britain
by Amazon

44368517R00169